Shady Park Secrets

REA KEECH

ISBN 978-1-7330524-0-5   **Hardback**
ISBN 978-1-7330524-1-2   **Paperback**
ISBN 978-1-7330524-2-9   **Ebook**

Library of Congress control number:
2019946572

Published by

Real
Nice Books

11 Dutton Court
Baltimore, Maryland 21228
www.realnicebooks.com

*Publisher's note: This is a work of fiction. Names, characters, places,
institutions, and incidents are entirely the product of the author's imagination
or are used fictitiously, and any resemblance to actual persons, living or
dead, or to events, incidents, institutions, or places is entirely coincidental.*

Interior sketches by Barbara Munjal.
Set in Sabon.

Shady Park Secrets is
Book 3 of the Shady Park Chronicles

Also by Rea Keech:

First World Problems (Book 1 of the Shady Park Chronicles)

"Keech (*A Hundred Veils*) takes on a literary classic in this novel, which follows the romantic and social trials and tribulations of Emma Bovant and her husband, Charles.... This tale should please readers who enjoy romantic drama, and may be of interest to fans of Flaubert."   — ***Kirkus Reviews***

Shady Park Panic (Book 2 of the Shady Park Chronicles)

"Keech's prose style is charmingly companionable, and he depicts the romantic entanglements of Anthony's personal life ... with a tone of sweetness and humor."   — ***Kirkus Reviews***

A Hundred Veils

Publishers Weekly BookLife Prize: General Fiction Finalist 2017

"Set in the lead-up to the Iranian revolution, *A Hundred Veils* is a rich portrait of cultural and personal discovery and forbidden love. Keech uses both humor and drama, as well as finely chosen details and rich description, to bring the characters and their world to life."
    — **Eleanor Brown**, best-selling author of *The Weird Sisters*

BookLife assessment of *A Hundred Veils*:

Prose: The writing is as economical and succinct as a film script. The narrative moves along swiftly, and yet it's studded with evocative detail.

Originality: This gripping book is a romance with humor and cultural insights that readers will find original and intriguing.

Character Development: The characters here are well developed and fully formed. Marco in particular feels vivid and real.

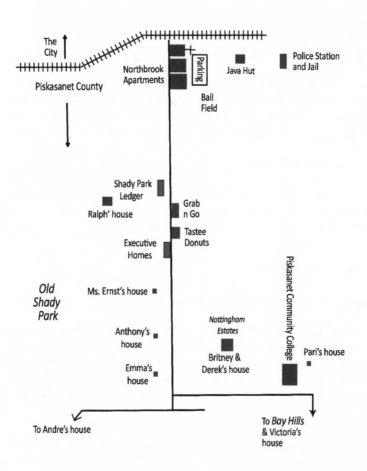

The City

Piskasanet County

Northbrook Apartments

Parking

Ball Field

Java Hut

Police Station and Jail

Shady Park Ledger

Ralph' house

Grab n Go

Tastee Donuts

Executive Homes

Old Shady Park

Ms. Ernst's house

Anthony's house

Nottingham Estates

Britney & Derek's house

Piskasanet Community College

Pari's house

Emma's house

To Andre's house

To *Bay Hills* & Victoria's house

Shady Park and vicinity

Riverside Village

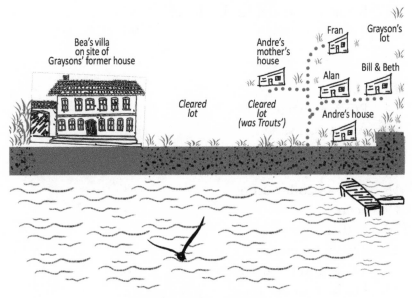

Bea's villa
on site of
Graysons' former house

Cleared
lot

Andre's
mother's
house

Cleared
lot
(was Trouts')

Fran

Grayson's
lot

Alan

Bill & Beth

Andre's house

Piskasanet River

List of Chapters

III   **183**

I

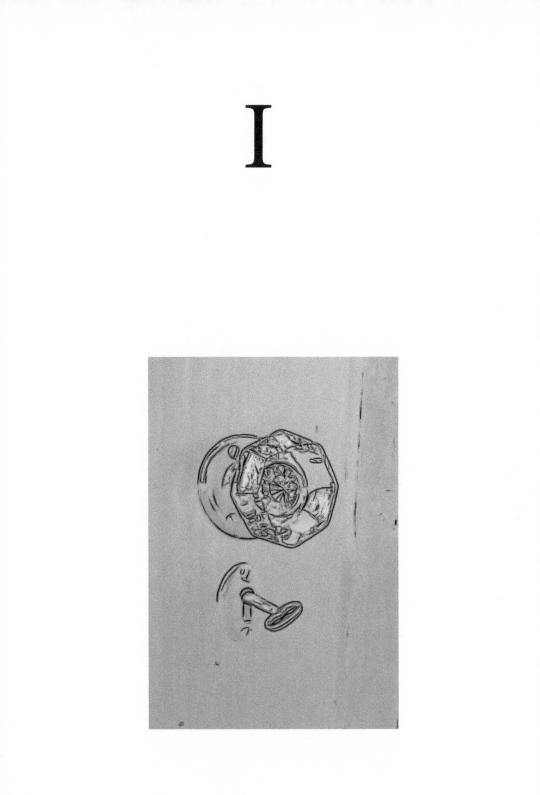

1

Awakening

*She had all her life long been accustomed to harbor
thoughts and emotions which never voiced themselves.*

—Kate Chopin, *The Awakening*

Nicole Ernst murmured softly, suddenly awake. She'd
never admit what she'd been dreaming. At first, she had no
memory of where she was. It was cold. The room was dark,
only a thin shaft of daybreak filtering in below a window
shade. She was lying on a carpet, her head on a thin cushion.
Somebody's arm was thrown across her.

The scent of rosewater gradually brought it all back. She'd
come to a vigil celebrating the longest night of the year. The
others were all asleep on the floor around the low table—she
couldn't tell how many were still here.

It was Andre's arm over her, she realized. He was a guest
she'd met that night at the Yaldā vigil. He was asleep. Instead
of removing his arm, she closed her eyes and lay perfectly
still. She'd hoped Ralph would be at the vigil and she let herself imagine for a moment it was Ralph's arm.

Nobody had actually been able to stay awake until dawn
at this night-long ceremony. They'd been sitting on cushions
around a low table set with pomegranates and rosewater fla-
vored pastries until, apparently, everyone had fallen asleep on
the carpet.

Nicole had been surprised at a young friend's invitation
to her mother's house for the Persian vigil. It was a Zoroastrian custom, according to Pari. "We eat special food, talk,

11

sing, recite poetry, stay up till dawn." The thought of talking, singing, and reciting among strangers made Nicole tremble. But Pari had said, "I'm sure our friend Andre will do most of the talking."

He had, in fact, monopolized the conversation, and Nicole imagined that habit might explain why at 37 he was still single. She was the same age as Andre and, like him, had never married. She went on dates arranged by her friends, but seldom on second dates. Her mother said that was OK—she was "particular."

Andre's arm pulled back a bit, his hand now draped across her breast. He was still asleep. And still she didn't move or wake him.

She'd *read* more about sex than she'd experienced it. Some articles claimed sexual pleasure might be enhanced if perceived as forbidden or secret. She lay motionless, abandoning herself to the outrageous thrill. She'd never imagined herself doing something like this.

Loud snoring burst out from the other side of the table. Andre groaned and sat up, holding the small of his back. He looked down at Nicole as if wondering who she was, rubbed his eyes. "Oh," he said, "the Yaldā ceremony. I guess I fell asleep." He searched the room. "Are we the only ones awake?"

Nicole's eyes gradually grew accustomed to the dim light. Pari and her friend Anthony were gone. Their Iranian friends were gone. Pari's parents were asleep on the floor. The feel of Andre's hand was hard to shake from her mind. "Just you and me," she said in a husky voice.

Andre cocked his head. "Nicole, right?" He rubbed his back. "I guess we could slip out, let our hosts sleep." Nicole nodded.

Her car, its yellow tennis ball on top of the antenna, was parked beside Andre's in the gravel driveway. He turned with his hand on the door. "Want to stop at the Grab 'n Go with me? I'll buy you a slice of pizza and some tea."

Nicole didn't eat pizza the first thing in the morning, and tea upset her stomach, but she said, "Oh. OK."

She pulled up to the Grab 'n Go between Andre's car and an old gray car with a red fender. It was chilly, late December, but the gray car's window was open. A young man with a black buzz cut sat in the driver's seat, absorbed in a magazine. As she passed by, the teenager turned. It was Willard Scherd, the high school student who'd been arrested last fall for bringing a gun to a board of education hearing and causing a panic in which she'd been shot.

Willard had on the same camouflage T-shirt he'd worn that night. She could see the tattoo on his arm. His eyes were trained on her in a blank stare. It was impossible to tell what he might be thinking. An icy tingle snaked down her back.

In the store, Nicole kept her eye on the doorway, afraid Willard would come in. She slopped some coffee into a styrofoam cup and was anxious to go home, but Andre lingered at the counter chatting with the manager. Nicole was afraid to leave by herself. She tapped him on the shoulder. "Can we go, Andre?"

"Go? Oh. Sure." It seemed to take a second for him to recall again who she was and that he'd come in with her.

He walked her to her car and held her coffee while she got in. As she backed up and drove away, she turned to wave, but Andre didn't see her. He was walking up to Willard Scherd's open window.

Her best friend Liz Costello phoned. Liz had taken Nicole under her wing the minute Nicole was transferred to Northbrook High School. "So tell me all about your exotic Iranian evening. Was Ralph there? I know you were hoping."

Nicole had first met Ralph at a parent-teacher conference

last spring when she was still teaching in Shady Park. She taught the seventh grade, and Ralph's son Bobby was in the fifth, but Bobby loved coming to Nicole's after-school book club. He insisted she meet his dad. Ralph's lustrous dark hair, thin moustache, and kind, coffee-brown eyes had held Nicole mostly speechless while he heaped Bobby's praises on her.

Ralph had given her his card. *Editor, Shady Park Ledger*. And he'd interviewed her three times after the incident last fall when she was shot in the leg. They talked about gun violence, the growing resentment of immigrants, teachers' need for academic freedom—and he finished by saying there should be more teachers like her.

"No, Liz. Ralph wasn't at the Yaldā vigil. It was interesting, though."

"That giggle—you sound like it was more than just interesting. You sound all throbby-spacey." It was how the teachers described high school girls when good looking guys talked to them.

"Actually, it got a little boring." Nicole mentioned the tea and pistachios and poetry recitations. "And then it seems we all fell asleep on the floor."

"Go on."

And then I woke up with a man's arm around me and I've been having erotic fantasies ever since. "Then we woke up at dawn and went home."

Liz and her husband treated Nicole as their project. They were fanatical about getting her married. "Remember what I told you. Your biological clock is ticking."

"The thing is, Liz, I'm waiting for the right guy."

"Meaning Ralph? At first, I thought he was into you, but he's never called you. So I don't know. And if you won't call him ...."

Ralph had given her his card, but probably that's what newspaper editors did. Nicole was too timid to call him.

"Nicole, with your looks, you don't have to wait around for a guy who might not even be interested in you. Really. That guy Harry that we fixed you up with? Want to know what he told Alfonse?"

"Not specially. I didn't—"

"You look finer than any woman he's seen on *The Bachelorette*. His words."

"Come on, Liz."

"I swear that's what he said. But he said when he took you home, you didn't invite him in. What's up with that?"

"I guess I'd heard enough about Game of Thrones and Instagram filters and—"

Liz shished out a laugh. "And how many Twitter followers he has? I know. Point taken."

"Anyway," Nicole said.

"Anyway," Liz repeated.

"So. See you at school Monday."

Smokey the Cat circled impatiently, tail on high, eager for Nicole to scrape the Salmon Paté, which he currently favored, into his bowl. A knock on the door made her jump, and the spoon clanked onto the floor.

She almost never had a visitor. She smoothed down her hair. When she cracked open the door, Andre stood there, blue eyes beaming. She let him in.

He began talking immediately, apparently resuming aloud a monologue that had been going on in his head. It was hard to follow, something about Plato's concept of universal beauty.

"How did you know where I live?"

"What? Oh, I knew it was in Shady Park. I drove around until I found a car with a yellow tennis ball on the antenna."

Nicole uneasily gripped her hands together. He didn't seem like a stalker, but you never ....

"In some languages," he was saying, "there are more words for colors than in others. In Japanese, for example, a single word can serve for blue or green—a perfect word to describe their brilliance. Sparkling, beautiful, changing in the light."

"I'm sorry. I don't—"

"Your eyes. I've been haunted by them since the Yaldā vigil."

It might have been the word "haunted." Nicole took a step back. But Andre's topic immediately shifted to the Zoroastrian insistence on preserving the purity of all nature, something Nicole could approve of with a tentative nod. She had a trellis over the path to her door covered with winter roses which she fed and watered conscientiously. Maybe Andre was just odd. And, after all, what he'd said about her eyes was flattering.

Smokey meowed from the top of a tower of multi-colored bins of school supplies stacked against the living room wall. Andre didn't seem to hear. He had now drifted from nature preservation to indignation at the real estate developers who, with the support of the county executive himself, had scraped the land bare in Riverside Village, where he lived.

"Oh, you're Andre Smyth? Smyth with a y? It was you who wrote those letters to the *Shady Park Ledger*? It seems they did some good. They stopped the construction." She noted a wrinkle on his brow and added, "I mean, some damage to the neighborhood was done, of course. I hope—"

"We have another mutual friend besides Pari—Emma Bovant. Emma was sorry you were transferred from Shady Park to Northbrook High. Her son Todd was hoping to be in your class." Andre closed his eyes, took a breath, and began, "Plagiarism has been a problem since before Guttenberg's press. In fact, ancient Chinese literature—"

So Andre had heard she was transferred after giving an F for plagiarism to an influential couple's daughter. Nicole remembered from the Yaldā vigil Andre's tendency to rattle on. She edged towards the kitchen as politely as she could. "Tea, Andre?" She remembered he liked it and luckily she had some on hand.

"Your leg. You still limp a little." He reached out and put his hand on her shoulder. Nicole flinched and stepped back, sliding his hand off.

Andre's face reddened. "Sorry," he said, wiping his eyes with the back of his hand. The whites of his eyes were turning pink. "Give me a minute," he panted, and stood there sniffling.

Nicole was devastated to think she'd misunderstood what he'd probably only meant as a gesture of sympathy. "I'm sorry, Andre. I didn't mean—"

Andre waved off the apology.

"It's just that you surprised me. I shouldn't have—"

He waved his hand again. "You don't have a cat, do you? I'm really allergic."

As if on cue, Smokey gave out a loud meow. He'd been observing the scene from a stack of plastic bins.

A bout of sneezing overtook Andre. He fumbled to button up his jacket. Nicole handed him a tissue. He was wheezing.

"Andre," she said. "This is terrible. I had no idea."

He shrugged. "No, I should have noticed you have a cat. There's something I came here to ask you. Maybe we can meet again at my house."

2

School days

Arts, sciences, no branch was made a mystery
To Juan's eyes, excepting natural history.
—Byron, *Don Juan*

It would be good to get back to the classroom, clear her mind. The Yaldā episode had hit Nicole like a freak rain shower, and she couldn't just shake it off like Liz's poodle.

Liz taught physical education. She was bent over one of the few desks in the teachers room that had a computer—in baggy red sweatpants with a white-toothed groundhog standing at attention along one leg and *Northbrook High* written across the butt. Nicole came up and saw *Cultural Alliance Club* on the screen.

"It's a new club I'm forming, Nicole. You know—learning about other cultures. I want to get it started after the Christmas holiday. Want to help?"

"Sure." Nicole studied Liz's face to confirm what she suspected. Higgy opposed creating this club. Principal Matthew Higgenbottom opposed doing anything he thought might set the parents further on edge after the recent shooting at a board of education hearing in his school. The community was calling for teachers to be armed and immigrants to be "sent back where they came from." All Higgy talked about these days was "facilitating community relations."

The young reporters Pari and Anthony, had discovered it was Derek Grosbeck, ,a real estate investor and intimate of the county executive, who'd accidently fired the shot that hit

Nicole in the leg. But some in the community still didn't believe this. Fake news, they called it. The mother of one of the students had come to the meeting in a hejab, and they were stubbornly convinced she was the one who fired the shot.

Liz handed Nicole a printout to copy for her classes.

"What about Higgy?"

"I checked. He can't actually stop us. As long as enough students sign up."

A few days ago Nicole would have been reluctant to stir up trouble. She'd already been transferred from the school she loved, Shady Park Elementary/Middle, as a punishment for accusing Britney Grosbeck's daughter of plagiarism, and she'd intended to keep a low profile.

But something about the whole Yaldā experience was changing her. She'd awoken Dante-like to find herself in an unfamiliar place, encountered Andre, and had survived. The Yaldā ceremony felt like the first sip of a revitalizing potion. "Right," she told Liz. "Let Higgy fret about it. The school needs a club like this."

"People must have been scared to death of dinosaurs back then."

Lyla looked up from her phone and giggled. "Dummy, there were no people back then."

The class roared in laughter. Nicole knew it was at Lyla calling Brett "dummy," not at the absurdity she was pointing out.

Brett reddened, said there had to be people then.

Head tilted, hands on hips, Lyla chided, "You weren't there. How do you know?"

Juan raised his hand. "Ms. Ernst, seriously, there weren't any people back then, were there?"

Before Nicole could answer, Brett insisted, "God created all the creatures on Earth together on the sixth day." His face still pink, he scanned the classroom with the satisfaction of a lawyer who'd just made an incontrovertible closing argument.

A girl in the front row turned towards the back of the class. "And what does your Koran say about this, Jamal? I'm sure we'd all like to know." It was Amber, whose mother had asked Higgy to put her daughter into a class that had no foreigners in it, something Higgy found impossible to do as long as Amber's mother defined "foreigner" as including children born here of recent immigrants.

The class laughed. "Jamal." "She still calls him Jamal."

Nicole intervened. "He prefers to go by his American name, Jim. We need to respect that."

Eyes lowered towards his desk, Jim answered, "Anyway, it's pretty much the same as in the Bible."

In the back row, Wally, who'd actually been reading his textbook instead of tapping at a cell phone, raised his hand. "Ms. Ernst. Our social studies text says, 'There is no scientific proof that the story of creation in the Bible is inaccurate.'"

"Well, Wally, all I can say is, what scientists do is, they look at fossil records and use carbon dating. I've planned a lesson on carbon dating for later this week. I think you'll find it interesting. Now let's get on with—"

Tobin, the Northbrook football team center, interrupted with a deep guffaw. "Carbon dating? Not for me. You'll never catch me dating any—"

"He's only interested in Ms. Ernst," Lyla shouted. Others joined in. "Tell her how hot you say she is, Tobin." "As if she'd ever hook up with a doofus like you."

Nicole sometimes yearned to go back to teaching the seventh grade, or preferably the third.

Principal Higgenbottom's forced smile came out closer to a sneer. "No, Ms. Ernst, I *can't* tell you when the currently approved textbooks will be made available again. If the county keeps changing its mind about which books we're to use, what am I expected to do? You tell me."

Nicole and Liz had been two of the many teachers in the county who'd worked successfully to get the recent alt-right Christian fundamentalist-flavored texts removed from the curriculum and replaced with the books used previously. She said, "It's just … it's been a while since the board mandate, Mr. Higgenbottom." Normally, she would have stopped there. But the more confident Nicole went on. "I wonder if you could call the warehouse and ask what the holdup is."

"So, Ms. Ernst, you're telling me how to do my job? I'm beginning to see why you were removed from your last position." He gave an annoyed tug to his tie. "You're already on thin ice here, young lady. It's my duty to warn you."

Nicole didn't understand.

"I had a call from the mother of a student in your morning class. Her daughter says you told the class the Bible isn't true."

"I did not say that." Nicole swallowed. "And how could a mother already know about something that happened in class only an hour ago?"

Higgy put on a squinty smile. "The girl posted it on Instagram, and her mother reads all her Instagrams."

At home, Nicole prepared for the next day's class. She spread books and papers on her fluffy living room rug. The Stone Age, the Bronze Age, the Iron Age. These weren't mentioned in the textbooks currently in her classroom. Pre-Flood and Post-Flood were the two ages of man described in the *Creation Science* chapters. Nicole used a book she still had from her high school days to draw up some posters. As she put in the time frames, she imagined objections coming from a few students. And she lacked textbooks to back her up.

She checked the time on her phone. The county warehouse in the Education Complex might still be open. She called. It was closing in a couple of hours. She threw on her coat, picked up her keys, and left.

The corrugated door was rolled up. Leaning against the outside wall was a powerfully built man, one knee bent and a huge tan boot braced flat on the bricks behind him. A cigarette hung from his mouth, and he held a copy of the *Shady Park Ledger* in his brown hands. The headlines read:

County Exec Indicted by State
for Misappropriation of Funds

Fed Demands State Restore Environmental Money
Diverted by Mauer

"You that teacher who got shot?"

Nicole nodded. Her leg felt better every day, but she must still be limping a little. "Nicole Ernst," she said. "Northbrook High. We still haven't received the books yet to replace the—"

"Fundamentalist books?" He held out a powerful hand. "Lloyd." He threw down his cigarette, folded the paper, and smiled, his deep brown eyes twinkling. "Nice to meet you. You up for a tour of the warehouse?"

She followed him along the cement floor of a cavernous expanse filled with skids of books piled twice as high as her head.

"Over here," Lloyd explained, "these are the fundamentalist books we've brought back, the ones that look brand new." He chuckled. "Guess the kids don't read their books much. But I have." He opened up a glossy-covered social studies book lying on a metal table in a corner of the warehouse. "*The Civil War was about one thing: states' rights.* You think? My great grandfather might disagree with that."

"So I guess those books over there are—"

"The old ones without lies." Lloyd spread out some papers on his table. "See here. All the delivery confirmations to the county schools. The only school holdout is Northbrook High."

"My school."

Lloyd held up a memo. "Principal Higgenbottom said not to deliver them until he gives the go-ahead." Lloyd glanced at Nicole and frowned, wiped a thick finger across his forehead. "Guess you need to get the fact-based books back into your class, huh? Tell you what. It might change his mind if I passed word up to the board of education that he's stalling."

"I don't want to get in trouble."

"Don't worry, Ms. Ernst. Nothing to do with you."

3

Fun with phones

We are in great haste to construct a magnetic tele-graph from Maine to Texas; but Maine and Texas, it may be, have nothing important to communicate.

—Thoreau, *Walden*

A straw wrapper circled and dove towards Nicole's head. Juan jumped up from his table and caught it before it hit her. Lunch monitor duty was different in high school. Advantages: less spilt milk, very little crying, so far no vomit to clean up. Drawback: the students dared to tease the teacher—and, at least with Nicole, tended to get away with it. Back in Shady Park, she was the one the kids looked to for help. Now it seemed like that had been turned around.

"Thanks, Juan."

He grinned, scrunching the straw wrapper in his hand. He wore a Baltimore Orioles shirt.

"Jim Delpak says you two are going out for the baseball team this spring."

Jim had quit the baseball team to avoid the bullying at school after the shooting incident. It was his mother who'd come to the board hearing wearing a hejab, an obvious sign she was a terrorist, many in the community still thought. She was the person Willard Scherd had aimed his gun at, though he never got the chance to fire it.

"I wanted to ask you about something else," Juan mumbled. His dark eyes focused on hers, hesitating. "A girl's been sending me texts."

Nicole glanced around. Three or four students had turned away from their lunch trays to see what kind of trouble Juan might be in. For eleventh-grade kids it was unheard of to talk to a teacher unless they had to.

Nicole motioned him out into the hall. He leaned back on the wall between two rows of lockers, hidden from the view of kids passing by. He waited, as if for Nicole to wind up and pitch.

"Well, if you don't like it, you could ask the girl to stop, I guess."

"She won't." Juan twisted nervously.

"Maybe block her?"

"I did block her on Snapchat. Then she started sending me text messages."

"You can't block those?"

"Yes, but she uses different Google Voice numbers. I can't tell it's from her until I click."

In Nicole's day, flirting was accomplished by slipping a note to a guy in class. Few kids had cell phones. She remembered her mother saying, "What do we need those things for?" Apparently, new uses for them were being invented all the time.

"It's … she sends pictures."

At first, Nicole thought his objection might be that the pictures took up too much memory on his phone. But Juan's face was bright red now. She cleared her throat. "Juan, show me. I need to know what you're talking about."

Juan clamped his hand over his pocket.

Nicole used her best Liz Costello voice. "Juan, hand it over right now."

Juan obeyed his teacher. And turned to face the wall.

As soon as Nicole took the phone, there was a *ping*. She tapped, and the naked body of a girl filled the screen. It was a young girl—just her neck down to her waist. Nicole covered it with her hand.

"Sorry." Juan pried the phone from her hands. "We don't do this in Guatemala."

"What kind of girl sends pictures like this?"

"An eighth-grader," Juan said.

"A girl in middle school?"

Juan's dark, handsome face flushed again. "Yeah, I don't really know her. I met her at a friend's house. Tell you the truth, I don't like her."

The bell for the next class rang, and Nicole and Juan both jumped. Juan swiped away the picture and jammed his phone back into his pocket. "Excuse me." He set off down the hall.

Nicole grabbed his shirt tail. "You have to tell your mother about this, Juan. Have her call the girl's mother."

Juan looked back. "I'm sorry, Ms. Ernst. I can't do that."

When Nicole walked into her classroom, Tobin was standing at the front, his Washington Redskins jersey rolled up to his armpits. He was flexing his abs and twitching his pectoral muscles.

"Show that to Ms. Ernst," Lyla taunted. "We're not interested."

Nicole's cheeks felt oven-hot. "Sit down, Tobin." Her back to the class, she shuffled some notes on her desk, then, with a full breath, turned. "Ahem. Today we are going to see what we can learn about carbon dating."

"Excuse me. Excuse me." It was Brett. "Those flyers you handed out, Ms. Ernst? About the Cultural Alliance Club? My father says this is the way terrorists filter our society."

"Infiltrate?"

"Whatever. He says the school should ban it."

"Let's get on with the lesson, shall we? So. About carbon dating. Does anybody know what it is?"

Lyla shook aside some strawberry blond hair. "It's how

you can tell how old something is."

"Could it tell how old my grandfather's Mayan coins are?" Juan seemed interested.

"Probably not," Nicole explained. "We can only date material that's organic."

"That's all we eat," Wally called out from the back of the class. Everything we eat has to be organic."

"Well, Wally," Nicole raised her voice over the tittering. "Organic means containing carbon. Bones, hair, skin, wood, dead plants—things like this."

"Yuck," Brett yelled. "Don't ever invite me to eat dinner at your house, Wally."

Nicole stifled a laugh. She knew even a smile could encourage them.

She wasn't planning to go into the chemistry of the process, but she'd prepared to draw a very simplified sketch of a spectrometer—carbon in, result out. She turned to the whiteboard. Back when Nicole was in middle school herself, parents had complained that chalk dust was harming their children. All the state's blackboards were hauled off to the dump. The teachers wrote on whiteboards with felt tip pens that had "easily erasable" ink.

Nicole's whiteboard was covered with unerasable black marks. She picked up a pen and started to draw in a relatively white section of the board. Unsurprisingly, the ink in the pen had dried up. There were five or six pens in the tray. She tried them all. All dry.

"All right, then," she told the class. Since you all have phones, please Google 'carbon dating' and go to Wikipedia to find a picture of a spectrometer." Since she couldn't write on the board, she wrote *spectrometer* on the back of her notes and held it up.

A hush fell over the class as they tapped at their phones. "Got it," Lyla said.

"Way to go, Nerd."

"Hold on. Wait. Spec-what? We should Google *dating*? You sure?"

"Juan won't take out his phone," someone yelled.

"He probably has nude pictures on it." Brett grabbed Juan from behind, wriggled his phone out of his pocket, and tapped it. "Oh, my God." He held it high in the air. The students gasped. It was a neck-down picture of a naked girl, sitting on a bed with a Teddy bear between her legs.

Juan stood and grabbed for the phone, but Brett kicked him away.

"Give Juan his phone back right now," Nicole yelled, "or I'm going to report you to the principal."

"We should report Juan to the principal," Brett piped. "Who's your girlfriend, Juan, huh? Bet you'd like to change places with that Teddy bear."

Nicole held her hand out, and Brett put the phone into it with a smirk. She handed it back to Juan saying, "You probably shouldn't bring your phone to school any more. You could get into big trouble." Hands on hips, she added, "And, girls, everybody, I hope you see how disgusting this activity is and never, ever engage in this kind of behavior."

As she let this sink in, Nicole noticed Trisha, a shy, polite girl, staring down at her desk, her face flushed.

"**M**s. Ernst, into my office, please." Higgy's eyes were slits. He pointed to a chair in front of his paper-strewn desk. "I had a call from the school superintendent first thing this morning, Ms. Ernst. But then I guess you know that."

"No," she trilled. "But that's wonderful, Mr. Higgenbottom. Are you getting Principal of the Year?"

"The books, Ms. Ernst. You know what I'm talking about. The superintendent put me on the spot, acted surprised when I said we hadn't asked for the replacement texts to be delivered here yet."

Nicole met his narrow gaze. It was amazing how bold you could be when you felt you were on the point of losing your job anyway.

"And you know nothing about this, Ms. Ernst?"

"No," she lied.

"Because a few months ago a student told his mother he saw you talking to a reporter from the *Shady Park Ledger* in the cafeteria."

"And the mother called you to complain about that?"

"Ms. Ernst, this school has its public relations guidelines, and I intend to enforce them."

"Yes, Sir."

"I'm sure you know that many parents in this community oppose going back to the previous textbooks."

"Well, Mr. Higgenbottom, I understand your dilemma. But it might be for the best, don't you think? The students won't have to keep reading that negroes came here from Africa as migrant workers. We'll be able to use the word 'slave' again."

"Don't get smart, Ms. Ernst. You've already been warned about denying the Bible."

"Mr. Higgenbottom, Mr. Higgenbottom!" Higgy's office assistant rushed into the office. "A huge van just pulled up to the delivery entrance. The driver wants to know where he should load the books."

Principal and assistant brushed past Nicole towards the door, leaving Nicole trying to keep a straight face as she followed. She'd been afraid Higgy was going to bring up the sexting incidents. Maybe he wasn't aware of them yet.

Liz was already standing by the delivery platform. "Higgy seems a little annoyed, wouldn't you say, Nicole? Something tells me he wasn't the one who gave the order for these fact-based texts to be brought back."

Lloyd stood by the van directing the crew. He looked up.

"Did that man wink at you, Nicole? He looks like he's enjoying this."

"Is there a Principal Higgenbottom here?" Lloyd gave Higgy a paper that Nicole assumed was a notice from the school superintendent.

The crew wheeled one load after another onto the ramp. "Now clean the fundamentalist books out of the classroom," Lloyd shouted. "Get them all."

Realizing the delivery couldn't be turned back, Higgy found Nicole. "I'm blaming this on you, Ms. Ernst. I'm going to write up an official reprimand."

"For talking to a reporter in the cafeteria a few months ago?"

He stomped away without answering.

Before she went home, Nicole found a pink note in her mail slot. It was from Andre. *There's something I need to talk to you about,* he'd written. Followed by directions to his house and a phone number.

Liz was watching her. "You look upset. Bad news?"

The ink was already blurring from her moist fingers. Maybe Liz noticed. "No," Nicole said simply.

Liz gave her a look. "Don't mean to be nosey. No need to tell me."

Nicole hadn't mentioned Andre to Liz. The whole thing was too ridiculous. It meant nothing. She should crumple up the note and throw it away. But for some reason she shoved it into her backpack.

4

Being normal

The things we feel are different about ourselves are the things that are rare, that give us our value—and these are the things we try to repress.

—André Gide, *The Immoralist*

Nicole's yard, front and back, was planted with day lilies, tulips, hyacinths, and azaleas, rather than grass. In the summer, to cut the little bit of lawn between the bushes she used a weed whacker. In the fall, a few minutes of trimming took care of everything. In the winter, there was no maintenance at all.

She picked up Smokey, who greeted her with a purr and a head butt on her cheek. The scent of his fur made her think of Andre. She slipped the pink note from her backpack and studied the address. River Road.

Recently, Nicole had read lots of news about the development project along River Road that was exposed as a scam and halted, but she hadn't driven there to see for herself what damage had been done by bulldozers making room for the planned "executive villas." In fact, she hadn't been there since she was in her twenties. The fishermen who lived along the river then were happy to have picnickers spreading blankets on the beach across from their bungalows and wading in the water. Andre was one of the few who were left. He wasn't really a fisherman, though. What was he?

She drove tentatively over the light snow, bracing herself to view the destruction of the retreat she'd enjoyed so much in her younger days. Then, as she turned onto River Road, her spirits soared. The snow had whitened the leaves of the tall trees lining both sides of the road. It felt like driving through an enchanted tunnel.

Under the thin snow, the gravel and oyster shell road still crunched the way she remembered. That hadn't changed. There were scraped, empty lots, but snow hid the dirt, and some shoots of trees had already sprung up here and there. Nature was making a comeback. Rays of sun filtering through the gray clouds cast a platinum glow over the landscape.

There it was, the infamous villa Bea Doggit had built—planned as the first of many. Nicole's car skidded slightly as she crossed the smooth surface that had been laid down in front of the villa. Icicles dripped from the rooftop of the now abandoned house. A few more snow-clad lots, and then—that must be Andre's house at the end of the road.

She noticed her hands beginning to feel slippery on the steering wheel and tapped the brake lightly. The car slowed without skidding, then came to a stop. She was alone on the road, her car the first to make tracks in the light snow. The river sparkled below on one side of the road, small patches of snow-covered ice drifting up from the bay. It was beautiful. But what was she doing here?

Andre had something to ask her but didn't want to talk on the phone. Nicole looked out the car window. Everything around her was white. There wasn't a sound. No cars. No people. She could have been hidden in a cloud. She eased the car forward, her heart racing.

Just past Andre's house was a place where cars could turn around on this dead end road. Still no tire tracks anywhere. Near the house she noticed a little car which must be Andre's, still covered in snow. It couldn't have been moved for at least a couple of days. She pulled up beside it and sat, engine still running, trying to think. Too late to turn back now. He'd probably already seen her arrive. She stepped out onto the snow. No footprints in his front yard, no path to follow towards his door. She wondered if anybody was in there. Then she noticed a thin line of smoke snaking up from a stovepipe on the side of the house.

Stepping through the snow cautiously, trying to keep most of the weight off her bad leg, she reached the house. The door hung askew, with newspapers stuffed into the cracks. There was a rap at the window. A grinning Andre called out, "Mind coming in the back door? It works better. I'll come around."

He appeared around the side of the house in high yellow boots and legs bare from boot tops to the bottom of tight corduroy shorts. "Careful," he said, taking her cold fingers into his warm hand as they retraced his tracks to the back door. Nicole saw another set of tracks to and from that door leading to another cottage in the trees behind his.

A wave of heat shimmered up when he opened the back door. "I stoked up the fire so the house would be warm when you got here." It was so hot Nicole felt flushed and had to take her jacket off right away. Andre held one hand as she bent to take off her wet sneakers.

She stood behind a white wooden chair at a porcelain kitchen table that looked just like hers except it was smaller. It was set for two. Andre picked up a thick book titled *Abnormal Psychology* from the chair so she could sit. She wiped her moist hands on her jeans. "I didn't tell anybody I was coming here." It was more a warning to herself than a comment to Andre.

Andre cocked his head. "Oh. I told my mother you were coming." He pointed to a dish on the table. "She made us a casserole for lunch. She lives back there, that little house across the path." He spooned out two plates of macaroni casserole and nodded for her to begin eating. As the domesticity of the scene increased, Nicole began to breathe more freely.

She hated macaroni casserole, but it made the visit feel more conventional. As opposed, say, to the yellow boots, bare legs, and abnormal psychology book.

His eyes were clear blue now, no tears or sneezing. But she noticed a black and red bruise across his cheek bone.

"Your face," Nicole said. "What happened?"

"Oh, it's nothing."

"It looks like you've been in a fight."

His fork held in the air, Andre began, "Physical violence, psychologists say, is a reversion to our primitive instincts." He put down his fork and spooned more macaroni onto her plate. Apparently, he felt that was a sufficient answer.

"Does it hurt? Can't you tell me what happened?"

He didn't seem to hear. The wheels of his mind were running on their own track. He said, "It's as if he's fighting things inside himself. Exteriorizing his inner conflict."

"Andre, who are you talking about?"

"It's a shame. That device he has to wear on his ankle. And he's not allowed to leave Piskasanet County."

Nicole put down her fork. "Who in the world are you talking about?"

Andre cocked his head as if puzzled she didn't understand. "That boy who was arrested."

Nicole remembered Andre walking over to a car after leaving the Grab 'n Go with her and talking to the driver. "Willard Scherd? Do you know him?"

Andre gave a tight-lipped nod.

"You mean you knew him before that Yaldā night?"

He stared at his plate, forking pieces of macaroni from one side to the other.

"How did you ever get to know him? He's a high school kid."

Andre continued with his own train of thought. "He needs love. He's tough on the outside. But he's soft inside when you get to know him."

Nicole's head was spinning. He was talking about the person who was about to shoot a woman he didn't even know simply because she was wearing a hejab. "Andre, when a man at the meeting reached for a gun to stop Willard from shooting that woman, the gun went off in the man's pocket and hit me in the leg. Willard Scherd is the reason I still walk with a little limp."

Andre sighed. She wasn't sure he'd heard her. "Willard's been expelled from school. I'm sure you know. I was wondering if you could write a letter requesting he be readmitted."

"That's what you wanted to ask me?" Nicole's voice was throaty. "Willard *was* let back in school after the *first* arrest, Andre. Then he carried a gun to school in his back pack. He's had his second chance."

Andre's blue eyes clouded. "I know. I thought maybe—"

"I just don't think he's ready to come back to school yet."

Andre only looked at the floor.

She said, "I still don't understand how you … where did you meet him?"

His mind was somewhere else. His lips were pursed as if he were trying to work up courage.

"Andre, what is it?"

He breathed out a sigh. "There's something I should have told you."

Probably lots of women on a date had heard these words before. *I'm married. I have a criminal record. I'm into kinky stuff.* But this wasn't a date, was it? She felt a chill and folded her arms. "Go ahead, I guess. Tell me."

"I don't know."

She was tempted to get up and leave, but her curiosity was getting the best of her. "You can tell me."

He pressed his finger tips together. "It's …. Don't hate me." His light brown eyebrows arched.

"Just tell me."

"All right. I'm gay."

The declaration made sense if they were on a date, she guessed. But since they weren't, why would he be embarrassed about it?

"I mean, definitely, if I could experience heterosexual love, it's with a person like you. Kind, understanding, a woman I could love."

Nicole's brain was short-circuiting. She kept her mouth shut while the neurons and dendrons tried to sort themselves out in her head.

"I'm sexually attracted to you," he added, as if to be perfectly clear.

Nicole tensed. She didn't know where this was leading. She didn't even know what she was doing here. She glanced nervously at the kitchen door, then back at Andre, her cheeks burning hot.

Andre lowered his eyes. "For a long time I had a close friend. Johan. A teacher. One day he broke up with me. And just disappeared. I've been a little crazy ever since." Andre hung his head. "I'd give anything not to be gay, to be normal." He dabbed his eyes with a handkerchief.

Nicole's throat thickened. "Hey, Andre, don't wish that. You are normal. That's a terrible thing to say." She put her arm on his shoulder.

He took her hand and kissed it. "I'm sorry, Nicole. "I think something about you reminded me of Johan. Things were getting mixed up in my head."

The vision of his troubled blue eyes stayed with her all the way home.

5

Sweet dreams

The dream has no way at all of expressing the alternative 'either … or.' It usually takes up the two options into one context as if they had equal rights.
—Sigmund Freud, *The Interpretation of Dreams*

Nicole started having strange dreams after going to see Andre. Higgy giving her detention. Brett's mother riding a dinosaur. Andre heaping more and more macaroni casserole onto her plate, grinning. She would wake up in the middle of the night trying to make sense of the dreams. Maybe she needed a break.

There were only a few more school days before the Christmas vacation. The students had stopped doing any homework more than a week ago. And as interesting as Nicole found carbon dating, she couldn't capture their attention. The girls sat at their desks drawing Christmas or other holiday cards. The boys mainly competed to see who could emit the loudest digestive gas noises. Only Wally was paying attention to Nicole. She taught the lesson to him. Better to light one candle?

Juan wasn't in class. She hoped he hadn't been traumatized by the phone incident. She still thought she'd been right to tell him not to bring his phone to school any more. It didn't seem he'd need it, anyway. He wasn't one of those kids whose mothers kept calling them all day long.

Then she saw him in the hall after class. He turned away and hurried down a different corridor. Angry? Or maybe ashamed? He shouldn't be. Nicole was fretting about this when she went to the teachers' room to pick up her lunch bag.

Higgy was waiting. He spoke with his lips stuck out like he was sucking a lemon. "Another complaint about your class I've had to deal with, Ms. Ernst. Unbelievable. A mother called to report you're letting your students pass obscene pictures around the classroom."

Nicole shook her head in denial but didn't reply. She knew Higgy didn't want to hear any explanation.

"You didn't take the student's phone away from him like you should have."

"Because he was keeping it in his pocket, turned off. It wasn't his fault somebody took it from his pocket and waved it around."

"No excuses, Ms. Ernst." He took another suck of an air lemon. "No matter. I called the culprit, Juan Moreno, to the office. He claimed he'd left his phone home today, so I sent him to get it. I have it now." Higgy pulled a phone from his pocket and slapped it into his hand. "I've already called Reverend Blatchford on the board of education. He's very concerned about this sexting among teens. It'll be interesting to hear what he has to say." Higgy turned abruptly and went back to his office, leaving Nicole standing with her lips parted.

She didn't have lunch duty that day, so she went out and sat in her car to choke down her ham and cheese sandwich. She texted Pari to thank her for the winter solstice invitation. An answer came back immediately: *Could I stop by your house after school today?*

If people were going to start dropping in to visit her, Nicole supposed she might do well to get a couch. For now, though, she and Pari sat at the kitchen table.

Pari had worked hard to get the fundamentalist textbooks out of Piskasanet County schools. She was younger than Nicole, and a relatively new reporter, but she'd already learned

how politics in the county worked and was a tireless opponent of corruption. It was largely her blog that had exposed
Beatrice Doggit for illegally voting with the board of education to change all the county science and social studies textbooks to the Bible-based books that she herself published and
profited from.

When Nicole described how panicky Higgy was that parents would complain now that the fundamentalist texts were
replaced, Pari seemed sympathetic. "I guess it's hard to run a
school with the parents looking over your shoulder."

Nicole agreed it wasn't a job she'd ever want.

Pari tossed her dark brown pony tail off her shoulder and
opened her notebook. She was just a kid, not long out of
college, but the notebook always made Nicole nervous. Pari
drew a line under something she'd written. "Still, we can't
have Piskasanet County kids being taught that God created
women to serve men, or that gay people are an abomination."

Nicole laughed. "Well, luckily most students don't read
the texts anyway." She stretched out her leg, and Pari asked
how it was feeling.

"Much better. I go for a checkup next month. It doesn't
really hurt any more. Just a little stiff."

Surprisingly, Pari even wrote that down. "Anything else
going on at school?"

Nicole thought of Juan—perfectly innocent, yet now it
looked like he was headed for trouble. She told Pari about the
nude pictures and his phone being confiscated. "I can't give
you his name. He's still 15 years old. I'm afraid Rev. Blatchford on the school board will blow this out of proportion."

Pari finished writing. Then she told Nicole, "Our editor,
Ralph, has a 10-year-old son. Bobby told Ralph there's some
sexting going on right here in Shady Park schools. Ralph's
looking into the legal side of this before he gives the story to
Anthony or me. It's kind of a delicate matter—these are just

kids. I'm sure Ralph'll be interested in what's going on in other schools, too." Pari took out her phone. "Mind if I call him?"

Nicole must have looked like she'd seen a ghost.

"Don't worry. Ralph wrote the book on being discreet." Pari called but had to leave a message for Ralph to "call Nicole Ernst about sexting at Northbrook High." She gave him Nicole's number.

Nicole checked her phone battery. 78%. She plugged it into the charger just in case. There was no telling when Ralph would call. Or which day.

Smokey meowed for his dinner. He liked to eat precisely at 5:00. Nicole usually ate with him, sometimes sharing a can of tuna fish, hers on bread with mayonnaise, but Smokey now favored Filet of Yellowtail. Nicole wasn't hungry right now. She wondered what time Ralph ate dinner. What he ate. She turned on the TV in her bedroom and sat on the bed to watch—no couch.

"WCTY weather, news, sports. Here. Now." Nicole preferred the City to the local Piskasanet County news. "Here with the latest on the snow is *meter-ologist* Victoria Whitman. Victoria, what can you tell us?"

A pretty young girl with long blond hair in a stunning purple dress said, "Ashley, it looks like it's going to be more of the same. Light to moderate scatterings over the area adding another one or two inches to what we've already had." She repeated this, with a map behind her this time, then as she started to read off the information posted at the bottom of the screen (for the visually impaired?), Nicole turned off the TV. She felt fidgety, unable to concentrate.

She slid open the nightstand drawer and picked up the card Ralph had given her. There was no reason she couldn't have called him all this time. Except what exactly would she say? I love the way your kind eyes focus on me when I talk? I love your smile when you talk about your son? Nicole felt bolder these days, but her cheeks burned even at the thought of saying things like that.

She must have drifted off because she had a crazy dream that Ralph—it seemed to be him—was examining a nude photo of her on his phone. She was mortified but, more than that, afraid he might not like what he saw. Then the phone Ralph was holding rang.

It was the phone on her table, waking her up. She was propped up against a pillow, notes on carbon dating scattered across her lap.

Her "Hello" came out in a trembling alto.

"Ms. Ernst? It's Ralph Novich."

"Hi. It's Nicole." She sat up straighter against the head-board. "Pari told me you might call."

She was surprised when he started chatting about the weather. "Bobby loves snow. Likes me to drive him up to the community college, go sleigh riding down the big hill with him. You ever been there?"

"Sure. I used to go sleigh riding down that hill all the time."

"Reminds me. How's your leg? Pari says it's getting better."

"Yes. Much better. Thanks."

"Guess you saw the Arm-the-Teachers bill never made it to the state senate floor?"

"Yes. Your *Shady Park Ledger* was a big help."

"You should thank Pari and Anthony for that." Ralph paused. Nicole imagined him touching the edge of his black moustache. He said, "Bobby talks about you a lot. We're both really sorry you got transferred up to Northbrook." He cleared his throat. "I still remember it was nice talking to you at that parent-teacher open house. And when I interviewed you."

"Oh. Yes."

"Christmas, or I should say Winter Holiday's coming up soon. Any special plans?"

"No. I'll be staying here. My parents are going on a cruise they've been planning for years."

It felt like he'd just called to chat. Was that something all newspaper editors did? To put you at ease or whatever?

"So," he said. "Pari tells me your principal—Matthew Higgenbottom, right? Two Gs, two Ts? Says he's going to turn your student's phone over to Reverend Blatchford on the education board."

"I'm afraid so."

"So you know the Reverend? I've done some checking on him. Young girls sending guys naked pictures—that's just the kind of thing he loves to hate."

Nicole's hands were sweaty.

Ralph went on. "Bobby hasn't seen any of the pictures the kids are sending. I haven't either. Pari tells me you have?"

"I've seen two."

Ralph waited.

"Do you want me to describe them?"

"If you don't mind. Your name will never be used."

"The pictures I saw looked like a girl only about 13 or 14."

She was pretty sure she heard Ralph gasp.

"Neither showed a face. Just the little breasts."

"Do you think you can get the student who received the pictures to talk to me? Off the record, of course."

"I doubt it. He doesn't seem to want the girl to get in trouble."

"I understand." He paused. "I'd like to talk to you in person, though. If you're willing."

Oh, she was more than willing. But if Higgy found out she

was talking to the editor of the *Shady Park Ledger*—"

"Ms. ... uh Nicole?"

"I'm here. Sorry, just thinking. My principal ordered the teachers and staff not to talk to the press. I know he can't do that, but he can make it hard for anybody who disobeys."

"I understand."

"But maybe if nobody knows ...."

"We can meet privately. Definitely."

"Let me think." She meant only for a minute. But Ralph said, "Sure, Nicole. I wouldn't want to pressure you. Think it over and give me a call any time."

Nicole clasped his hand to her racing heart, a sensual delight flowing through her body. It was Andre, or seemed so at first. Then a moustache caressed her lips, and it seemed it had been Ralph all along. As the thrill intensified, she called out his name.

Slowly, reluctantly, she was drawn back into consciousness. When she opened her eyes, she felt Smokey's tail twitching across her face. She squinted in the morning light, then closed her eyes again, hoping to re-enter the dream. It wasn't possible. But the experience had been so vivid it lingered in her mind as if it had been real. The line between fantasy and reality remained blurred until long after she took a shower and dressed for school.

6

Squatters

*Love is the flower of life, and blossoms unexpectedly
and without law, and must be plucked where it is found,
and enjoyed for the brief hour of its duration.*
                    —D. H. Lawrence, *The Rainbow*

It was the last day of school before the holiday. Nicole
had a demonstration to perform for her class. She'd brought
a glass from home and filled it halfway with water from the
fountain in the hallway. The water always came out rusty at
first because nobody under 40 years old—except Nicole, it
seemed—used water fountains any more. They carried their
own water in plastic bottles. Nicole tried to imagine the first
time a business proposal was presented to sell bottles of water. The guy must have been laughed out of the conference
room. Yet somehow the ad agencies had managed to convince
the public that water is better if you buy it in stores.

She let the water in the glass stay rusty. "Here's something to give you a basic idea of the theory of carbon dating,"
she told the class. Most were listening because of the prop.
"What if I tell you this glass was once full? OK?"

"Drink it," Brett called out. But most of the class waited
in silence to see what she was up to.

"How long do you think it took the water to evaporate
down to this level? How would you figure that out?"

Wally raised his hand. "See how much evaporates in one
day. Then measure—"

"How 'organic' the water is," Brett shouted.

Nicole ignored this and continued the discussion with Wally. Some in the class kept listening. More of them than usual, actually.

After class, she caught Juan in the hallway. He stood head-down, as if waiting to be scolded.

"Juan, the principal says he took your phone. I'm so sorry."

Juan backed up against a row of lockers and spoke in a murmur. "I should have thrown it away. Now he's going to give it to a school board member."

"It's not your fault you get the pictures, it seems to me."

"But now this guy has the phone. What if the girl keeps sending pictures? I mean I'm sure she will. I finally set a password, but I don't know how secure that is."

"How about canceling your phone service?"

"I keep trying. Press this number, press that number. When I get a person to talk to, they say they can't handle cancelations. They give me the same 800 number to call that I called in the first place."

"Tell you what. Here. Take my phone and call the girl right now. Tell her the situation."

"OK. She's in school. I'll have to leave a message." His message was, "Some preacher guy has my phone. For your own good, you need to stop sending pictures right away. I'm serious."

"Juan, I'd like to drive you home today. Do you mind? Don't tell anybody. My car's the one in the teachers' section with the yellow tennis ball on the antenna."

She assumed he lived in the Northbrook Apartments, where most of the immigrant families stayed, and she was right. On the way, she stopped at the Econo Mart and led him through the aisles until she found what she was looking for. "Here, Juan." She took a $9.97 Tracfone from a display next to gift cards, scented candles, and Chinese batteries. "An early Christmas present." She read from the package. "Phone calls and text messages only. No pictures. New phone number. Fifty minutes startup airtime. Pay as you go. No contract."

"A burner phone," Juan laughed. "Thank you, Ms. Ernst. My mother said I should bring *you* a Christmas present. I told her students don't do that in the States. I'm sorry. I should have brought it. It was cookies she baked."

"Maybe I should move to Guatemala."

"Yeah, but there are some disadvantages there, too, nowadays."

Back in Shady Park, Nicole stopped at Nielsen's open-air vegetable and flower market, which sold nothing but holly wreaths, poinsettia, and Christmas trees this time of year. She was hoping to find a tree small enough to fit in her car. Every year it seemed less worth the trouble to put up a tree. Maybe she'd settle for a wreath on her door.

"Ms. Ernst. Ms. Ernst." Bobby Novich ran up to her. "Dad, it's Ms. Ernst."

Ralph peeped out from behind a huge Christmas tree. "Ah. Ms. um Nicole." He let the tree fall back against the rack. "So glad to run into you like this." To Nicole, it seemed he held her hand longer than what a conventional handshake required. It might have been her imagination.

Bobby pulled at Ralph's jacket. "Dad, can Ms. Ernst come to our house tomorrow for Christmas Eve?"

Ralph studied Nicole as if giving her a chance to decline before he said anything. She looked at him with pursed lips and widened eyes. She had absolutely nothing to do on Christmas Eve. She usually went to her parents' house. If not, Liz would invite her over. But this year Liz and her husband were visiting friends.

"Dad's afraid to ask you," Bobby taunted. "Aren't you,

Dad?"

Ralph nodded.

"I'd love to come."

Bobby gave his dad a high-five.

She hung a wreath on her door. Done. Now to the Hair Salon, then to Dress Barn before they closed. She hardly ever bought new clothes because she never liked anything she saw. No ... no ... no. Then, there it was. A simple black dress with thin white piping on the collar and front, not formal but a little dressier than casual. She looked in the fitting room mirror. The neckline was lower than what she usually wore. It looked good, though. She leaned in closer. Maybe some new earrings.

Smokey added some gray hairs to her outfit which she brushed off on the way to the car. There was a light sprinkling of snow, not predicted by Victoria Whitman. She looked in the rear view mirror and brushed some flakes from the outward curls of her new "fringed layered" hairdo. Ralph had given her the address. "Right behind the *Ledger* building."

There was no driveway, just a graveled space beside the house where a car was parked. Nicole drove across the sidewalk and parked next to it. She noticed an old garage far in the back yard—probably designed to house a horse-drawn carriage. A basketball hoop now hung over its door.

The brown cedar shake house was three stories high, probably built not long after the First World War. It looked like it had been made for a family of eight. Nicole imagined the boys in knickers, the girls in pinafores, and the mother in a rocking chair on the wide wrap-around porch, knitting or crocheting. But the only people who lived there now were Ralph and Bobby.

The large windows were curtainless, but the house sat high, allowing passers-by a view of nothing but a tarnished chandelier hanging from a high ceiling. The gray wooden stairs sagged and creaked as Nicole mounted to the porch, which not only sagged and creaked but slanted. There was a thick door knocker, but Nicole preferred to announce herself with a quieter rap of her hand. She heard floors creak inside, then, with two separate yanks, the heavy door swung open, rattling the knocker anyway. Bobby called out, "Dad, she's here." He had to put his hip to the door to get it to close all the way.

"Take her coat and show her to a seat," she heard Ralph call out from a darkened room at the other side of the hall. "I'm almost finished."

Bobby led her into the living room, their steps resounding on the bare wide-planked floor, towards a red velvet Victorian couch with elaborately carved mahogany crest, arms, and legs. It looked like something ladies would be expected to sit on with back straight, knees together, and hands on lap clutching a tiny beaded purse.

"I usually sit on this," Bobby remarked when Nicole seemed to hesitate. He pounced onto an orange beanbag chair, squirmed deep into it, and said it was "way more comfortable." He got up. "Want to try?"

"This is fine, Bobby." She sat on the couch and could feel the springs contract bouncily with a low, twanging sound. No beaded purse, but she did keep her knees together, mainly because it was a little chilly in the cavernous, near-empty room.

"Dad really likes you."

Nicole's face felt warm.

"Ready?" Ralph called out from the other side of the hallway. A lighted Christmas tree suddenly materialized in the dark room. Bobby clapped. So did Nicole.

Bobby led her into the large, dark room to admire the tree. The only items besides the tree were two green World War II army surplus desks, one with a laptop on it, and one piled with newspapers. Bobby knelt in front of some wrapped presents. "These are for me. This one's for Dad. From me."

"And I brought one for you, Bobby. It's in my coat pocket."

"Can I get it?"

When Bobby ran to the coatrack, Ralph said, "You look, um. In this light, you—"

Bobby came back. "I'm sure it's a book." He held it up. "Can I open it?"

Tree lights glimmered in the depths of Ralph's questioning eyes. Nicole nodded.

"*Treasure Island*. Thanks, Ms. Ernst."

"I hope you like it. No aliens, vampires, monsters, or super heroes. But it does have pirates, and they're real."

"There's no Reading Circle any more after you left my school, Ms. Ernst. I wish you would come back. Can we read it tonight, Dad?"

Ralph hedged. "Maybe. We'll have to see."

They ate at a table with a red and white checkered tablecloth in an echoing dining room lit dimly by wall fixtures that Nicole assumed had been converted from gas lights. "We mainly eat at the kitchen counter," Bobby explained, "even on Christmas Eve."

Ralph had cooked chicken alfredo lasagna. "One of the few things I learned how to make," he admitted. Bobby added, "We often dine on gourmet fried chicken from the Grab 'n Go."

Ralph touched one end of his thin moustache. "I have wine. I don't know if you—"

"I'd love some."

Ralph beamed, pouring two glasses of Chianti from a basket-clad bottle. It felt like they were eating in an Italian restaurant.

"My mother's Italian," Bobby told her. "She lives in Virginia now."

Ralph spilled some drops of wine on the tablecloth. Nicole rested her hand on his back as she dabbed up the wine with her paper napkin. Ever since that Persian vigil at Pari's house she kept surprising herself.

The lasagna was great. Nicole even took another small helping. And a second glass of wine. Bobby said, "Ms. Ernst, there's something crazy going on at my school."

Nicole waited.

"These pictures some girls are sending."

"Your dad told me about it. They're not sending them to you, I hope."

"No. Mostly to seventh and eighth graders."

"You haven't seen the pictures, your dad says."

"Not until yesterday." Bobby's face turned red. "I didn't tell you yet, Dad. When I was walking to the bus, an eighth-grader showed me one. It was, you know, boobs."

Ralph's eyes widened. "Who, Bobby? Who showed you that?"

"She told me not to tell. She just said, "Want to see something? Then she turned her phone right off."

"She shouldn't be doing that, Bobby. I think you should tell the principal."

Nicole agreed.

Bobby shook his head. "I don't want to be a snitch."

"Hmm." Ralph seemed more sympathetic to this line of argument than Nicole.

"Anyway," Bobby said, "it was just boobs."

Ralph's smile turned to a frown. "Nicole, do you think Bobby could get into trouble. I mean for not reporting this to his principal?"

"I guess not."

Ralph stood up. "Oaky doaky, then. Well. What do you say we read some of that book? Maybe Ms. Ernst will read a little."

Nicole took *Treasure Island* to the Victorian couch, expecting Bobby to sit next to her, but he wiggled into the beanbag. Ralph avoided the couch, too, and sat in a tattered wing chair. "We never use that couch," Bobby informed her. "It's from Mom's mother. Mom left it here even though Dad said he didn't want it."

"Right," Ralph said. "Let's start the story. I loved that book when I was your age."

Not long after Nicole started reading, Bobby's eyes drooped. Soon he was asleep.

"Come on up to bed, Buddy." Ralph shook him. "Won't be long, Nicole." At the top of the stairs, he turned and called down, "Would you mark that place? Bobby and I want to hear you read the whole book."

Could he be serious? That would mean …. She went into the kitchen to wash the dishes, surprised to see nothing but a wrench, hammer, and can of Plumber's Putty on the kitchen table, surprised also by the long cast iron, wall-mounted sink—so old it was rough when she ran her hand over it. Nobody had these any more.

The sink, the mostly empty rooms, the bare floors, the old-fashioned flowered wallpaper everywhere—Ralph and Bobby seemed like squatters living in an abandoned house. She couldn't believe she was here.

"Hey, no." Ralph pulled her from the sink. "Leave the rest. Please, Nicole." He turned her around, drying her hands on his starchy white shirt front, holding them there. "I was thinking … sometimes I sit on the porch a while at night. Do you want to?"

They put on their coats. The air was clear. Specks of snow melting off the leaves were lit by the single street light. The street was hushed by the snow, not a soul outside at this time on a Christmas Eve night. They sat on a wooden swing hanging from the porch roof. "Peaceful, huh?" Ralph said. "This is my time to think."

"What are you thinking now?"

"Crazy things."

"Did you used to sit here with your wife?"

"No, I only started doing it after she left. Sometimes, actually, I think of you."

Nicole shivered. He put his arm around her. "Too cold out here?"

She shook her head and snuggled closer. "Would you have asked me here if Bobby hadn't said anything first?"

Ralph sighed. "Probably not. I wanted to but never did."

Nicole felt mischievous. "You wanted to? Why?"

Ralph sputtered. "Why? Because, you know, because you're ...."

"Hmm?"

"So pretty and stuff. Bobby's words."

"Kids, huh?"

Ralph gazed into the distance. "Bobby said something else. Want to know what it was?"

Nicole studied the street light reflection in his eyes.

"He said I should try to get you to stay here tonight so you'd be here on Christmas morning."

Nicole took a sharp breath. Things were moving faster than she expected. She started to say she'd come back the next morning. But would that give Ralph the wrong message? Maybe she'd never get another chance. She thought of a phrase she'd read recently: *the flower of love blossoms unexpectedly and must be plucked where it is found.* The new, bolder Nicole took over. She lifted her head, and Ralph kissed her.

His bedroom had a musty smell. He pulled down the window shade and kicked some dirty clothes into a corner. The room was lit only by the street lamp streaming faintly through some rips in the shade. They kissed again, Nicole thrilling to the touch of his soft moustache on her lips. Ralph seemed bolder now that he was sure she wanted his kisses. He said, "You're beautiful, Nicole. Your eyes, your hair shining in the lamp light." His hands touched her arms. "Your skin is so smooth."

Nicole put her arms around his neck, holding her breath, letting him delicately unbutton her dress. This was really happening. He unhooked her bra, with some help, and stood back holding her hands. "Beautiful," he said, as if admiring a statue. He tossed his shirt onto the dirty clothes pile.

"I like the way you look, too, Ralph."

Ralph turned the skeleton key in the door.

"Hello. Hello. Merry Christmas. Are you guys still asleep up there?"

Nicole sat up in bed, heart racing. "Ralph, who's that? Some woman."

Ralph rubbed his eyes.

"Hello. Ralph. Bobby."

Ralph jumped out of bed, pulled on his trousers, struggled with the key. "Stay here a minute." As if there was anywhere Nicole could flee to. She heard Bobby running downstairs after his father. It probably wouldn't be the first time an ex-wife dropped in to see her son on Christmas. Nicole raced to put on her dress. She listened at the door. Christmas music, tinny sounding as if from a small radio or even a cell phone. Excited conversation that she couldn't make out. She peeped out the door, listening. She couldn't stay upstairs all day. Besides, her car was parked in the yard. She looked down the hallway and saw a bathroom, where she did her best to straighten herself out in front of the cracked mirror. Now there was nothing to do but walk down the stairs.

A dark-haired woman with frameless glasses said, "Oh."

"Beth," Ralph said, "this is my friend Nicole."

"Oh," Beth repeated. "Oh. Merry Christmas."

"My sister," Ralph explained. "Beth always comes here to eat Christmas breakfast with us. Which she brings with her."

"And cookies," Bobby said. "And egg nog. You're staying, aren't you?"

Ralph gave Nicole a good-morning kiss on the cheek.

"Oh!" Beth said. Nicole's mouth formed an O, too, but the word didn't come out.

Ralph's older sister lived nearby and came every day to stay with Bobby after school until Ralph got home. "Makes me feel less like an empty nester," she told Nicole. "I'm getting better at shooting hoops, too."

"Come sleigh riding with us, Aunt Beth."

She couldn't. Had to get back home.

"You're coming, aren't you, Ms. Ernst? Up on the community college hill?"

Nicole glanced at Ralph. The problem was, all the kids in Shady Park knew about that hill, including her own former students. Teachers were recognized everywhere they went. If word spread as far as Northbrook that she was a friend of the *Ledger*'s editor, her principal would have more evidence to accuse her of violating his policy against teachers talking to the press.

"Is there really enough snow?"

"We don't need much," Bobby insisted.

There was barely enough snow, but the slope was crowded. Nicole should have realized Pari and Anthony would be there, too, since Pari's house was just beyond the trees at the bottom of the hill.

"Won't be much reporting for the *Shady Park Ledger* today," Ralph quipped. But Anthony snapped some pictures with his phone, said he'd load them onto the newsroom server that evening: "Christmas Sleigh Riding in Shady Park." He got the names of everyone in the pictures.

Pari took a picture of Nicole, Ralph, and Bobby. It was really cute. But Nicole asked her not to put it in the paper.

Pari smiled. "No worries. Here, let me send it to you, though."

Two kids in matching red earmuffs planted themselves in front of Nicole.

"Hi, Ms. Ernst."

"You like sleigh riding, Ms. Ernst?"

"Are you coming back to teach in Shady Park, Ms. Ernst?"

They looked back and forth between her and Ralph as if it was obvious what they wanted to know. But they didn't ask.

A woman about her age came up with her dark haired, hatless son. It was her friend Emma and Todd.

"Nicole! I didn't expect to see you here."

"Hi, Ms. Ernst."

Pari and Anthony knew Emma and her family even better than Nicole did. "Hey, Todd," Anthony said. "That sled looks fast."

"It is. Where's your sled, Ms. Ernst?"

"Oh, um, I'm sharing ...." She pointed to Bobby's sled. Emma gave a significant nod.

So much for keeping things on the downlow—her students' term.

Nicole knew walking back up the hill would be a challenge for her leg and said she'd just watch. Ralph liked to lie on the sled and take Bobby on his back. "More steady this way." Then Pari started riding on top of Anthony. After a few trips, everybody insisted Nicole take a turn.

"Come on, Ms. Ernst."

"Yeah, come on."

She badly wanted to take a turn. It didn't make any sense to be just standing there. Besides, a fine rain was starting to fall. Everybody would be going home soon. "I'll ride the 'steady way,'" she said and plopped onto Ralph's back. From the corner of her eye, she saw Pari and Anthony staring in disbelief.

It was a wild, rainy ride down. She held Ralph tight, her legs hugging his as the sled bumped and rocked first up onto one runner, then the other. Every bounce sent a memory of last night through her body. When they came to a stop, she didn't want to get off. She gave Ralph a surreptitious kiss on the cheek before she did.

She slipped after only a few steps back up the hill. "Here," Ralph told her. "Don't even try. Hop up, piggy back." He trudged up the hill planting one foot after another, Nicole trailing the sled by its rope. It was raining harder by the time they got to the top. Bobby, Pari, Anthony, and some others applauded when he put her down.

7

Lusts of the flesh

"I have a Master to serve whose kingdom is not of this world: my mission is to mortify in these girls the lusts of the flesh; to teach them to clothe themselves with shame-facedness and sobriety ...."

—Charlotte Bronte, *Jane Eyre*

Before she got in her car, Ralph invited her to come back to his house for leftover lasagna.

"I'm soaking wet," she apologized. "And tired. I need to go home, warm up in the shower, and get into some dry pajamas."

"I'll bring it to your house, then. My sister invited Bobby to stay over with her."

"She did?"

"Uh-huh. And ... I want to see you in your pajamas."

Recalling those huskily uttered words transformed her shower into a heightened sensual experience. She wiped off the steamy mirror and dried off slowly, observing her body with fresh eyes. Ralph's eyes.

A knock at the door. She'd wanted to put on the silk raspberry nightgown she'd bought long ago. It was somewhere in the bottom drawer. She dug through skimpy tank tops, tight shorts, push up bras—the pile of clothes she was too shy ever to wear—but couldn't find it.

Another knock, louder.

She didn't want Ralph to think she'd fallen asleep or anything, so she tightened the towel around her and went to the door.

Andre stood there, eyes glaring in the portico light like the daemonic incarnation of her lust.

Nicole felt her skin turn to goosebumps. Andre didn't seem to notice she was half naked and shivering from the cold air. "I can't come in," he was saying. "The allergy is worse in winter, possibly because the dryness of the nasal mucosa—"

"Andre, I can't keep the door open. You'll have to come inside, or, better, come back another day."

He held a handkerchief over his face, ventured a step through the doorway, and mumbled, "This is important."

"Just move a little so I can close the door." When this didn't seem to register, she gave his arm a tug.

Andre was still mumbling through the handkerchief. "Sponsors of immigrant families are simply responsible for their financial welfare, of course, but bonds develop which—"

"Andre, I'm expecting somebody. I'll call you tomorrow. Right now I'm going to have to ask you to leave."

"But—" His objection was cut short by a wheezing gasp and rattling sneeze. Still holding his handkerchief to his face, he nodded sadly and left.

With a sigh of relief, Nicole threw herself down on her bed. Smokey climbed onto the towel covering her legs and settled down, purring, assuming they were in bed for the night. He seemed annoyed when Nicole sat up staring at her phone, wondering why Ralph hadn't come by yet. He'd said he'd be right over.

She smiled at the picture Pari had texted her. A happy family, it looked like. And that's how she'd already started to feel. But maybe she was moving too fast. According to Liz, when you dropped pebbles into a man's emotions, they didn't always send out ripples like stones in a pool of water. They often just sank without a stir.

She decided to wait a little longer before calling Ralph.

Then, as soon as she'd decided that, she called.

"I did drive over," Ralph explained. "There was a car out front. Somebody was just going in the door. Figured you had company. Didn't want to intrude."

"Oh. It was just—"

"I know you've been told not to talk to the press. That's why I turned back."

"It was nothing. I'm alone now."

"Oh. OK. I'm on my way."

"And, Ralph, forget the lasagna. I'm not hungry."

She opened the door still wrapped in her towel. Why not? She'd already met Andre like this—with nary a ripple set off in his emotional pool. Maybe Ralph ....

The paper bag he'd brought slipped out of his hand. He pulled her close, and the loosened towel dropped onto the rug. He'd kissed her the night before—in the dark bedroom of his curious house. The unfamiliar setting intensified the thrill. But the pleasure was mixed with trepidation. When they made love, she'd sensed it in him, too. Tonight felt different.

His belt buckle was cold on her stomach. "I want to look at you, too," she coaxed. They didn't make it beyond the white towel on the floor. Nicole abandoned herself in a way she'd never thought possible and finished gasping, her breast resting on the fine black hair of Ralph's chest.

"Am I too heavy?" she purred.

"No. This is fine, just like this."

"For how long?"

"Forever."

Smokey's meow woke her up. They were in her bed. She had one leg thrown over Ralph. After a momentary pulse of confusion, the memory of their night of love-making flooded back. "Go away, Smokey," she whispered. "Too early for breakfast."

Ralph stirred, blinked, patted his head for his missing reading glasses. Smiled. "Nicole."

She rested her head on his chest. "Hi, Ralph."

Unbelievably, she was stirred again by the feel of his hand on her back, on her hip, on her leg. And she knew he could tell. It was 10:00 before they got out of bed. Smokey was outraged. He'd tipped over his bowl. Nicole gave him some Ocean Whitefish in Sauce Normande, his current favorite, and made a cheese omelet for her and Ralph. Sitting across from him felt like they were on their first date. "So," she grinned, "tell me about yourself. Novich. What kind of name is that?"

"Slovak. My father emigrated from Bratislava to Pittsburgh. He started a Slovak-Czech newspaper there after the Second World War. *News from Home.* That sort of thing."

"How did you end up in Shady Park?"

"The paper folded. Only the old people could read Slovak. My father didn't want to work in the mines. He brought us here to live with his cousin. He got a job delivering the *Shady Park Ledger.*"

Nicole filled his coffee cup.

"Great coffee," Ralph said. He pulled at the tip of his moustache. "I meant to bring some Dobosh cookies my sister made. Guess I forgot."

"Unless they were in that bag you dropped on the floor last night. You know, when you came in and saw me dressed only in—"

"Dropped?" Ralph's cheeks reddened. "I'll go check." He came back with the bag, partly torn. "Looks like the cat took a bite of one."

"I'll eat that one." They were chocolate covered and delicious. "Hope you saved some for Bobby."

He gave a quick nod and checked his watch. "Guess I

should get in to the newsroom. They'll be wondering where I am. I'm never late."

Nicole swallowed a lump of disappointment. "No holiday for the press, I guess."

"Not until after New Year's. All these after-Christmas sales, you know."

"Mm."

"I did want to tell you what I've learned about Reverend Blatchford. The guy who has your student's phone?"

"I've seen him at board of education meetings. Little man, bow tie, natty dresser."

"Right. He's not with any church. Doctor of Divinity from some school in the Midwest. He ministers to incarcerated people, mainly to delinquent girls at the Wilcox Center in the neighboring county. Maybe you've seen some articles in the *Ledger* about the Wilcox? Overcrowded. Girls sleeping in the hallways. Petty shoplifters mixed in with hardened prostitutes. They won't let reporters in there any more."

"Sounds terrible."

"I'd like to know more about what goes on there." Ralph finished his coffee and gave his moustache a tweak. "Maybe you can help. You're not a reporter. They'd probably let you in."

Nicole must have looked doubtful.

"For example, if you said you wanted to give Rev. Blatchford some information you have about sexting in the schools."

"What are you getting me into?"

He narrowed his eyes. "You're right. It's too much to ask."

The woman from the Department of Juvenile Services sounded nice on the phone. "Yes, Reverend Blatchford is counselor and chaplain for the department. The best way to talk to him would be at the Wilcox Detention Center for Girls. I could set that up for you."

The snow had melted, and the rural road to "the Wilcox," as people called the detention center, was filled with puddles. Nicole had to slow down to a crawl when she drove through them because if she splashed water up, she knew her fan belt would slip and the power brakes and steering would stop.

On one side of the red brick building was a vacant asphalt recreation area enclosed by a high chain link fence with inward-facing barbed wire at the top. A basketball hoop without a net stood at one end, and Nicole was shocked to see a hopscotch grid painted on the asphalt at the other. Ralph had told her girls as young as 12 were held here.

In the small parking lot in back of the building, she passed a space marked "Chaplain" with a long black Lincoln in it and another marked "Wilcox Center Director" with a Corolla like hers. Most of the other spaces were empty. Not many visitors, apparently.

She rang a bell at the door that sounded more like an alarm and waited what seemed like forever for someone to answer. A guard with an annoyed scowl let her in. She was frisked in the entryway and had to drop her purse and cell phone into a basket before the guard gave her a *Visitor* tag on a chain and called the director. "Yolanda, a Ms. Ernst to see the Reverend."

Yolanda had yellow hair, tawny skin, a bright red lipstick smile, and glasses hanging from her neck on a chain. She escorted Nicole through a clanking metal door and down a long hall with a rancid smell reminding Nicole of her high school locker room. The hall was empty, and yet continuous high-pitched yelling rang out from somewhere that Nicole couldn't identify.

They stopped at the door to Yolanda's office. "Here's what I'm thinking," Yolanda said. "The Reverend's counseling some girls now in the all-purpose room. We can watch from the second floor balcony until he's finished." She gave what Nicole thought was a cagey glance. "It might be the best way to see how he operates."

They walked up a metal stairway that echoed like the emergency exit in an apartment building, then past one narrow green door after another, each with a book-sized window at eye level. "The dorms," Yolanda explained. Through one door that was open, Nicole saw two foam mats on wooden slabs with only a few feet between them. Clothes hung from pegs on the walls. "We've had to double up," Yolanda explained. "Lots of pot arrests with the new administration."

They leaned over a rail and looked through a chain link barrier down onto a group of young girls, most but not all in blue uniforms. Rev. Blatchford—red bow tie, round black-frame glasses, a custom fitted suit, and shiny black shoes that squeaked on the tiles—stood lecturing the girls. "The Lord," he was saying, "is disgusted by prostitution, fornication, lascivious behavior of all types. I am here to help you preserve your bodies as temples of the Holy Spirit."

The girls without blue outfits looked quite young.

"Newcomers," Yolanda whispered. "We don't have uniforms to fit them. You'll see. The Reverend takes special interest in what he calls setting them on the right path."

Reverend Blatchford squeaked up to the first girl and laid his hands on her shoulders. "Peace be with you." She rose and left, and he did the same to the next uniformed girl, skipping over the youngest ones. Nicole counted six of these.

"I ask our newest arrivals to remain," the chaplain said. Raising his eyes as if hearing a voice from above, he approached the first girl and put a hand on her forehead. "Lord, pour out your grace. Help the sinner to open her heart to you and your servant in Christ. Move her to reveal all lustful, lecherous, pornographic images with which she has besmirched cell phones, websites, computers, or the cloud."

Each of the new girls received this prayerful laying-on of

hands. Rev. Blatchford then took sheets of paper and pencils from his table and distributed them to the girls. "If you want to be forgiven, you must reveal the location of your lascivious pictures and videos so that the Lord may wipe them away." He passed a basket around. "And please don't forget to include your password. Cast your sins into the cleansing fire."

Yolanda took Nicole into her tiny office. "The chaplain assigned to us is very ... enthusiastic," she noted with a deadpan expression focused on Nicole. "Especially in counseling girls associated with pornographic material."

Reverend Blatchford came in, a drop of sweat trailing down one side of his face. He folded his hands, looking Nicole over when Yolanda introduced her. "I understand you have some information about what is being called 'sexting' in the schools," he said. "Let's go into my office where we can discuss this in private, shall we?"

"It's a simple thing, really," Nicole said. "I wanted to make sure you recognize that if a student, a young man, for instance, receives a lewd photo of a girl without requesting it and neither keeps it nor passes it on, he's done nothing wrong."

The chaplain gave her a disappointed half smile. "You bring me nothing?"

"I just thought that needed to be said."

"If you ever come across such a case," the chaplain said, "I hope you'll bring the photo or video to me. I'm making it a point to gather and destroy the lustful material produced by our misguided youth."

Yolanda looked at Nicole with raised eyebrows. "It's his Crusade against Lusts of the Flesh."

8

The password

He found the rock, and having said, "Open Sesame,"
gained admission, where he found more treasures
than he expected.

—*"Ali Baba and the Forty Thieves,"*
A Thousand and One Nights

Nicole texted Ralph in her car: *Went to the Wilcox. De-*
brief tonight?

His reply popped up immediately: *My place at 8:00? Spa-*
ghetti.

There was another text from Liz she hadn't noticed:
Missed you this Christmas. Hope you haven't been too lone-
ly. Nicole texted back: *Far from it. Details later.*

Now to find out what Andre's visit was all about. He
wouldn't have come to her cat-infested house if he didn't
think it was important.

"Hello?" Andre's shaky voice sounded like he wasn't very
familiar with how telephones worked.

"It's Nicole. Nicole Ernst. I said I'd call you back."

"Nicole?" There was an audible yawn. He cleared his
throat. "Sorry. I stay up late reading books, and sleep late."

"There was something you wanted to tell me? About
sponsoring immigrant families?"

"It's a shame. I didn't hear about it in time to go with him
to the station."

"Who?"

"Juan Moreno. He says you're his teacher."

"I am. Go with him to what station?"

"The police station. They called him in for questioning about child pornography."

"What? How do you know this?"

"I'm sponsoring his family so they can live here. Taught his parents Mateo and Esmeralda how to drive. Well, not officially. They had to take professional lessons. His father is building a house behind mine. Esmeralda's taking English lessons at—"

"Wait. Where's Juan now?"

"Home. They let him go—for now, they say. The police called his school. They said he was going to be suspended. I wanted to tell you there's no way he's done anything wrong."

"Of course not." Nicole's hands were shaking.

"I don't know how suspensions work," Andre said. "I was hoping maybe there was something you could do."

"Yes. I mean, I don't know what, but I promise you, I'm not going to let this happen."

"Hey!" Andre yelled so loud it hurt Nicole's ear. "Hey!" He seemed to be rapping on the window. "Hold on, Nicole. Here they are now. All of them, Mateo driving. He needs to slow down."

She heard the kitchen door open. Apparently, Juan's family were frequent enough visitors to know the front door didn't work. Andre was still on the phone. "Nicole, why don't you come down here? I think Juan would like to talk to you."

It was almost 6:00 by the time she got to Andre's. The Morenos' massive brown 1970s-vintage car was parked at an angle next to his house. The trunk didn't seem to close all the way. Nicole saw Andre's beaming face in the house window. He circled a finger in the air and mouthed 'Back door.'

Right away, Nicole knew she'd seen Juan's mother Esmeralda before. Deep brown eyes and dark flowing hair. Where was it?

"Shady Park school science fair," Esmeralda told her. "I came to help Chip Grosbeck set up his project. Was working for Ms. Britney then."

Nicole vaguely remembered seeing Esmeralda there. But she would never forget that science fair. That was the night the Shady Park principal pressured her into changing Chelsea Grosbeck's plagiarized F to an A. Then, even though she'd given in, he had her transferred the next school year to Northbrook High. It was all because of pressure from Britney Grosbeck. "You say 'was' working for Britney?"

"Jes. She fire me. Now I work for Mrs. Michelle Whitman. No bus to Bay Hills, but we have a car now." She smiled at Andre. So did her husband, a wiry, handsome man with black hair.

Nicole glanced at Juan, and he lowered his eyes.

"I'm short on chairs," Andre announced. "Anybody mind sitting on the floor?"

Nicole took Juan's arm, held him back. "Can we go outside for a minute?"

Head down, he followed her.

"Juan, the police! You must have been scared."

He nodded, avoiding her eyes.

"Why did they question you? You've done nothing wrong."

Finally, Juan made eye contact. "They asked me about the pictures, how I got them, what I did with them. They said having pictures of girls under 18 is child pornography."

"Did they have your phone?"

"I don't know. They kept asking me for the password."

"You didn't tell them?"

"No. That's why they called the principal. He told me I was going to be suspended if I didn't give him or the police my password."

Nicole tried to see this from Juan's eyes but couldn't. "They already knew the pictures were on there, so—"

"I erased them, but by now, there might be more."

"It's the girl's own fault if there are. You gave her a warning, remember? Using my phone."

"I can't give them the password, Ms. Ernst. They'll find out who she is. She's just a kid."

Inside, Andre had spread blankets on the floor in front of a glowing pot bellied stove. There was a box of donuts in the middle of the circle, and they passed around a teapot to fill the mugs that Andre had set out for everybody. It felt like some kind of pow wow.

Esmeralda took a sip of tea and began. "Why do American girls send naked pictures of their bodies?"

"Mo-om," Juan groaned.

"I wonder also," his father said. They seemed to be going around the circle. If so, Nicole was next. She passed, lifting her tea mug without comment.

Andre: "There are several species of fish—carp, mullet, bass—that jump up out of the water. Nobody knows why for sure. There are several theories, but I have my own. It's just because they can."

Several in the circle reached for a donut to mull this over.

Esmeralda: "Because they can. Yes. And maybe they are like *pavos reales* spreading their feathers." She tapped Juan's arm. "Peacocks," he translated. "Can we talk about something else?"

Mateo: "For impress a *cónjuge*. Yes, I see."

Nicole and Andre looked at Juan. "A mate," he grumbled. "Can we stop this discussion, please?"

Andre ignored him. "But it's the male peacock who displays his plumage to attract the female," he noted.

Nicole thought it was time for her to speak. She put down her mug of tea without drinking any. "Juan's one of my best students. On the last test, he was the only one to locate every country on a map." She saw Esmeralda's lips soften into a smile.

The topic of conversation thankfully changed, but then the phone in Nicole's pocket went off. She had it set on buzzer as well as the Marimba text alert so she wouldn't miss any text from Ralph. She leaned towards Andre, holding his shoulder as she worked the phone out of her tight hip pocket.

An extreme close-up of a girl's nipple appeared above the message: *I know U changed Ur phone.*

As she drove home, Nicole's mind was a blank. She remembered leaving in a hurry, but she didn't remember saying anything, giving any excuse. She didn't know whether anybody had seen the picture on her phone. She didn't even remember putting on her coat. At a stop sign, she looked down to check. She was wearing it. It was already 7:30. She'd be late even if she went straight to Ralph's. But she had to stop by and feed Smokey.

Smokey was waiting in the dark. Nicole turned on a lamp, fed him, and with trembling hands took another look at her phone. The nipple picture was texted from a number reported as *Restricted*. Nicole didn't know you could do that. The girl who sent it might be young but she was savvy.

Nicole peeped at herself in the mirror on her closet door. *Frazzled*—the only word to describe how she looked. The "fringed layered" outward curls at the tips of her hair were reproducing themselves randomly in this damp weather. She wiped some powdered donut sugar from her blouse. OK. Never mind. No time to change. But should she bring an overnight bag? She feared that would be presumptuous.

In front of Ralph's door, she took a breath before knocking.

"What's the password?" she heard Bobby call out. She

wasn't as amused as she should have been.

"Pieces of eight," she squawked. "Sorry I'm late, guys. I stopped by a friend's house."

Ralph took her coat. "Same friend who visited you last night?"

"Yeah, actually."

Ralph was quieter than usual during dinner. Nicole too. She had a lot to tell him, but most of it wasn't for Bobby to hear.

Bobby brought *Treasure Island* to her after they'd eaten. "I hope you'll read some more tonight, Ms. Ernst."

As soon as Bobby had finished his homework, he ran upstairs to change into his pajamas. "Story time!"

Nicole kissed Ralph. "Thanks for letting me into your life."

"Nicole, you can't imagine—"

"You guys coming?" Bobby stood at the top of the stairs, waiting.

Nicole sat in a chair, and Ralph lay down next to Bobby. She remembered her mother reading this to her when she was Bobby's age. The language was dated but had a charm she loved. She began doing Jim's, the Doctor's, and Black Dog's voices. When she looked up at the end of a chapter, both Bobby and Ralph were asleep.

She walked softly down the stairs, put on her coat, and went out on the porch to call Liz. "Yes," Nicole told her. "Ralph. We're … seeing each other." She laughed at the phrase she never thought she'd use. She told Liz the latest on Juan. Liz was furious. "We can't let Higgy suspend him. We have to get together to make plans."

The door opened, and Ralph came out onto the porch.

"I have to hang up now," Nicole said. "Bye."

Ralph said, "I thought you'd left."

"I just came out here to call a friend." Ralph stood there

shivering, arms folded across his shirt, until she said, "I have so much to tell you. Can we go in and get warm?"

Sitting next to him on his bed, she started with her trip to the Wilcox Center. "I mean, his Crusade against Lust or whatever is good, I guess. But he gives me the creeps." She told Ralph about Juan being questioned by the police, who wanted the password to his phone. "If he insists on protecting this girl who's sending him pictures, it looks like he's going to be suspended from school." She told him about getting a text and picture herself from the girl. Ralph just shook his head. He seemed less interested than she'd expected.

"What's wrong, Ralph?" She recalled some things he'd said earlier: *Same friend who visited you last night?* And *I thought you'd left.*

"I don't know." He fingered his moustache. "I guess maybe I'm a little insecure."

"About me?"

"My wife made me this way. I loved her, and now she's gone." He leaned back on his elbows and looked towards the door. He told Nicole his wife had kept up with a previous boyfriend after they were married. "Handsome, light hair, blue eyes. Turns out she was in love with him, not me. She couldn't marry him because he was her first cousin." Ralph stared at the floor. "She was always going to see him, and he was coming here. Bobby called him Uncle Bob. I overlooked it because he was her cousin, and that made her more open about seeing him."

Nicole put her hand on his knee.

"He was a fundraiser. That's what he called himself. For lobbies, political candidates. Plenty of money. Then he got a job in northern Virginia and moved there."

Nicole felt the sadness in his eyes. She didn't know what to say.

"Guess she couldn't stand being away from him. She left

me and moved to Virginia. Filed for a divorce. They're living together, I hear."

Nicole slid a leg over his lap and pulled his head to her breast. "Ralph," she said, "Don't worry about me. I'd choose an editor over a fundraiser any day. And, Ralph, I've always been more attracted to dark hair and eyes."

9

Point of honor

But if it be a sin to covet honour,
I am the most offending soul alive.

—Shakespeare, *Henry V*

A former railroad line running through Shady Park and on to Colonial City in the south had been converted into a bike trail, which was used mainly not for cycling but for local moms walking briskly, trying to stay thin and at the same time keep up with local gossip. Nicole's house backed up to the trail. It was an old wooden cottage with a moss covered roof sheltered by oak trees. Like some others along the former railroad track, it was said by local historians to have been a former slave quarters, long ago rehabilitated in the craftsman style and modernized—according to 1950s standards.

She met Liz on the trail behind her house. Since school was out and the moms were home with their kids, the teachers had the trail to themselves. Liz, in her red Northbrook sweatpants, had to slow her pace so Nicole could keep up. The more details Nicole gave her about the past few days of her life, the slower they went. Finally, they stopped altogether and sat on a bench.

"So let me get this straight. You and Ralph are actually together now? You're all throbby-spacey over him, and I haven't even met him yet?"

"How about tomorrow night. New Year's Eve. Ralph said Anthony and Pari, his two reporters, are going to a Vietnamese restaurant just opened by a guy they know. I said let's go, too. I know he doesn't like to go out much. But he just flipped his glasses up on his head and nodded yes. How about you and Alfonse meet us there?"

"OK. I guess he can miss the evening football bowls. What's the place called?"

"The guy's name is Tran, right? So he calls it Tran's America. Sounds like he's planning to open branches all across the country. Which he might, according to Anthony. He says they work all day long and save every penny they make."

A group of lacrosse players came jogging by in their blue and gold Shady Park High uniforms. "There's Northbrook's competition." Liz sized them up. "So, anyway, back to Juan. You mean if he just reveals who the little bitch sending him pictures is, he'll be off the hook?"

Nicole shrugged. "That's what Higgy told him."

"You don't trust Higgy, do you?"

"Not really. I'm sure he doesn't want to suspend one of our best students, a kid who's never been in any trouble. But Higgy's, you know—"

"Wimpy."

"Yeah. He's petrified of the security moms and education moms."

"Well, it was the security moms who got rid of the last Northbrook principal before you were transferred there. He went on TV to explain that undocumented immigrant kids had a right to attend school. The moms lost that battle but got him sacked anyway."

Nicole was holding her phone. "You want to see the picture that girl sent me?" She tapped.

Liz burst out laughing. "OH. MY. GOD. That's hilarious. It looks like something from a medical textbook."

"I don't know if anybody at Andre's saw it. I just shoved it into my pocket and left."

"Wait a minute. Let me see your phone. The number the

picture was texted from should be …. What's this? *Restricted?*"

"I checked. You can go to a website and send a text anonymously. No way I can find out who sent it. Maybe the police can."

The phone buzzed and chimed. Liz jumped. The screen said *Esmeralda Moreno*.

"Let it ring," Nicole said. "It's Juan's mother calling. Do you think she saw the picture?"

"Just answer it."

Nicole gave Liz a unsure glance but swiped to answer.

"Hello, Ms. Ernst. This is Juan's mother. I am sorry to bother you. Mr. Andre gave me your number. I have just receive a call from Juan's principal, Mr. Higgybot. He said Juan going to be suspend unless he cooperate with police. I don't know what can I do."

"Oh." So far no mention of the item Nicole had received on her own phone. That was good. "Can you persuade him to give the police the password, Mrs. Moreno?"

"No. He doesn't want police to find the girl. He doesn't like her, but—"

"Then I don't understand. If he doesn't like her, why won't he tell the police who she is?"

"He thinks it is not honorable."

"Ah." Nicole had no answer for that. She tapped a finger on the bench, thinking it over, and all she could say was "He's a good boy, Mrs. Moreno. I guess we can't force him to do what he thinks is wrong. When school starts back, I'll try talking to the principal."

Esmeralda was upset and had been talking loud. Liz heard the whole conversation. When the call was ended, Liz said, "Nicole, you know you won't have any luck talking to Higgy."

Nicole agreed. "The best thing would be if the girl herself

came forward, apologized, and said she'd never do it again."

Liz's eyes rolled up the way they did when she was scheming. "The girl's in Shady Park Middle School, you say? That's the principal who got you transferred, right?"

"Mr. Prosterner. Yes."

"Judging by how you describe him, I'd say he's as scared of the moms as Higgy is."

"Even more. He makes Higgy look like Braveheart."

"Uh-huh. And don't we know just the mom to do battle with him? That virago who shoved you at the guns-for-teachers signing a couple months ago. The woman who made you change her daughter's grade. Let's light a fire under her butt. If Britney Grosbeck can't pressure the Shady Park principal into finding out who the sexter in his school is, no one can."

Liz flipped through Nicole's contacts. "You might still have Britney's number in your phone. Maybe from when she called you to complain about the grade? Here it is. Don't worry. I'll wait and use the school phone to make the call. And I'll disguise my voice."

Anthony and Pari were trying to drum up business for Tran's restaurant. Their friend Emma Bovant and her family were coming for New Year's Eve, too. Nicole knew Emma and her son Todd from when she was teaching in Shady Park. Emma was also a good friend of Andre, he'd told her. Nicole hoped Andre wouldn't come.

The young reporters had written an article about Tran's America's opening a couple of days ago. Dr. Reginald Bland, podiatrist, had his office between the new restaurant and Pet Supply World. The article quoted him saying he was coming on New Year's Eve. "Reggie" Bland was the chair of the Piskasanet Board of Education.

Tran and his wife Thieu beamed as the customers poured in. They bowed to each customer, Tran in a tuxedo—"my wife sew for me"—and Thieu in a long black, silky dress with a split partway up the side, which Tran pointed out she also sewed herself. French chansons played softly, and each table was lit by a candle that cast a flickering glow over its white cloth.

Most of the tables were full. Anthony's publicity had worked. Nicole noticed little Dr. Bland and Mr. Prosterner, her former principal, sitting with their wives at a large table. Then another man came and joined them. It was Reverend Blatchford, also a member of the board. Nicole hoped the Trans were ready for so many customers.

Tran apologized for not having a "rikker risence" yet. "But good coffee after eat." The menus were in Vietnamese and French. Ralph and Bobby stared apprehensively. Finally, Ralph said, "Ah. Here, Bobby. Chicken." He asked Tran, "Can we get it fried?" Tran breathed out a long "Haaaaa," which seemed to mean "No, but I can't bear to say so." In the end, Ralph just pointed to something and said, "We'll have that."

Latino waiters in white coats brought the food. Tran's little son Henry came up to Bobby and Todd. "Want to come back and see the kitchen?" Without a word they were off. Ralph shrugged at Emma and her husband Charles, who was the only one who hadn't been able to decide yet what to order. Nicole saw Emma nudge him and whisper something. She heard only one word, "organic," and saw Charles smile.

Liz's husband Alphonse said his dad was always talking about some food they'd eaten "back in Nam." He stuck his finger on the menu. "I think this is it. Want to try it, Liz?" Nicole waited to see what Emma would choose and ordered that. So did Anthony and Pari. "I hope this place isn't too exotic for Shady Park," Pari wondered. "Ralph, how about we do an article explaining the menu?"

The food was on the table when a woman carrying an

armful of papers brushed by Thieu at the door and rushed from table to table. It was Britney Grosbeck. She dropped a flyer on Nicole's plate and spread several others onto the table. Nicole peeled it off her noodles with her fingernails and held it up.

An American eagle and crossed U.S. flags were printed over the words "Back To Christian Heritage Society," and under that was "BTCHS."

"An unfortunate acronym," Alphonse noted.

Honor your American way of life, the flyer said. It was a plea by Bea Doggit to bring back the fundamentalist textbooks Nicole, Liz, and others had fought to get replaced. Bea's battle had already been lost, and these flyers seemed to be left over. In huge letters at the bottom, somebody, probably Britney, had printed with a wide felt tip pen: "STOP LEWD TEXTING IN OUR SCHOOLS."

Liz gave Nicole a glance. "It worked."

Thieu stood with her hand over her mouth in disbelief at the disturbance Britney was causing. Tran followed Britney, tapping her politely on the shoulder. But Britney was unstoppable. Every table got a flyer. When she dropped one on a plate of spring rolls where Dr. Bland, Rev. Blatchford, and Principal Prosterner were sitting, Liz nodded grinning to Nicole. "The Eagle has landed."

Spending New Year's Eve with Ralph and Bobby was a new adventure for Nicole. They'd sung Auld Lang Syne along with everybody in the restaurant before they left. Back in Ralph's house, they stayed up to watch the Times Square ball drop on the little TV in the study room-slash-Christmas tree room. Ralph kissed her at midnight, then clasped Bobby and held him while Nicole gave him a kiss on the cheek. He poured three glasses of eggnog from a carton he'd bought at the Grab 'n Go. Happy New Year.

The three of them crawled up the stairs, exhausted.

"You're going to read a little to us before we go to sleep, aren't you, Ms. Ernst?"

Us. She loved that. Ralph was content to lie there and let her read to him, too. It only took a few pages before all three of them were asleep. The next thing she knew, Ralph was standing over her chair, jostling her awake. "Time for bed," he said. The street light crept weakly through the misty air into the window, giving his eyes a mischievous glow.

Every time was better than the time before.

10

Working the base

LADIES AND CHILDREN NOT ADMITTED.
*"There," says he, "if that line don't fetch them,
I don't know Arkansaw!"*
—Mark Twain, *The Adventures of Huckleberry Finn*

Nicole had to go home to feed Smokey. She offered to bring Bobby along to see her cat, but Bobby's aunt had planned to take him bowling.

There wouldn't be any mail because New Year's Day was a holiday. Instead, she found another BTCHS flyer on the path to her house. It had the same logo and heading, but this one was different. It announced a *Prayer for Purity* gathering that evening at the Bay Hills branch of the Church of the Invokers of Jesus. Beatrice Doggit was to speak on "The War on Our Values: A Plea for Supporting Our County Executive."

At the bottom of the flyer, in boldface type, was this notice: REV. AUGUSTUS BLATCHFORD WILL GIVE EVIDENCE OF NUDE AND PORNOGRAPHIC PICTURE TRAFFICK-ING IN OUR SCHOOLS.

She texted Ralph. *Check your mail, would you? See if you got a flyer.*

He called her back. "Yeah, I got it. I'd like to cover this, keep track of what Bea's up to, see what the Rev has to say. But I need to work on a *Ledger* holiday advertising supplement this evening. And Anthony and Pari are working on the county executive trial." He paused. "I wonder."

"What?"

"I mean, not as a reporter, but maybe if you went and brought back some observations."

Nicole could feel her heart beating. "Are you serious?" She didn't know if she hoped he was or wasn't.

"Of course, your name would never appear in the *Ledger.*"

Ralph was crediting her with more nerve than she really had. But she wanted to do it. She would do it. She said, "Could I take my friend Liz with me?"

Horses grazed in the rolling fields marked by endless white fences. "Oh, I get it," Liz remarked. "That's why they call the Bay Hills congregation the 'Horsey Invokers of Jesus.'" The road wound up the side of a cliff overlooking the bay until a huge gold cross appeared at the top of the hill. "Prime real estate," Liz commented. "They call it a church, but these are the folks who—"

"Whatever," Nicole interrupted. "We're not here to judge. Just to get the facts."

"Miss reporter," Liz scoffed. "Where's your notebook?"

"No notebooks," Nicole said. "As far as these people are concerned, we're just two more Horsey Invokers."

"I see, Miss Undercover Reporter."

Nicole turned into a huge lot that had men in white uniforms showing them where to park. "Jeez," she laughed. "Like at a baseball game."

People greeted them with religious refrains as they entered the church, which looked more like a sports arena inside, except the seats were padded and arranged in a semicircle around a high stage. Nicole and Liz took a seat as close to the exit as possible.

A microphone squealed, and Bea Doggit walked forward, one foot in front of the other like a model on a runway. "She looks even sexier than she did at that infamous board of education hearing," Liz whispered. "I hope there's no gunfire this time."

"Shh, I want to listen."

"May Jesus pour his bounty on everyone here," Bea began. "May he bless us with increasing success. And may he assist us in our struggle to preserve our heritage in his name." She paused for the Invokers to bleat out a round of hallelujahs.

"You may be wondering," Bea went on, "why our beloved Pastor Mitchel Rainey is not here this evening. Well, Pastor Mitch has heard the call to begin a cable television broadcast from Reno, Nevada." There were murmurs and low hallelujahs. "You can still hear him on channel 854, mornings at 8:00 and evenings at 10:00, except on weekends."

"Got that?" Liz whispered. "I'm sure you'll want to—"

"Shh. Please." Nicole felt it her duty to notice every last detail to bring to Ralph.

Bea went on, "Our vestry and board, with the help of the Lord and your generous donations, has vowed to maintain this Bay Hills church as we search for a pastor with enough charisma to step into Pastor Mitch's shoes. We'll hear much more about that in the coming weeks, I'm sure. As for the branch of the Church of the Invokers of Jesus down in Northbrook, the lease on the building will be over soon, and the church and its daycare center will be closed."

A heavyset man with a rather large head and a checkered sport coat walked onto the stage.

"No," Liz muttered, "I don't want to buy a used car."

Nicole gave her an elbow.

"And now," Bea said, "our beloved County Executive Andrew Mauer has a few words to say."

Anyone who read Anthony and Pari's articles in the *Shady Park Ledger* knew that Mauer was indicted for wrongdoing by the county, state, and Federal governments. But the Horsey Invokers didn't seem to care. They jumped up with a round of applause.

"They're cheering for a guy who diverted Federal environmental funds to a project that he benefitted from," Liz whispered. "His trial comes up in a couple of weeks. He's sure to be convicted."

"They're his base," Nicole whispered back. "They love him because he hates the same people they do."

Mauer waved his arm back and forth until the cheers died down. "This is heart-warming," he said in a high pitched voice. "As long as I'm in office, I'll never let you down."

Bea stepped forward. "And we won't let our executive down, will we?"

Cheers rang out.

"The Bay Hills church," Bea announced, "is proud to sponsor a petition demanding that the governor pardon Executive Mauer, who's always been on our side—pardon him, that is, if he's found guilty."

The men who'd been directing traffic in the parking lot whisked through the aisles passing clipboards through the congregation for signatures while Andrew Mauer kept repeating, "I am ever so grateful. Thank you. Thank you." He raised his voice. "And I want you to know that I have done nothing wrong."

There was a round of applause.

"And even if I am wrongly convicted," Mauer said, "I hope to be pardoned and come back here asking to be re-elected." He threw the Invokers a kiss and left the stage.

"And now," Bea said when the crowd quieted down. "What I expect you've all been waiting for."

A dead hush settled over the congregation.

"The Reverend Augustus Blatchford has come to us with shocking information about ungodly behavior here in our public schools."

Rev. Blatchford—short, thin, bowtie, slick hair—was a less imposing figure than the county executive, but the Invokers listened with rapt attention. "Let us pray," Blatchford intoned. "Oh Lord, you who said, 'Let the children come unto me,' help us to watch over them. Help us to see what errors they have fallen into so that we may guide them."

He stared straight ahead. "Parishioners, parents—like many of you, I have witnessed what sexual education in our schools has done to our children. It has emboldened them—it pains me to say this—it has emboldened them to expose their bodies to others." He lifted his eyes. "Yes, naked pictures of girls as young as 12 or 13 are being transmitted in cell phone messages and through something called Snapchat. Do you find this hard to believe? I tell you I myself have seen—the Lord must excuse me for speaking plainly—detailed photos of girls' breasts, vaginas, every imaginable part of their precious bodies. I have seen pictures of naked girls posed in sexual positions with suggestive expressions on their faces."

A murmur spread through the congregation, and Rev. Blatchford paused to let his words sink in.

"I'm sure you will agree," he continued, "this must be stopped. I have prayed for guidance and found there is only one way to put an end to this sinful activity. We must track down and delete all the Snapchat, YouTube, Instagram, Facebook, and cloud storage accounts on which these obscene pictures are sent or stored. And, to do this, I am asking your help."

Rev. Blatchford paused while a screen dropped down behind him, an email address flashing upon it. "We don't want to involve the police. No, the reputations of our little ones are too precious. So here," he pointed to the screen, "is where I am asking you to send any links to nude pictures of children you discover. I can assure you, the transmission is secure. No one but you and I will be able to view it or know who sent it.

Embarrassing? Yes, of course, it is embarrassing. But I have found this is the only way."

This time, it was more like whispers flying through the congregation. Nicole heard one woman hiss, "This is insulting. What makes him think we have information like that?" The woman next to her lisped, "But if somebody does find it, it's better than turning your child in to the police, I guess."

Bea came back on stage and stood next to Blatchford. "Reverend Augustus, we weep to hear what you describe, but we are blessed by your offer of help. I know you agree with me that this problem wouldn't exist if the righteous textbooks my company produces had not been rejected." She lifted her head towards the lofty ceiling. "And if anyone here thinks it is time to remove your children from the schools in which they learned these lewd practices and enroll them in a private school, then you may contact my friend Britney Grosbeck." Another email address flashed on the screen. "Britney is accepting donations towards building Evergreen Academy in our county—a school, I might add, that has agreed to use the textbooks rejected by the county schools."

At a signal from Bea, the congregation stood and broke into song. Nicole's phone vibrated. It might be a text from Ralph, she thought, and slipped it from her pocket to take a peep. As soon as she tapped the Message button, a nude picture popped up—a young girl lying sideways on a bed, her arm held out to snap a picture of her whole body except for the face hidden mostly behind a pillow, only two long strands of purple tinted hair showing.

"Text from Ralph?" Liz asked?

"No. Let's go."

Before going to Ralph's, Nicole stopped by to serve Smokey some Cod, Sole, and Shrimp Paté in Florentine Sauce and fix a snack for Liz. "So who texted you?" Liz still wanted to know.

Nicole showed her the picture. Liz's gasp made Smokey jump and arch his back. "I'm guessing you're not going to forward that to *blatch-latch@hushmail.com*?"

"It's from *Restricted* again. I don't like the way I'm getting involved in this, Liz."

"Me, I'd like to find this girl and shake some sense into her."

When Liz went home, Nicole drove to Ralph's. After Bobby was asleep and she and Ralph were in bed, she told Ralph, "The Horsey Invokers are strong supporters of Andrew Mauer. They don't care what misdeeds he's committed. Everybody there seemed sure either he wouldn't be convicted or he'd be pardoned and re-elected."

Ralph was stroking her back. She couldn't be sure he was really listening.

"And Bea Doggit?" she said. "Seems like she's planning to hawk her books to private schools since the public schools rejected them."

"Mm."

"And guess what text I got while I was there. A picture."

Ralph's hand was still moving. "Hmm? Picture?"

Nicole found herself excited again.

Ralph trailed his fingers down her side. "You say you got a text?"

"Tell you about it later."

11

Rookie reporter, rookie lover

All you have to do is write one true sentence.
Write the truest sentence that you know.

—Ernest Hemingway, *A Moveable Feast*

Ralph left for the newsroom early the next morning before Nicole had a chance to finish telling him about the Bay Hills church meeting. "How about writing something up, Nicole? You can email it to me."

It was the last day of the school's winter holiday. Bobby's aunt came to take him to the City zoo. Nicole went home to feed Smokey. And to write.

She took a yellow legal pad, two pens, and a pencil from a red plastic bin. She lined them up neatly on the kitchen table. She pulled a dictionary from the shelf under her nightstand. She set that squarely beside the notepad. Maybe she should make a cup of coffee before she started. This had to be good. She pictured Ralph flipping down his black frame glasses and scrutinizing her story with a poised pencil.

Just start writing something. That's what she told her students. *Don't sit there staring at the paper.* In all her years in school, she'd never frozen up when writing an exam or research paper. But now? She traced an invisible sketch of Ralph's face on the notepad with her eraser. *Just start.* She took a breath and wrote, "Yesterday the congregation attending a prayer meeting in a Bay Hills church heard that—"

She started with Rev. Blatchford requesting they forward any nude pictures of children they discovered to a secure email account he apparently maintained. With that, she was on a roll. Just telling what these guys said was enough. She left out the resigning pastor's TV channel number, the Rev's email address, and the name of the private academy Britney was trying to start. This wasn't a promotional article.

She used her laptop to type it up and thought of attaching a link to the nude picture she'd received in the church. She hadn't had a chance to show it to Ralph yet and wanted him to know the pictures were getting more daring. She opened it on her phone, then pursed her lips. No way. Bad idea. She shut off her phone and emailed her report.

Ralph called immediately. "I'm looking at your report now. Good spelling."

"Well, I am a teacher."

Ralph gave a cynical chuckle.

"Don't know about 'lustful instincts.' Might have to paraphrase. I'll run this by Pop, our publisher, before we print it."

"Before you—"

"Great job, Nicole. Good reporting. You should come work for us."

It was like getting an A on a paper.

"I'd like to find out what Reverend B's doing with those pictures. Maybe you could look into it."

Nicole clenched her fist and gave a silent "Yes." After she hung up, she texted, *I'll bring dinner over tonight.* Was she presuming too much? She and Ralph talked only about the immediate future, never about the long-term future.

She drew a blank trying to think of what to cook. From her mother, she'd learned to make sauerbraten and Wiener schnitzel. That's about it. She was determined to make something Italian—and make it authentic. She clicked on her laptop, pitying people who lived in the days before Google.

"Chicken scarpariello," Nicole announced, lifting the

cover from the chafer. She shifted her eyes from Ralph to Bobby, bracing for a reaction.

"Smells good."

"Mmm."

Ralph spooned some onto Bobby's plate with a grin, and Nicole gradually unclenched her hands under the table.

"Are you Italian, Ms. Ernst?"

"No, Bobby."

Ralph held up a forkful, eyed it critically. "Looks as Italian as anything we've ever had." He swallowed. "Tastes like the real thing, too. We should know. Right, Bobby?"

Nicole cleared her throat and asked Bobby about his trip to the zoo.

Bobby swung his arms like an orangutan. "They look like Principal Prosterner except covered with red hair. I asked one for a hall pass. That cracked Aunt Beth up."

But at the reference to his aunt, Bobby's face turned serious. "I told Aunt Beth about the picture that girl showed me on her phone. She asked why I didn't tell my teacher. Do you think I should? I don't want to."

Ralph was putting a second helping of chicken scarpariello onto his plate. "The girl didn't send it to you, right? Just showed it to you on her phone?"

"Yeah, is it really my business what she has on her phone? That's what I figure."

"What do you think, Nicole?"

"Hmm. I think there's a good chance Bobby won't have to tell. Remember that flyer Britney Grosbeck dropped on everybody's table New Year's Eve? *Stop Lewd Texting in Our Schools*? She dropped one on Principal Prosterner, Dr. Bland, and Rev. Blatchford's table. That had to put all of them on notice. They know they'll feel Britney's wrath if they don't find out who's sending those pictures. I don't think you'll need to be involved, Bobby."

Bobby scratched his head, looking confused. "Mrs. Grosbeck, you say?"

"Right. She has two kids at the school, Chip and Chelsea. Maybe you know them?"

"Yeah, I do." He stared at his plate. "What's *lewd*?"

"Like the picture that girl showed you," Ralph told him. "Or maybe something worse."

"What do you mean 'worse'? More naked?"

Ralph nodded. "Mmm."

Bobby frowned. "I can see showing your boobs, maybe. But—"

Ralph changed the conversation to *Treasure Island*.

She woke Ralph up. "You fell asleep before Bobby. You missed part of the story."

He blinked. Nicole could swear he wondered for a split second who she was.

"Yo-ho-ho," she chanted.

He took her hand, and they tiptoed into his bedroom. In his house, there were no closets, only antique-looking armoires. Both of them in Ralph's room were full. Nicole dropped her clothes on the floor, piece by piece—something she'd never do in her own house. Ralph sat naked on the bed watching— something else she could never have imagined. She stepped close enough for him to touch her.

Loving Ralph transported Nicole into a new dimension. She felt like a different person and was still panting as they lay side by side, Ralph running his fingers through her hair. "What are you thinking?" she asked him.

"How beautiful you are." Maybe looking at her made Ralph think of the photo she'd mentioned the night before. "Did you say you got another picture on your phone?"

Nicole realized she was lying in the same position as the girl who'd texted her the photo. She nodded.

"You didn't show it to me."

"No."

"You're not going to?"

"It looks just like this. Me lying here like this."

"Hmm."

"You don't need to see the picture. You can look at me all you want."

"And kiss you?"

She nodded.

"All I want?"

"Uh-huh."

She felt his moustache tickle her breast.

Bobby had school the first day after the winter vacation, but at Northbrook High it was an administrative day for teachers. Nicole had arranged for Juan's mother Esmeralda to meet with her and Higgy in his office. She'd written a letter for Esmeralda requesting Higgy withdraw Juan's suspension.

Esmeralda sat on the edge of the chair rubbing her hands on her skirt as they waited for Higgy to come in. Nicole put her hand over Esmeralda's to calm her. "I know what behavior can justify a suspension, Esmeralda. Juan's done nothing like that."

Brian, Higgy's office assistant, came in before Higgy. "The principal will be here shortly. This morning the county board of education called all principals to a "legal advice conference." Brian held up his fingers in air quotes. His thin blue tie with narrow end hanging lower than the wider end was caught on a pocket protector with pens of three different colors. He was Liz's informant about what went on in behind-the-door board sessions. Brian knew Nicole knew, but they never talked about it. "So if you don't mind waiting here a bit," Brian said and went into his glass cubicle.

Esmeralda was sniffling. Nicole reached her a tissue from

Higgy's desk. Like certain professionals—grief counselors, psychiatrists, oncologists—principals, too, Nicole mused, needed to keep Kleenex handy. "Cheer up, Esmeralda. We'll get through this."

"Juan says he wants to quit school. He wants to help my husband Mateo make a construction business."

Nicole was stunned. Juan was probably her best student.

"We tell him stay in school, but—"

"He can't quit until he's 18. You should tell him that. Besides, he can help start a family business much better if he stays in school long enough to learn about finance, government regulations, advertising, things like that. Things he could learn in college."

"Is what me and Mateo tell him."

Higgy slipped through the open doorway and froze when he saw an attractive dark-haired woman sitting there with Nicole. He'd probably forgotten the appointment. Either that or the "legal advice conference" had set him on edge.

Brian stuck his head out of his cubicle. "Your ten o'clock appointment, Mr. Higgenbottom. I asked them to wait."

Higgy sat down behind his desk and stared. "Yes?"

Nicole dropped a paper on top of the pile on his desk. "This letter from Mrs. Moreno explains why we both think her son Juan was suspended unjustly."

Higgy picked it up, scanned it. "The password. I don't see the password to his phone here."

"That's the thing, Mr. Higgenbottom." Nicole slipped a marked copy of county school policies from her backpack and read. "A student can be suspended if he disrupts a class or poses a threat to others." She pointed to the regulation. "Juan has done neither of these things. He's one of the most polite students in my class."

"This sexting is definitely a disruption. I've just come from a meeting where a prominent board member, the Reverend Augustus Blatchford, explained how serious this problem is. We've been given a mandate to help him put an end to it."

"But Juan has never sent a text or picture of a sexual nature."

Esmeralda put her hands over her face.

"All he has to do is give Rev. Blatchford the password to his confiscated phone. The suspension will immediately be revoked."

Nicole pretended to page through the school policies. "No … no … I don't see that here. I don't see 'password' mentioned anywhere. I don't see where suspension can be used as a tool to force a student to do something he's not required to do. Passwords are designed to protect someone's privacy. That's a right backed by a higher code of law than—"

"We just need to know who the girl is who's sending him the pornographic pictures. The minute he gives us that information, he'll be off the hook. That's all we want from him."

"The police didn't seem to think he was required to tell who she is. They let him go. It seems to me you're using suspension as a threat."

Higgy looked to Brian's cubicle to see if he was listening. He was. In fact, he was holding up what seemed a copy of school board policy, pointing to it, and shaking his head.

"Now, let me be clear," Higgy said. "No one's using suspension improperly. I'm going to look into this. Mrs. Moreno, I'll let you know my decision tomorrow."

"He is a good boy," Esmeralda blurted out. "Please." Tears gleamed in her deep brown eyes.

Higgy was visibly moved. She was a beautiful woman, and tears were streaming down her face.

"Yes. Yes. I know him. Please don't cry." He fumbled for the box of tissues and handed it to her. "I have to worry about community relations, you understand. Parents are demanding—"

Esmeralda burst into sobs.

"Mrs. ... there's no need to .... Please. Well, then, I *have* made up my mind. No suspension. You can tell Juan he's not suspended."

Bobby's first day back at school in Shady Park was exciting, too. He gave Ralph and Nicole a breathless account. "Chip and Chelsea's mom parked her SUV right behind the principal's car, blocking him in. I heard her yelling in his office. She wouldn't move it unless he called a school assembly and let her talk."

"Britney Grosbeck's the chair of the PTA," Ralph told him. "But there's no excuse for acting like that." He frowned at Bobby as if to warn him not to block the principal's car in and yell at him if he ever became the chair of a PTA.

For her part, Nicole was relieved that Britney seemed to be taking up the task of outing the sexter. "What did she say at the assembly?"

"She told us she's holding Principal Prosterner responsible to find out who's sexting at our school."

"That's good," Ralph said. "If he finds out who it is, you won't have to worry whether you should turn her in."

Bobby's brow wrinkled. "She said anybody who knows who's doing this and doesn't tell is just as guilty."

Nicole put her hand on his shoulder. "I don't agree with that, Bobby."

He seemed satisfied. The frown was replaced by a mischievous grin. "She said, 'I *won't* have *my* children associating with a *low-life* who would *do* this.'" He sounded exactly like Britney.

After dinner, Bobby went to his green metal desk to do his homework, and Ralph went to his to proofread some articles for the *Ledger*. Nicole got a call from Liz: "Guess what. I'm pregnant. About six weeks into it, the doctor says."

"Liz, that's wonderful. I can't believe it. You said you'd pretty much given up."

"You're next, you know."

Nicole's heart raced. It's what she wanted maybe more than anything. Yet here she and Ralph were taking precautions to prevent it. She knew what Liz was going to ask.

"So when are you going to take things to the next level?"

Nicole didn't know how to answer.

"I don't want to nag, Nicole. Sorry."

In bed later, Nicole mentioned to Ralph how happy Liz was.

"Would you want a baby?" he asked.

"Yes." Maybe she should've given a more qualified answer, been more careful not to alarm him. But that's what came out. It was the truth. She looked away, unable to meet his eyes.

"Huh," Ralph said. "Something to think about."

12

The black spot

... I saw him pass something from the hollow of the hand that held his stick into the palm of the captain's, which closed upon it instantly.

—Robert Louis Stevenson, *Treasure Island*

In the teachers' room, Liz tapped Nicole on the shoulder, lowered her voice. "I got the scoop from Brian about the board's 'legal advice conference.'"

They huddled in a corner.

"Rev. Blatchford monopolized the discussion. Gave lots of examples of sex pics he's seen. Makes you wonder."

Nicole gave an eyes-closed nod.

"Professor Shandule on the board suggested not allowing phones on school grounds at all. Simple solution, he said. He was sure the teachers would like it."

"I would. That's for sure."

"But the rest of the board said the moms would never permit that."

"Uh-huh. 'Community relations' trumps common sense."

"Finally, the board's lawyer told them they need to be able to prove they were taking steps to stop sexting in the schools."

A bell rang. Liz headed for the gym. Nicole was excited about once again being able to use textbooks that contained the word "Paleolithic." Hurrying towards her classroom, she nearly bumped into Juan waiting for her in the hall.

"Ms. Ernst, thank you. My mom thanks you, too. I didn't

mean to cause you trouble." He tapped his pocket. "No phone. I'm not bringing a phone to school any more." He grinned. "Not even my new burner phone."

On her classroom shelf, Bea's fundamentalist texts had been replaced with books that contained pictures of archeological excavations. These always interested her students. Especially the skulls. Brett held up his book, pointing to one. "Looks like a bushpig girl I met at a party last week."

Lyla sang out, "So that's what getting blind drunk can do to your vision?"

"All right," Nicole said. "That's enough. I need you to turn to the next page. Primitive artifacts."

After class, a pink message note was waiting for Nicole in her mail slot. The receptionist who put it there must have just changed the ink cartridge in the Xerox machine. There was a black thumb print on the note. It said, "Meet Principal Higgenbottom in his office as soon as you get this."

Sitting next to Higgy was a gaunt man, bald on top, with salt-and-pepper hair coiling down to his shoulders. He held a shaky hand out to Nicole. "Trevor Steinborn. Board attorney."

"On the advice of Mr. Steinborn," Higgy said, "the school superintendent has contacted all principals. We're to report any instances of sexting in our schools. And report what we're doing to try to stop it." He leaned towards Nicole as if she might be hard of hearing. "Teachers are ordered to report any instances to their principal."

"As for me," Nicole said, "I don't know of any case other than the one you're aware of."

The attorney glanced at Higgy, then peered at Nicole over the top of his half-glasses. "This case you speak of—I understand you could help expose the, uh, sexter."

Nicole folded her arms and said nothing.

"Mr. Higgenbottom has explained the situation. We're hoping you'll convince your student to reveal the password on his confiscated phone."

Nicole told the attorney Juan's reason for not giving it out. "Now he's broken off contact with the girl. She can't send him any more explicit pictures or texts."

Mr. Steinborn's bushy eyebrows met. "But, you see, what's to keep her from sending these things to other people?"

Higgy agreed. "Right, I want to report we've made sure this won't happen again. So, Ms. Ernst, you can make it easier on yourself if you get Juan to tell his password."

The attorney cleared his throat, eying Higgy. "What Mr. Higgenbottom means is you don't want to create an atmosphere where sexting can thrive by showing you won't turn sexters in. Of course, creating such an atmosphere would be grounds for termination."

Nicole said, "I've told my students it's disgraceful. That they shouldn't do it."

"This is a start," the attorney said. He frowned as he regarded Higgy. "Perhaps termination will not be necessary if Ms. Ernst cooperates fully from now on. In your report, Mr. Higgenbottom, you can say that with the confiscation of the cell phone the one case of sexting at Northbrook High as been put to rest."

Higgy's jawline relaxed at those last words.

"Well," Mr. Steinborn said, checking his watch and jotting down a note. "I'm glad we've been able to work this out." He snapped his briefcase shut.

Nicole's phone pinged. Expecting a text from Ralph about dinner, she tapped the Message icon. The page opened to her last message—the girl lying naked in bed.

Higgy's crimson face radiated fury. "Give me that phone, Ms. Ernst."

She slipped it into her backpack.

Attorney Steinborn sat blinking, speechless. He'd seen the picture, too.

Higgy reached toward her backpack, then held back. "I have no choice, Ms. Ernst. This is atrocious. Mr. Steinborn, please convey my request to the superintendent that Ms. Ernst be fired."

The lawyer muttered, "I ... the teachers' union ... due process, of course ... yet this does seem to be cause for—"

"And I'm going to report this to the police," Higgy growled.

II

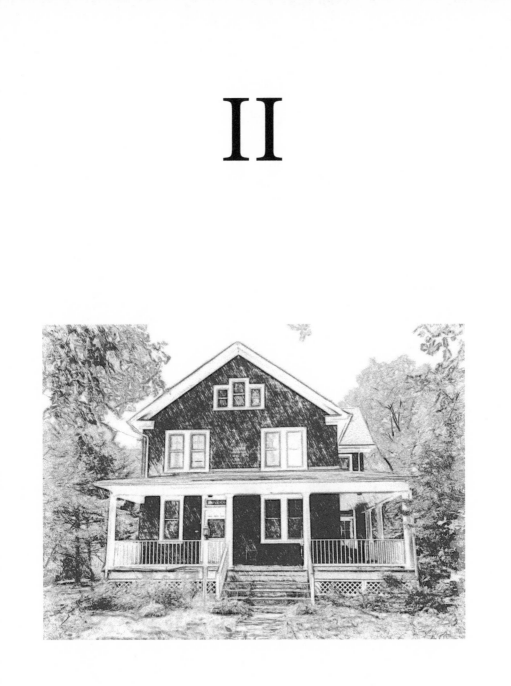

13

Game over

... Things without all remedy
Should be without regard. What's done is done.

—Shakespeare, *Macbeth*

Bobby was dribbling a basketball around the dining room table. The pounding and clattering of plates didn't seem to bother Ralph—this was a man's household.

Ralph pulled his glasses from the top of his head, dropped them on the table, and kissed her. "Don't worry, Nikki, you're going to be all right." It was the first time he'd called her that. She liked it.

"Maybe you were right to just quit."

She leaned into his arms and confessed, "The thought of going through with all the hearings and stuff was too depressing. Besides, it would probably drag out forever. And they'd still end up firing me. I'm sure."

Bobby stopped dribbling. "Does that mean you're coming back to teach at Shady Park?"

It was what she wanted more than anything, but she had to say it didn't seem possible.

Ralph took off his tie, draped it over a chair, kicked off his shoes, and put on sneakers. "Why don't you come with us to Bobby's game tonight? Take your mind off things."

"Please, will you?" Bobby tugged at her hand. This was another first. She felt raised to a level beyond father's girl-friend.

Shivering boys, some in yellow T-shirts, others in green, all in shorts of random colors, swarmed into clusters on the shiny boards of the middle school basketball court. Ralph hunched with a circle of Robbie's Yellows. He was the coach—something he'd never mentioned to Nicole. This was a Ralph she hadn't met yet. He was no basketball expert. She was sure of that. He'd told her he never played any sports in high school or college. Yet here he was, sans coat, tie, and reading glasses, down on one knee, sleeves rolled up, barking encouragement to a kids' basketball team. A new thrill rushed through Nicole as she watched his dark eyes sparkle with self-assurance.

The coach of the Greens was a towering 20-something man in a State basketball jersey over a white T-shirt. Notepad in hand, shooting the other team quick, sporadic glances, he bent over his Green huddle giving, in a conspiratorial voice, what must have been last-minute instructions, now and then drawing diagrams on his pad.

A tall teenager in a black and white striped referee shirt stood under a basket, taking a few shots. At a long table in front of the stands, mothers and fathers fussed over something until a burly man with hair like a porcupine gave a signal to the coaches. The three conferred while the referee carried the ball on his hip towards the table, impatiently fingering the whistle around his neck.

Some of the parents in the stands mumbled annoyance at the delay. People at the table stood and turned towards them. "We could use some help," the porcupine man shouted, hands to his mouth. Catching Nicole's eye, he curled his fingers inviting her to come down onto the court. She started to shake her head no, then saw Bobby pointing her out to his team mates.

"It's Ms. Ernst," some of the boys called out, and parents near her turned to look. A few recognized her.

"Looks like they need you down there," the man next to her said.

"Timekeeper," porcupine man called out. The parents slid aside on the benches to let Nicole climb down. Luckily her hurt leg supported her weight well enough to get her to the court without holding onto anybody's shoulders.

Nicole hadn't been on a basketball court since her high school gym classes. She'd always been nervous then, and this was worse. Rows of people had their eyes focused on her. Kids on both teams were grinning. They knew her but had never seen her at a Shady Park basketball game before. Some of them, Greens as well as Yellows, clapped.

A woman at the officials' table saw her. "Ms. Ernst. Perfect. We need you to keep the time." They sat her at the end of the table in front of a red clock with buttons marked Start, Stop, and Reset. The scorekeeper told her, "Start the clock when the ref whistles; stop it when he whistles again. The clock stops for time-outs, then at the end of each half. The instant it does, hit the buzzer." OK, Nicole thought, this is something I can do.

Ralph's baritone voice sounded, "Remember what we practiced, guys." The ref blew the whistle, and Nicole, her finger already on the Start button, pushed. She rested her finger on the Stop button as Bobby's team threw in the ball. It sailed in a high arc to the other side of the court. And Bobby caught it. She sneaked a look at Ralph, wishing she could sit next to him, share his excitement.

"Aw, come on, guys," the Green coach bawled. "You got to block passes like that." He stood on the court shaking his head a few seconds after the ref motioned him to sit down.

The boys were a *little* more disciplined than she remembered the girls in her gym class being. It was more than running after the guy with the ball, even though there was a lot of that. Bobby could dribble well. When a rebound was passed to a little fellow who couldn't, she wondered why they didn't give it to Bobby to bring down the court. But she saw Ralph nodding his approval. When the little guy stopped and the Greens surrounded him, he bounced the ball to Bobby, who was standing in the open halfway down the court. It looked like something they'd practiced. Ralph gave a single clap. "Way to go, guys."

The tremendous number of double-dribble and walking penalties kept Nicole busy with the clock. She wondered why they were so strict on these kids when college players and pros in the games she'd watched were allowed to double-dribble, palm the ball, and walk as many steps as they wanted. She'd asked Liz about this, and Liz had said, "Pro and lately even college basketball is more an entertainment than a sport. The audience likes shots and baskets. They don't like the action being stopped."

Emma once told Nicole that Little League baseball scores were comically high. Basketball apparently was the opposite. Not many of the boys could get the ball through the hoop. A few boys on each team did most of the scoring. At the end of the first half, the score was Green 6, Yellow 5. Bobby had made a foul shot. Ralph waved his boys in with a wide smile, gave every one a high-five.

The Green coach said, "Take a knee, guys. Some things we need to discuss." He singled out the tallest player. "Tim, I counted three rebounds you missed. No excuse for that. We're depending on you."

Towards the end of the second half, the score was Yellow 11, Green 10. Bobby had scored a two-pointer right under the basket. Nicole controlled the urge to cheer. Her task was to keep the time accurately. She concentrated.

There was half a minute to go in the game when Tim on the Green team caught a rebound and, rather than passing it to any teammates standing in the open, dribbled down the court himself. Ralph waved for his team to take up their defensive positions under the Green basket, which forced the tall guy to stop at about the foul line and set up for the shot that would win the game.

Nicole saw this much out of the corner of her eye but no more. She was focusing on the clock. It ran out, and she hit the buzzer. A roar broke out in the stands. She looked up and saw Tim slam the ball down on the court. He hadn't had time to take the shot. Bobby's yellow team won by a score of 1.

All the officials' eyes were on Nicole. They'd seen her come in with Bobby and Ralph. If the buzzer had rung maybe a second later, the green team might have won. She twisted the red clock for them to see its hand on the zero, then felt silly since that didn't prove anything.

Ralph dashed onto the court and gave Tim a pat on the shoulder. "Tough luck, Tim. I'm sure you would have sunk it."

He signaled his team to line up and congratulate the green team on a good game, and, while they did, went and said something to their coach. The green team coach just shrugged.

On the way home, Bobby started giggling as soon as he climbed into the back of the car.

"BLAAAZZ—You heard the buzzer, guys. Ms. Ernst says stop this game right now." He used his schoolmarm voice. "This foolishness must stop immediately, or everybody's staying after class."

Ralph laughed until the car started to swerve. "Yeah. Way to go, Teacher."

Nicole didn't mind being teased. "I do feel sorry for Tim, though. I hope he doesn't think—"

Bobby stopped laughing. "Don't feel sorry for him. He's the guy who keeps calling my friend a terrorist."

Nicole was shocked.

"Yeah, after that Northbrook High shooting when you were wounded? Tim started picking fights with Carlos."

"But why?"

"He says Carlos is a foreigner. His dad says foreigners are terrorists."

Ralph interrupted. "To be clear, one of Carlos's grandparents is Puerto Rican, so Tim's father considers him a foreigner."

"Tim's father says his skin's the 'giveaway.' But I can't see much difference."

"Anyway," Ralph said, "Let's hope Tim gets to know Carlos better now that he's playing basketball in the league with him."

When Nicole got into bed with Ralph that night, she closed her eyes and could still see him on the court, encouraging the kids, making sure they had a good time.

"Thanks for taking me along tonight, Ralph. It really lifted me up." She kissed his cheek. "You're a great dad. And a good coach, too."

He chuckled. "And you, Nicole, are a fantastic timekeeper."

14

Private instruction

... quoth Adams, "I prefer a private school, where
boys may be kept in innocence and ignorance."
—Henry Fielding, *Joseph Andrews*

The house felt emptier than usual after Ralph and Bobby left the next morning. Nicole winced at the echo of her footsteps. Now what? She'd planned a lesson on Cro-Magnon man for the day. She had drawings that always held the kids' attention, at least for a little while. Teaching was all she knew. And now that had been taken away.

She went to her house, scraped half a can of the tuna fish into Smokey's bowl, and used the rest to make herself a sandwich for breakfast. She turned aside to avoid Smokey's insulted look while she ate. There was a loud knock at her door. She swallowed and opened it.

It was like opening the door on Halloween and seeing someone in a gruesome costume. The close-cropped head rose from a full white cervical collar or neck brace. She took a step back. But this wasn't a costume. It was Willard Scherd. The brace lifted his chin so that he seemed to be looking over her head. "Ms. Ernst?" he rasped.

Liz knew Willard well, but Nicole had never had him in her class. She put her foot behind the half-opened door and felt her pocket for her phone. She'd left it on the kitchen table.

"Andre called you," Willard said. "No answer." He didn't try to force his way in. He just stood there. "He couldn't come with me," he explained. "Cats." It sounded as if his throat had been crushed.

"Andre sent you?"

"Yellow tennis ball. How to find your house."

"Go away. I mean it." Nicole pushed on the door, but Willard didn't budge. He said, "Please." It came out like a whimper. He had on only a loose-fitting camouflage jacket and was warming his hands in the pockets.

"Quick, then. What do you want?"

"No more guns. Police took them all. Even Dad's. Still can't get back in school."

Nicole had read in Pari and Anthony's report that one of Willard's bail conditions was that all the guns—and there were many—must be removed from the Scherd premises. His father had fought that and lost.

"Andre says get private instruction, get my diploma."

"Instruction from me?" Nicole couldn't believe Andre might have suggested that. Rather than flatly refusing, she hedged. "I'm not a teacher any more." It choked her up to say it.

Willard backed up in small steps. He was obviously in pain. Nicole softened. "What happened to you?"

"I'm not a pansy. I'm a fighter. Hooah!" The exclamation came out as a pitiful gargle.

"Nobody thinks you're a pansy, Willard."

"Andre, neither."

Observing his moist eyes, Nicole opened the door a little wider. "What are you talking about?"

"I'm as tough as my brother. Tough as my father." He pulled a jacket sleeve up on his arm, and Nicole jumped back. But he was only showing her his enormous flexed, biceps.

"The court says I have to live at home. Can't leave Piskasanet County." He pulled up one leg of his baggy army fatigues to reveal an ankle tracking device. "Huh!"

"Tell me how you got hurt."

"My father. I took Andre to my house to see my setup." When Nicole frowned, he said, "My games, my workout stuff."

Nicole pointed to his neck. "Your father did that to you?" She recalled the bruise on Andre's cheek. "Did he hurt Andre, too?"

"I can fight, but can't fight my dad. Never hit him. Calls us fairies. I still won't hit. Stand and take it! Like a man."

Nicole knew the court had ordered psychological counseling as a condition for Willard's bail. "Have you been, um, talking to anybody?"

"Andre."

"Talking to Andre? But I mean somebody trained in … trained especially to help people."

Willard's voice was scratchy. He had a hard time getting out an answer.

"Would you like a drink of water?"

"Please."

"Stay here. I'm going to close the door. I'll bring it out to you."

He was waiting there when she brought him the glass. With the neck brace, he had to basically pour the water into his mouth. "A psychologist," she said. "I meant have you seen a psychologist?"

"I'm not a psycho. My dad says nobody's making him send me to a shrink."

"If you don't, the court could revoke your bail. I'm pretty sure."

"No way. And I won't be in jail long. The county exec will protect me. Wrote him a letter."

She knew County Executive Andrew Mauer had been elected on a pro-gun platform. "You mean you asked the exec to argue for a light sentence?"

Willard didn't seem to take this in. He held the empty

glass out to her. Half the water had spilled down his front. It was chilly and he was shivering. He turned in small steps as if every movement hurt his neck.

"Can you drive with that thing on?"

"Not supposed to." He set off stiffly towards his car. "Fight on!"

Nicole watched him work himself onto the seat and drive away. In seconds, she was warming herself under a blanket on her bed and calling Andre.

"Hello?" he said.

"Andre, it's me, Nicole. Why did you send that boy to my house?"

"Boy? I don't …oh, yes, Willard. I thought if he asked for your help with the suspension in person—"

"As if I would let him into the house even if you came with him."

Andre drifted into a long monologue about abnormal psychology, the diagnosis and treatment of various psychoses, the efficacy of traditional forms of therapy—on and on. Nicole was too tired to interrupt. She listened, hoping he would get around to the subject of Willard again. But Andre kept branching off in unexpected directions along his mental railroad. Finally, Nicole asked, "Andre, did Willard's father hit you? What were you doing in Willard's house?"

"Hit? Oh, just a tap. Can I call you tomorrow? I have a call waiting. I need to talk to my friend Charles now. It's about Willard."

Nicole was cooking dinner at Ralph's when he came back and Aunt Beth brought Bobby home. They were already worried that she'd lost her job. She decided not to mention the visit from Willard. Instead, she listened as Ralph and Bobby talked about basketball plays. Ralph said he got a lot of ideas from the *Ledger*'s sports reporter, Sam.

That night, she told Ralph, "It's not just money. Maybe you don't know what it's like to lose your job. I lost mine twice. First, I lost the Shady Park job I really loved. Kids, parents knew me in the neighborhood, talked to me everywhere I went. I had, I don't know, an identity. Then, even at Northbrook, I felt the kids were starting to respect me. And I lost that, too." She was crying and buried her head in Ralph's chest.

"I do know what it feels like not to have a job, Nikki. I saw what my father went through when the Slovak paper closed. He was a writer, an editor, and then nothing. I'll never forget seeing him sitting in his chair, staring out the window."

Nicole clung tighter to him. Ralph gazed out his own window. "Anthony and Pari say I'm too cautious. They say I favor local news over investigative reporting."

Nicole had never heard the young reporters criticize Ralph. It seemed to her they knew it was his job to be careful.

"I want them to investigate. I know we need those reports. But what keeps a paper alive is local stories, advertisements. I saw what happened to my father when his newspaper died." He wiped a tear from Nicole's cheek. "Anyway, I know a little bit how you feel."

A light rain was beginning to patter on the tin porch roof below the window. For Nicole, it was a soothing sound that reminded her of listening to the rain on her tent when she went camping as a girl. The rain was out there, but she felt warm and dry inside.

"I guess you could get a job in a private school," Ralph said, stroking Nicole's hair.

"What? Oh, That would be a last resort."

"Mm," Ralph agreed.

She was lying in his arms, almost asleep, when he said, "I've been thinking. You say Principal Higgenbottom is afraid of public criticism. It gives me an idea. I don't want to say any more, but there might be something I can do."

"Something you can ...?" Nicole heard him but drifted into a deep sleep before his words fully registered.

15

A fishy crusade

Why hadn't Javert arrested Jean Valjean?
Because he was still in doubt.

—Victor Hugo, *Les Misérables*

Her phone rang. "Nicole, what's going on?" Liz was breathless. "A police detective was here asking about you. Juan's substitute teacher told him you're not coming back. I can't talk long. I have the 11th-grade boys playing basketball."

"It's OK, Liz. Yeah, I quit."

"I can't believe it. Why, Nicole?"

"Long story, but basically that picture popped up on my phone while I was talking to Higgy and the school board lawyer."

"What picture? You mean the Headless Nude Reclining?" A shrill whistle blasted in Nicole's ear. "Foul," Liz called out. "Sorry, Nicole, I have to go. Call you after school."

As soon as she hung up, Nicole's phone rang again. "Ms. Ernst? This is Detective McGinn with the Piskasanet County Police. I wonder if you could come in to the station. I'd like to ask you a few questions."

She'd never been to the police station, she told him, her voice quivering. The detective told her it was half an hour's drive up North-South Highway. "Take the first road after the Northbrook Apartments and follow along the railroad tracks about a mile."

"OK." She waited for more directions. "Then?"

"You'll probably recognize it. It's the building with police cars parked out front."

Just what she needed today, dealing with a sarcastic cop. She started to write a note for Ralph, but what could she say? I've been arrested?

"Yes?" The gold badge on the desk clerk's large blue-uniformed chest gave Nicole a chill. She had to wait on a bench under some *Wanted* posters until the detective, a thin man in a tight suit, came to take her into his office. She sat at a gray table across from him. "I wonder if I should call somebody?" she asked.

"Up to you. I understand you're Juan Moreno's teacher."

She took out her phone, intending to call Ralph, but decided not to. She didn't want the police questioning him—or Bobby.

Detective McGinn sat back in his seat, thumping a pencil on his notepad. "That your phone? Mind if we examine it? I guess you know, we're investigating some instances of sending and receiving sexually explicit pictures, including by your student."

Nicole handed him her phone with a trembling hand.

"May I have your password?"

"I don't use one."

The detective raised an eyebrow, then left the room with the phone. Nicole had already deleted both the Anatomical Boob and the Headless Nude Reclining. The detective came back without the phone. "We need a while to check it out. What can you tell me about this sexting, Ms. Ernst?"

She told him everything she knew. "Juan was an unwilling receiver of the pictures," she insisted. "I think it's a girl who has a crush on him. He's done everything he could think of to get her to stop."

"Why doesn't he tell us who she is if he doesn't like getting her pictures?"

"I think he feels sorry for her. He doesn't want to get her

in trouble."

The detective wrote something on his pad. "Kids sending these pictures to each other, that's one thing. But your principal says he saw a picture of a naked woman or girl on *your* phone. Do you have an explanation for that?"

Nicole gave him all the details, hoping they didn't sound contrived.

Detective McGinn studied her, tapping his pencil on the table. Nicole wiped her sweaty hands on her pants. Muffled shouting came through the walls from some other part of the building. Scenes of jail cells she'd seen on TV flashed in her head. She pictured herself holding her hands out to be cuffed.

"Ernst," McGinn mused. "I'm thinking. My daughter Erica had a teacher in Shady Park she liked a lot. I think her name was Ernst."

"Erica McGinn. I remember. I taught her in the seventh grade."

"She's in Shady Park High now. Says she's heard of kids sexting. Mostly girls to guys. And I think you may be right. It could be a new, nasty type of flirting."

Nicole let out a breath that was embarrassingly loud.

"Still, we have to take it seriously. I guess you've heard Britney Grosbeck is causing a stir about this in Shady Park. She's called here twice, demanding to know what we're going to do about it. And a board of education member has called quite a few times."

Nicole thought of Bobby keeping his secret. And Juan. And her. She wondered if they were doing the right thing.

A young man in jeans and a red State University sweatshirt came in with Nicole's phone. "The texted pictures have all been deleted. We can get them back, but it'll take a while. We can't retrieve the phone number the pictures were texted from if they weren't saved as contacts."

"Thanks, Matt."

Nicole felt her face flushing. "Well, you can be sure any indecent picture I received wasn't from one of my contacts."

When Matt left, McGinn glanced down at the phone, then studied Nicole. "I don't think you're a pedophile, Ms. Ernst. But we never know. Anybody, even the person you'd least suspect, could be into kid porn. Teachers, cops, even religious leaders." He twisted his mouth. "We have to investigate all complaints."

Nicole stared at her lap, ready to be hauled away. Instead, Detective McGinn said, "You can go for now, Ms. Ernst. But we'd like to keep your phone for a while."

Nicole stopped at the Econo Mart on the way home. The contract on the phone kept by the police was almost over. She didn't care if she got it back. It was only a few years old, but her students called it "Paleolithic." She wanted a new phone with a new number—like the burner phone she'd bought Juan in this same store. No camera, no pictures, no apps, just phone calls and texts.

When she got home, her friend Pari was waiting outside her house. "I couldn't get you on the phone," she said.

"Oh. Yeah."

"You seem upset."

They sat at the kitchen table, Smokey weaving around their ankles. He seemed lonely now that Nicole was spending so much time at Ralph's. Nicole had a lot to fill Pari in on. In a quavering voice she told her she'd quit her job and had been contacted by the police. She held a tissue to her face. "I'm not crying. I'm just …. So anyway, was there something you came to ask me?"

"I only wanted to see how you're doing. I guess I found out."

"Ralph doesn't even know yet about the police. I can't call him. His number was in my old phone. You never have to remember anybody's number any more, just tap their name on your phone."

Pari tapped her own phone. "Here it is. You can type it in. And if you come over to Anthony's apartment sometime, he knows how to download all your other saved numbers from the cloud."

Nicole tried to smile her thanks.

"Now what else?" Pari said. "You need a job. You've met my dad, right? At the Yaldā vigil? He works at Piskasanet Community College. He hires adjunct instructors. I'll talk to him. The semester starts in a couple of days. No time to waste."

As soon as Pari left, Nicole dialed Ralph from her new phone. *Your call cannot be completed at this time. It may take several hours for your service to be activated.*

At dinner, Ralph took Nicole's hand under the table. "I hated to leave you alone here today. You must've found a way to keep busy, though. I tried calling you several times. No answer."

"The police took my phone. Yeah, I've been busy." She told Ralph and Bobby the whole story of her interrogation, leaving out the words "pedophile" and "porn."

Bobby said, "Wow, did they read you your rights?"

Nicole shook her head, smiled. "Didn't even print me."

Her footsteps echoing through the empty house the next morning, Nicole found a packet of instant oatmeal in Ralph's kitchen cabinet and settled for that. She texted Liz and her parents the number of her new burner phone. Then a text from Pari popped up: *Dad says come in for interview at the college as soon as you can.* She'd have to get dressed. And Smokey must be starving. She rushed home.

She'd settled for oatmeal. Smokey was going to have Pate of Sea Bream in Salmoriglio Sauce. Before she could open the can, there was a knock at the door. Detective McGinn with his notebook. She let him in and pulled out a kitchen chair. "Can this wait a minute, Detective? I really need to feed the cat."

More scenes from TV shows and movies came to mind where the suspect offered the detective a cup of coffee or a drink. Nicole didn't feel like doing that. She sat down.

Flipping back a page in his notebook, Detective McGinn began, "I understand you made a visit to Reverend Augustus Blatchford at the Wilcox Center. Reverend B says you're 'on his side'—his words. What does he mean by that?"

Nicole told McGinn about Reverend Blatchford demanding to know the websites the girls had posted to and their phone and social media passwords. "On his side? I guess. Actually, I tried to convince him that receiving an unwanted nude picture of a girl, as long as you deleted it right away, didn't make you guilty of anything."

"Uh-huh. Like Juan Moreno?"

"Yes."

"And you?" The detective's eyes focused steadily on her face. Nicole didn't feel a need to answer.

"We're keeping Juan's phone. And yours. We've recovered naked pictures on both. One that we retrieved from your phone shows the girl's hair. Don't know if that's enough to ID her."

Nicole repeated she had no idea who the girl was.

"Right. Juan wouldn't tell you. And you don't remember who sent the pictures to your phone?"

"It said *Restricted*."

McGinn nodded as if he already knew, then turned a page in his notebook. "Let me get back to Reverend Blatchford. What's your opinion of him?"

She was in trouble already, Nicole thought. She might as well give an honest answer. "It's good to oppose kids sending nude pictures of themselves. We should make sure this doesn't go on in our schools. But ...."

McGinn raised an eyebrow.

"But I have my doubts about his Crusade against Lusts of the Flesh. You could put it like that." She thought she detected a slight grin on McGinn's face. He closed the notebook.

16

Pop psych workup

Now when Cyrus had thus returned, after his danger and disgrace, he set about planning that he might never again be under the shadow of his brother.

—Xenophon, *The Anabasis*

When the detective left, Nicole breathed a sigh of relief. But she still needed a job. It would be embarrassing to go ask her friend's father. She made a cup of coffee and skimmed the Employment section of the *Shady Park Ledger*. Plenty of jobs as long as she wanted to be a telemarketer. She flipped back to the front page.

Mauer Faces Prison If Convicted

Pari and Anthony shared the byline. Anthony was her boyfriend and had a few more years experience at the *Shady Park Ledger* than she did. They often worked together as a team. The article explained that County Executive Mauer was accused of diverting Federal environmental funds to a sewer line project contrived to force poor residents in Riverside Village to sell their houses when they couldn't afford the frontage fee. The district attorney said Mauer's motive for doing this was to obtain a significant discount on a villa to be built on a prime lot in the Riverside Paradise project. The project was forced into bankruptcy when the scandal was revealed. Finally, the article quoted an anonymous "longtime resident of the village who had stood to lose his house" before the scheme was unearthed: "That Riverside Paradise project ignored all the laws and regulations."

Nicole wondered if it was Andre they'd quoted. She knew the *Ledger* had printed his letters before. At that moment, her phone rang—Andre.

"Charles thinks Willard should work on getting his GED," he began *in medias res*. "Might help with his sentencing. Have you ever tutored for the General Education Development exam?"

"How did you get my new number?"

Andre didn't seem to hear the question. "Because Charles is giving him a psychological workup—"

Two could play this game. Nicole cut him off. "So Willard's father hit you? Is that what you're saying?" She knew it was too much to expect a straight answer, and didn't get one. Andre went on, "Since getting back into school is out of the question, maybe you could tutor Willard in your house?"

"You can't be serious. Did Mr. Scherd give you a blow to the head? Because that's what it seems like."

"… basic arithmetic and reading. What? Oh, hit? The court placed him in his parents' custody. But Charles and I think Willard should spend as much time as possible away from his home."

Nicole couldn't argue with this. She wondered if jail might even be better than a home with a father trying break your neck. "What's Willard's father angry about, Andre?"

Andre's answer was cryptic, but Nicole was getting better at interpreting him. He said, "Expressions of affection between individuals of the same sex are accepted in many countries. Soldiers in the Middle East hold hands just as naturally as girls do in the States, and—"

"Wait. What are you saying?" She cleared her throat. "You never told me how you met Willard. I saw you talking to him at the Grab 'n Go after the Yaldā vigil. Was that the first time you met?"

"No."

She held off asking any more questions while she tried to picture Willard holding hands—with anybody. The only vision she could conjure up was of Willard pointing a gun at a woman he didn't even know. Willard setting off a panic that ended with Nicole being shot in the leg. Maybe Andre knew a softer side of him.

"I went to your school," he said. "They told me you'd quit. I can't say I blame you. I tried teaching once. Absurd regulations. Classes have to begin exactly on the hour. No spontaneous field trips. A teacher named Liz gave me your new number." In the background, Nicole heard something that sounded like "Shh!" Andre lowered his voice. "So could you come and look at some of the GED materials I've found here?"

"Where?"

"I'm in the Shady Park Library."

Nicole had to admit that working towards his GED would be a good thing for Willard. The library was only a short walk from her house. She should probably be going to the college to ask Pari's father for a job, but thinking about that made her nervous. She decided to put it off one day and instead went to help set Andre up to tutor Willard himself. No way she was going to tutor him.

She found Andre at a table in the reading room and immediately had her doubts. Andre had pulled one math test preparation book from the shelf, but next to it he'd piled some supplementary material: *Social and Sexual Equality in Denmark*; *The Work Ethic Myth*; and *Readings in Eastern Philosophy*.

A text from Liz popped up on Nicole's phone: *I'm at your house. Where are you?*

Nicole texted: *In the library. Could use your help.*

When Liz found them in the reading room, her eyes hung

on Andre as she introduced herself. She turned to Nicole with a raised eyebrow and sat down, uncharacteristically silent. Andre went back to thumbing through a book he thought would be perfect.

"We were talking about Willard Scherd," Nicole whispered. "I told Andre I don't really know him, but he was in your gym class."

"Right. He was peculiar. 'Tell that guy to keep his hands off me,' a couple students complained. He wasn't rough, though. He never hurt anybody."

Nicole told her about the neck brace. "He says his dad called him a pansy." She didn't mention Andre's bruise.

"As long as we're giving him a pop psych workup," Liz noted, "I should mention his big brother's in the army fighting in Afghanistan. Willard talks about him a lot, like he's trying to be as tough as his brother." She got Andre's attention. "By the way, Willard's a quiet young man. Keeps to himself. I can't imagine how you met him."

Andre ignored the question. "The GED exam shouldn't be a major obstacle if somebody like—"

Nicole cut him off. "I think you should tutor Willard yourself, Andre. He'd probably listen to you better than he would me."

Liz agreed. "So what are those books there?"

Andre grinned when Liz started leafing through the Eastern philosophy tome. "I understand reading is part of the GED test. I thought Willard might as well read something interesting."

"Uh-huh. He finds *Combat* magazine interesting. Maybe you could make some reading comprehension drills based on that."

Andre shot Liz a look of disdain. Then he put his finger to his temple. "You just gave me an idea. My copy is in Greek, but the library should have an English version."

Nicole and Liz left Andre in the library to do more research.

"Not a bad looking guy," Liz commented. "Stick a moustache on him and he'd rival—"

"Come on, Liz."

"Of course, he's a little wacky. An interesting choice for a GED tutor. You have to wonder what he'll teach him."

Nicole wondered, too. She didn't say anything.

"You're not limping. I notice." Liz gave her a pat on the back. "Doesn't hurt any more?"

It was the first time Nicole herself noticed she wasn't limping. And, no, it didn't seem to hurt any more. She did a little skip. Then ventured a hop. OK, that hurt just a little. But not much.

On her street, she saw a gray car with a red fender parked in front of her house. Nicole put out her arm. "Hold on, Liz. I think that's Willard's car."

"You're kidding? Is he stalking you?"

In slow, deliberate steps, Willard made his way from Nicole's front door back to his car.

"Probably wanted to ask me to tutor him."

"Good thing you weren't home."

Willard slid gingerly behind the steering wheel.

"Poor thing," Nicole said. "I know it hurts him to move with that neck brace. He shouldn't be driving."

The car took off, weaving down the street. "He can't see where he's going with that thing on," Liz said. "He's going to crash."

"He lives in Northbrook. He's heading the opposite way."

"Towards Colonial City," Liz said. "I have to pick up a rock fish at the seafood market there for dinner. Let's follow him, see where he's going? Come on, I'll drive."

Clouds were forming, darkening the sky even before the early winter sunset. But it was easy to keep Willard's slow-moving gray and red car in sight. From the bridge over the Piskasanet River, Nicole watched the gulls diving for alewives. It was fun being the passenger for a change. She could take her eyes off the road and see things she never noticed while driving.

Traffic was pouring out of the city as state employees rushed home. Liz followed Willard when he turned from the busy Capital Boulevard onto a narrow street just before Colonial Circle where there were more pedestrians than cars. A rowdy group of happy-hour couples burst out of the Blue Crab Tavern, arms around each other, walking unsteadily along the sidewalk. A tall, thin man in a threadbare overcoat carried a bottle of something in a brown bag, talking to himself. On the other side of the street, a young woman in heavy makeup walked coatless, balancing on high platform shoes.

Willard's car crept along, then pulled to the curb. As Liz drove past him, Nicole couldn't tell what he was doing. He seemed to be just sitting there. "I'll make another turn around the block," Liz said. At the stop sign, a young man with a gold earring rapped on Nicole's window. "Anything you need?" Nicole didn't make eye contact.

A lot of streets were one-way, so it took some time before they were able to circle back. This time around, the street lights were glowing dimly. Willard's car was still parked there. Liz slowed down to a creep, and Nicole saw a well dressed man with a wool cap pulled over his wide forehead slip out of a parked black sedan and rap twice on Willard's window. The window slid down, Willard twisted stiffly to face him, and the man burst out laughing and quickly returned to the sidewalk.

"Seen enough, Nicole? I have to get to the seafood market."

"And I have to feed my cat."

Nicole texted Ralph. *You guys like fish?*

Maybe it was because they couldn't make sense of what Willard was up to that Nicole and Liz talked mostly about fish recipes on the way home. "I don't even know what Ralph has in his kitchen to cook with," Nicole admitted.

"You haven't actually moved in yet?"

"Well, no."

"That biological clock is ticking. Just saying."

Ralph's sister helped Nicole cook the fish, and the four of them ate together. They were eating French pastries that Ralph brought from Tran's America when Nicole got a text from Andre. *Just checking. They don't teach ancient Greek any more in high school, right?*

Nicole texted *No* and shut off her phone.

"Anything important?" Ralph asked.

"No. Just a silly friend of mine."

Ralph pursed his lips.

17

Dangerous books

*There is more than one way to burn a book. And the
world is full of people running about with lit matches.*
—Ray Bradbury, *Fahrenheit 451*, Coda

Professor Shandule's office was halfway down a narrow
second-floor corridor. The sign beside the open door said
Professor of English, Coordinator of Part-time Faculty. The
white-haired professor was slumped over his computer and
didn't notice her until she knocked.

"Professor Shandule, I'm Nicole Ernst. If you're busy,
I—"

"No. Come in." With a slight squint that told Nicole he
didn't remember her, he pointed to a chair. Pari had told her
he hired and supervised over 100 part-time teachers and tu-
tors. He couldn't really keep track of all of them.

"I'm a friend of Pari's. We met at the Yaldā vigil. I want
to thank you and your wife for inviting me. It was very interesting." She was relieved to see a smile of recognition appear.
Couldn't blame him for forgetting her. She'd hardly said a
word that night. "I haven't taught adults before," she began.

"Would you like to?" He said this as if he were offering
her a cup of coffee.

"Yes. Another friend of mine, Emma Bovant, said she
loves working in the tutoring center." Nicole handed him a
folder from her backpack.

Prof. Shandule glanced at the first page, then closed the
folder on his desk. "M.A. from State. That's good."

"In, um, anthropology, as you see."

"English would be better, I admit, but ...." Prof. Shandule slid a worn list from the top of his in-box. "Tutoring, you say? Yes, but let me see."

Pari had told him something else. The college administrators held her father responsible for finding a teacher for every class listed in the register that had at least 15 students signed up. To cancel a class for lack of a teacher meant a loss of money for the college.

"Classes start on Monday," Prof. Shandule said. "English 101. He handed her the list of unstaffed courses. "As a part-time instructor, you can teach up to three classes. Have a look."

It seemed that he was offering her the job. She tried to imagine herself teaching English 101 and drew a blank.

Prof. Shandule must have read the doubt on her face. "I've written a course plan with the assignment for each day of the semester," he assured her. "All you have to do is follow it. Do you see any classes that fit your schedule?"

She had no schedule, but she didn't think it necessary to mention that. "I'd like to do daytime classes," she said. "Whatever ones you need me for."

He took the list. "How about this, this, and this?" He pointed to classes at 9, 10, and 11 on Mondays, Wednesdays, and Fridays.

She managed a nod, then filled out and signed some papers he gave her.

Prof. Shandule got up and went to a shelf. "These are the books. What I tell new teachers is to do the lessons on the syllabus yourself before each class. Keep one step ahead of the students."

Nicole balanced three heavy textbooks on her lap. It was like the scene in a movie when the sergeant piles the recruit with equipment and tells him to get on the plane.

The college tutoring center was in the next building over. Nicole wanted to see if she could find her friend Emma. She took a shortcut through the cafeteria and found Emma eating lunch with one of her students, a petite woman who looked familiar.

Emma put down her sandwich. "Nicole! What a surprise. Do you remember Thieu? Tran's wife. Owner of the Tran's America Restaurant. One of my best students."

Thieu stood up to shake Nicole's hand, smiled, gave a little bow. "So happy to meet you, Teacher." She waited for Nicole to sit down, then excused herself. "Must study for next class." She bowed and left.

Tutoring people like Thieu was the kind of job Nicole had in mind when she'd gone to Prof. Shandule's office. Emma had told her it was the best job she ever had. But she doubted there would be students like Thieu in English 101.

Nicole told Emma she'd lost her job. She didn't mention the Headless Nude Reclining or the police. She only said, "The principal accused me of something unjustly and I quit."

Emma nodded. "Andre told me. He drops in on Charles and me now and then. To talk." Her eyes twinkled. "And ... talk. Lately, it's all about Willard Scherd."

"I saw him recently. He had a neck cast on."

"I know. Andre told me it was Prof. Shandule's wife, Mastaneh, who put it on him at the hospital. She's a nurse. My husband Charles works there, too. Patient Trauma Counselor.

"Right. Andre told me he's counseling Willard. I wonder how that's going?" Nicole remembered Willard insisting he was "not a psycho."

"Charles can't talk about his patients. I know he's working hard at it, though."

"Andre's been reading abnormal psych books himself. He says he 'recognizes certain aberrant behavior patterns resulting from domestic abuse.'"

"Uh-huh." Emma smiled. "Charles also got Willard to sign up for the GED course here at Piskasanet CC. He isn't attending, though. He doesn't like being in a class. He wants Andre to tutor him one-on-one. Or you, for some reason."

"Not me. Sorry." Nicole was still angry about Willard bullying Jim Delpak, the son of the "hejab woman" he'd aimed the gun at. And about the threatening phone calls he'd made to that family's house. And the hate graffiti he'd painted on their door.

As if Emma could read her mind, or face, she assured Nicole, "Willard has a court order to stay away from the Delpak family. I have it from Andre that he's promised to comply."

Thieu whisked back to the table. She put a package wrapped in white paper in front of Nicole. "For you. I call my husband, and he bring. Cleam puff. Mrs. Emma already have." She bowed. "*Now* I go to study."

Nicole and Emma picked up their cream puffs. Emma said she would take hers home to her son Todd. Nicole said she would take hers to Ralph's son Bobby. And then she had to explain all about that.

Ralph and Bobby laughed over Grab 'n Go fried chicken when she described her "job interview" with Prof. Shandule. Nicole confessed doubts she could teach college freshman English.

"Let there be *nooo* doubt about this matter," Bobby droned in Principal Prosterner's voice.

"What he said," Ralph added.

That night and the next day, she concentrated on preparing for her new classes. She followed Prof. Shandule's instructions—studied all the assignments on the syllabus and did all the exercises. She actually learned a few obscure points about grammar and punctuation. The students were to write a research paper. And one novel was assigned. *The Scarlet Letter*. That should be interesting.

She stopped in Prof. Shandule's office half an hour before the first class with some questions. He gave precise answers about grading papers, leading discussions, and sticking to each day's scheduled assignments. Other questions he seemed to care less about. Was what she was wearing OK? What should they call her? What should she call them?

"That's all up to you." He smiled. "As for me, I'd like you to call me Mark."

Nicole was nervous. She dropped her pen on the floor.

"And be confident," Mark said. "A word of advice. Do not say 'this is the first time I've taught at the college.' They don't need to know that."

Nicole swallowed, nodded.

She walked down a hallway that was much quieter than in any K through 12 school. It was the ten-minute break between classes, and a row of students sat on the tile floor, leaning back against the wall, holding their phones in front of their faces, not talking to or looking at each other. A chill ran down Nicole's back. These students didn't know each other yet. Weren't they excited about a chance to meet new people? Instead, they were desperately clinging to previous friends through social media. Social media, Nicole thought, was destroying social skills.

This wasn't like middle or high school. No bells to signal the start and end of class. The walls of Room 126 were bare, the whiteboards blank. A wooden lectern faced the rows of desks. Some students were already there, apparently those who wanted either back row seats or front row seats. A middle-aged woman in a tan wool dress and a perm smiled at Nicole from a corner desk as more students drifted in and sat self-consciously among strangers, still comforting themselves with their phones. She remembered a comment Prof. Shandule had made. "It's like they're sucking their thumbs." He advised telling them to turn off their phones in class.

The students trained their eyes on her with the same mix of hope and dread Nicole had seen in middle schoolers sizing up a substitute teacher. She introduced herself, called the roll to get their names, and described the course, handing out the schedule Prof. Shandule had drawn up for each day of the semester. Going over it stirred up defensive instincts in some.

"Do we have to buy the books? What if we can't afford them?"

"I don't understand. No extra credit? What if our grades are too low to pass? We'll fail the course?"

"What if we're absent on a day a paper is due? It says there's a penalty for late papers. That doesn't seem fair."

"Do you take off for spelling? How about grammar? That doesn't seem fair."

"What do you mean by logical organization? Can you really judge that? Are you going to grade us on our ideas?"

The woman with the perm rolled her eyes. She looked at her watch as if her time was being wasted.

The students' objections, Nicole realized, were partly the first-world millennial sense of entitlement talking, but she felt sure their concerns also came from subjective, arbitrary, prejudiced grading they'd experienced in the past. They were truly worried. It wasn't going to be as easy to teach them how to write well as it was to teach the difference between a Paleolithic and Neolithic artifact.

Thanks to Prof. Shandule, she was prepared for most of their questions. After class, a young man in a V-neck sweater, white shirt, and tie came up to her with a different problem.

"I scanned the list of books and texted it to my mom." He pointed to *The Scarlet Letter* as if he was afraid to pronounce the words. "She says I can't read this book. It's about adultery."

"It's not in *favor* of adultery."

He shrugged. "She says I can't read it."

The instructions on the syllabus were to take one episode from the novel and discuss it from today's point of view. That would work for any novel, Nicole figured. "All right then. How about reading Dickens's *A Christmas Carol* instead?" While he wrote it down, she added dryly, "See if your mother approves of that."

That night Nicole opened *Treasure Island*. They were on the chapter where Jim Hawkins climbs up the rigging to escape a pirate. Nicole hadn't remembered the story featured so much shooting and killing. She was starting to regret choosing it. After all, she believed America had too many guns. She'd read statistics that show even a gun kept for self-defense is more likely to harm an innocent person than to provide protection. She was a walking—and until recently, limping—example of that.

Bobby, of course, loved the story. Would reading about a heroic boy who shot bad guys turn Bobby into a Willard, obsessed with finding and destroying enemies? It hadn't done that to Nicole, or to Ralph, or to just about anybody who read the book. Should she take it away from him like Chad's mother in the belief that keeping a child from knowing about something bad is the best way to keep him from doing something bad?

"There's a lot of shooting in this story, isn't there, Bobby?"

"Yeah. What if you had to load pistols one ball at a time nowadays? That'd be cool."

"You think so?"

"Yeah. I saw pistols and muskets like that in the City Museum. It's neat the way they work."

Actually, Nicole was fascinated by them, too. Her father had an old flintlock pistol in a glass case. It was beautifully carved, with inlaid mother of pearl.

"Plus," Bobby said, "I'd feel a lot safer."

"What do you mean?"

"Because not just anybody knows how to shoot them. And even if you do, you have some time to think about it first."

Nicole had learned long ago that kids have a lot more common sense than they're given credit for. She continued with the story.

18

Roman collar crime

Conceal me, what I am, and be my aid
For such disguise as haply shall become
The form of my intent.

—Shakespeare, *Twelfth Night*

Ralph sat at his desk looking over a report by Pari and Anthony while Nicole sat at Bobby's desk getting ready for her next English 101 class. Her phone rang. Andre. "I'll take this out in the hall, Ralph."

"Aristotle, they say, was Alexander the Great's tutor," Andre began. "A philosophical mind confronting a young man with a warlike nature. So my challenge in tutoring Willard might not be—"

"Andre, I'm busy now. Could we talk about this later? I have to hang up."

Ralph came into the hallway. "Same friend who texted you the other night?"

"Mm."

"Same friend who went to your house? And—"

"Yes. His name is Andre Smyth. He's written letters to the *Shady Park Ledger*. You might know him."

"That guy? You enjoy listening to him? I mean, Anthony and Pari came to like him, but he drives me crazy."

"He's ... different."

Ralph flipped his reading glasses down from the top of his head. The better to see her with? He shoved his hands into his pockets. "Yeah. Pari claims he's good looking."

Nicole shrugged.

"How long have you known him?"

"Pari invited me to her mother's house last month. Andre was there." The more she thought about it, the stranger it seemed that she knew Andre. It was hard to account for. But there it was.

Nicole continued to return to her own house every day to feed and play with Smokey. She would lie on her bed and read, sometimes falling asleep for half an hour or so. She felt guilty about her new free time, especially since she often did nothing more than drift into thoughts and dreams about her nights with Ralph.

Bobby had asked if she was going to move in with them.

"Your dad hasn't asked me yet," she'd told him.

As the days went on, Ralph never did ask. Maybe it was because he and the *Ledger* staff were consumed with the trial of the county executive, which was due to start soon. But there was also his admitted "insecurity," which basically meant fear she might do what his wife had done to him.

Was insecurity the reason he asked her if he should shave his moustache? (No, he shouldn't.) Did insecurity explain why he started hogging the bathroom mirror, arranging and re-combing his hair (and creating no perceptible difference)? Asking her if she preferred this or that shirt when they were virtually identical?

As for Nicole's own appearance, the scar on her leg had almost disappeared. She'd gone to the doctor for a follow-up. He peered at her calf through Coke-bottle glasses, poking her with a blue-gloved finger. "That hurt? That hurt there? OK here?" She said her leg didn't hurt at all any more. It was just a little stiff. "For the stiffness, there are exercises you can do. I can refer you to a physical therapist." Sure, she thought, but without medical insurance, how am I going to pay for it?

There was a knock at the door. "It's Detective McGinn, Ms. Ernst. May I come in?"

He slapped his notebook on her kitchen table as if her were playing the first card in a game of War. "I've been thinking about our last talk." He paused to study her face. "We were talking about Reverend B, if you remember. You mentioned he was collecting secure website addresses and passwords."

Nicole nodded gravely.

"We're concerned about things some girls who were sent to the Wilcox have told us about the Rev. To tell the truth, I don't think a lot of them should have been sent there. I argued with our prosecutor, but he felt he had to press charges." The detective looked towards the window. "Politics—I guess you know, Ms. Ernst, there's a lot of pressure these days to lock people up. For marijuana possession, petty shoplifting, sexting, things like that. Not for white collar crime."

The detective reached down, and Nicole noticed he was petting Smokey. He immediately rose in her estimation.

"Our prosecutor," McGinn explained, "keeps his eye on public opinion. Reverend B is popular. He writes op eds in the *Ledger* alarming parents about 'the debauchery being countenanced in our schools.' I guess you've seen those. And the Back to Christian Heritage Society holds him up as a kind of savior."

Nicole had skimmed a few of Reverend B's op eds but had never finished reading one. Yet there were letters to the editor praising them, and Ralph said his op eds increased the circulation.

"The thing is, the Rev has been on our radar for a while. We've gathered from the Wilcox girls and others that he must have a ton of naked pictures and videos of minors by now. And we'd like to know what he's doing with them."

It was exactly what Nicole had been wondering, although she'd told herself she was probably being too cynical.

"The prosecutor says leave him alone. 'We don't want people saying our office supports debauchery in the schools.' He says if the cops get any evidence to support the claims of the Wilcox girls, he'll talk to us then."

So far, Detective McGinn hadn't mentioned anything about Nicole's phone or the Headless Nude Reclining photo. He wasn't talking about Nicole at all. She started to relax the hands she'd been clenching on her lap under the table.

"So. The Reverend Augustus Blatchford. You've had some interaction with him. We think his lifestyle—clothes, cars, boat, trips abroad—is above what can be afforded on the salary of Chaplain for the Department of Juvenile Services."

Nicole had heard from Ralph that Reverend B wasn't associated with any church. Instead, he visited jails, had an office in the Wilcox Center, and lived in a house provided by Juvenile Services.

"We don't think he keeps any *material* at the Wilcox. We have a contact there. We hear he empties his desk completely when he goes home. He lives in a white-columned house on the water in Colonial City that he calls the Rectory." McGinn scoffed. "At taxpayers' expense, I might add. I've knocked on his door, but his servant, doorman or whatever, says it's a private residence and no one is admitted. I show my badge, and he asks for a search warrant."

Nicole was gripping her hands under the table again. She said, "Yes. I was told he doesn't do any interviews at the Rectory. That's why I went to see him at the Wilcox."

"I figured," McGinn said. "We've staked out the house. No visitors. Just grocery delivery kids, repairmen, dry cleaners. That's in the daytime. But every couple weeks he hosts a cocktail party. I guess he calls them soirées. We know his doorman checks the invitations."

Nicole wondered why McGinn was telling her all this.

He went on. "Guys in tuxes. Mostly men, but a few women in evening dresses. That's who my men observed going to these parties. Lots of out-of-state tags on the parked cars. We ran them. Didn't come up with any flags."

Nicole met McGinn's intense eyes.

McGinn cleared his throat. "He's having one of these soirées tomorrow night. We'd like to send an officer in disguise, but that's not possible. The Rev won't invite anybody unless he already knows them." The detective bit his lip. "That's where we're hoping you come in."

Nicole gasped.

"The thing is, the Rev already knows you. He told our contact at the Wilcox he likes you. He said he thought you had some material to give him but were afraid and changed your mind."

"That's not true." Although she remembered implying that when she made the appointment. "I mean—"

"I believe you, Ms. Ernst. But since he thinks you have kiddie porn pictures or videos, that might be a way to get invited. It would be a big help to the police department."

Her first thought was, even if she agreed, which of course she wouldn't, what could she possibly wear to a "soirée"?

McGinn leaned towards her. "We don't think you'd be in any danger. But if you even start to feel threatened, we'd want you to walk out right away."

The word *threatened* echoed in her head.

"Another thing. You live alone, so it should be easy enough to keep this secret. If the public, the *press*, anybody finds out about this, the whole operation fails."

Nicole remembered that Ralph's number was in her contacts on the phone the police were still holding. The detective didn't seem to have noticed that yet.

"I know this comes as a surprise, Ms. Ernst, but you might be the key to finding out what this guy's really up to. What do you think?"

Nicole took a breath. The detective waited, eyes on hers. A picture of Reverend B laying his hands on those girls' heads flashed before her. She agreed.

"Ms. Ernst, this is a great service you are doing."

"But how am I going to get an invitation?"

"As I said, we have a contact at the Wilcox. I can have an invitation for you on my desk by tomorrow afternoon."

It was Friday evening. Ralph fingered the tip of his moustache. "It's important, but you can't tell me where you're going tonight?"

"I will later. I promise."

"If it's Andre again, it won't hurt my feelings or anything if you just tell me."

"It's not. Don't worry, Ralph." She ached to tell him more, but couldn't. "I'll be out late, so I plan to sleep at my own house." She took his hands. "Trust me, Ralph."

Swallowing her guilt, she dressed hurriedly at her house and drove to Colonial City for the soirée. The skirt of her black satin evening gown glimmered as she walked under the street light. Across the street, men in tuxedos, several sporting what Liz's husband called man purses, made their way up the long flagstone steps to the former colonial river mansion. A black man in a white jacket stood outside checking each guest's invitation. He found Nicole's name, glanced at the little purse she held, and knocked on the door with a brass-headed mahogany stick.

Inside, two more men in white waiter's jackets stood at either side of the long hall. One took her new gray cape, and the other led her to the parlor entrance, where the Reverend Augustus Blatchford, grinning and bowing, held out his hand to the guests as they filed in. "Ms. Ernst, I'm pleased you got my invitation. An honor to have you." He waved her towards a group chatting and sipping cocktails. "Please." Debussy's

"Prelude to the Afternoon of a Faun" played softly in the background.

In seconds, a circle of men vied for Nicole's attention. She was definitely the youngest woman there. The few other women seemed to be neither wives nor girlfriends but career women of one kind or another, unrelated to the men. Nicole refused a Manhattan from a swarthy young man in a pink cummerbund who managed to maneuver her away from the others. He signaled a waiter to come her way with a tray of hors d'oeuvres, which she also declined.

"Such a pleasure to meet someone new," he said.

She held out her hand. "Nicole Ernst."

"John."

"I didn't really know what to expect."

"You're not familiar with the routine? I'll be glad to help." He caught Reverend Blatchford's eye, and Blatchford nodded. "This way, then." John took her arm and led her to a doorway in the rear of the parlor, through which a man in a crew cut re-entered the room, eyes shifting back and forth. He looked like he'd been crammed into his tux and was already anxious to leave.

Beyond the rear doorway was another hall with two closed doors, and beside each stood a man in a white jacket. The old man at the first door gave a slight bow. "Mr. John. Ms.—"

"Nicole."

"The acquisition room is occupied at present, Sir." The doorman took a pen and paper from his vest pocket. "If you'll be coming back, I can schedule you next."

"Just showing our new guest around." John took her arm again and stopped before they reached the other door. He lowered his voice. "Acquisition—that's where you preview and can buy a product. Down here is Presentation, where you offer a product for review and sale. I don't know which—"

"Presentation, I think."

He led her to the white-coat man at that door. "A new guest," John said. "Here to make a presentation."

"Welcome. The room is free." The bright light contrasting with the dim hallway made Nicole squint. A blank movie screen hung on a green wall. Tables with laptops and speakers stood at each side of two gray safe boxes.

John released Nicole's arm. "I'd like to have a drink with you after you've made your presentation."

"You're not—?"

"Presentations are always made alone."

Nicole's hands were shaking. She considered turning and running. But the man at the door closed it behind her. It was too late.

A German shepherd beside the door jerked up its head, ears pointing at her. A bald man in a wrinkled business suit sauntered towards her, blinking, his face so pale he looked half dead. His pointy goatee gave the impression that his hair had melted off his head, run down his face, and was dripping off the end of his chin. "What have we brought?" he asked with a mistrustful tilt of the head.

Nicole snapped open her little purse. "Um, flash drive."

"Under eighteen?"

"Eighteen? Oh. Yes." She had no idea what was on the flash drive and hoped this was right.

The bald man took a step closer. "Under fourteen?"

"I'm pretty sure."

"Non-pro? Never posted?"

She nodded, noting her escape path to the door.

The pointy-beard man held out his hand for the flash drive. "This way." He went towards a different laptop than the one he'd been watching. "Still or video?"

"Video." Thank goodness Detective McGinn had told her that much. He'd told her to take whatever she was offered for it.

The goatee man inserted the flash drive. A man's voice blared in a wheedling tone from the speakers, and Goatee lowered the volume. Then there was a little girl's voice. Nicole peeped at the screen and had to turn away. She felt like she was going to throw up and braced herself on the table.

"Yes, indeed," the man said. "Looks like the real thing." He fast-forwarded, stopping every now and then until he reached the end. "Twenty minutes," he said. "All right. Anything else?"

Nicole shook her head. She felt like something was stuck in her throat.

"$250."

Nicole stared. The man went to a safe and came back with cash. Nicole stuffed it into her purse and waited.

"Anything wrong?"

"Can you transfer it from the flash drive onto your computer and give me my drive back?"

"Shiiiit," the bald man hissed. "I just give you $250 and on top of that you want your cheap drive back?"

"Yes. I'll wait while you transfer the file."

He looked like he might cancel the deal, but he took another look at the laptop screen and changed his mind.

John—she was pretty sure that wasn't his real name—was flushed with drink when she got back to the parlor. "What took you so long?" he asked, too loud. Several guests raised their eyebrows, and Reverend B came over. "John, please don't embarrass our new guest. We appreciate your business, but now I'm going to have to ask you to leave." Reverend B nodded to a doorman, who escorted him out.

"You're doing the right thing, Ms. Ernst, in turning over material of this sort to me. As I said at the Wilcox, I believe I'm in a position to do something about it. And I know you recently lost your job. Please consider any remuneration you received as my compensation for your trouble."

Nicole drove straight to the Grab 'n Go when she left. Detective McGinn pulled up next to her and she got into his unmarked car. He smiled. "You look fantastic, Ms. Ernst. You're a good sport. The department owes you a debt of gratitude."

She handed him the flash drive from her purse.

"Yes! I was afraid they wouldn't give it back."

"He almost didn't."

"To tell you the truth, I don't know exactly why we needed it back. It's now got the Rev's IP address or something. Young Matt handles that. He swore if you could bring the drive back, we can nab him."

"Oh," Nicole remembered. "The money."

McGinn counted it, put it on the dashboard, wrote her a receipt. He stared at the pile of bills. "So that's the payment for ruining a little girl's life. Don't worry, Ms. Ernst. We got that video from the FBI. It'll stay on the Rev's computer but can't be transmitted or copied again."

Nicole agreed to meet him at the station the next morning to give a full report.

19

Secrets

Nothing weighs on us so heavily as a secret.
—Jean de La Fontaine, *Fables*

Ralph called before she got out of bed. "Wanted to be sure you're OK. It's Saturday. I thought the three of us could, I mean, do you have any plans for the day?"

Unfortunately the first thing on her agenda—going to the police department to be formally debriefed—also had to be kept secret. "Um, there is something I have to do this morning."

"I don't understand why you can't tell me where you went last night."

"I'm sorry, Ralph. I have to keep it secret." There was a catch in her throat. "You'll know soon. I promise."

"I worry, you know. You going to stay with me tonight?"

"Sure. There was just something I had to do last night."

Emotional wounds. That's what the love advice columns that sometimes appeared in the *Shady Park Ledger* called it. Ralph's sad experience with a wife who kept another man in her life the whole time they were married made him worry too much. Of course, it didn't help that Nicole wasn't telling him what she was up to.

McGinn recorded her description of everything that happened at the Rectory. Nicole threw in every detail she could remember. She thought she might later write a news report for Ralph after the police finished their investigation and gave her the go-ahead. McGinn clicked off the recorder. "Sounds like a sordid operation. I have to ask, weren't you a little scared?"

"I was scared to death. And disgusted."

McGinn poured her a cup of coffee and opened another folder on his desk. "I need to ask you one more thing." He pointed to a picture in the file. "This Willard Scherd. He told his lawyer he's been in touch with you." McGinn waited for her nod. "He's been granted bail on certain conditions. Our prosecutor asked me to read you a list. Could you let me know if you have any reason to believe Scherd has done any of these things?"

Nicole answered *No No No* for everything on the list, until there was one that made her heart jump—"solicitation for prostitution." She'd never talked to Liz about what Willard might have been up to in Colonial City when they followed him there, but she had a suspicion that might have been it. It didn't seem like any money was involved, though. So she might be wrong. As she remembered the incident, the man just laughed at Willard and walked away. She didn't want to add to Willard's troubles, so she decided not to tell about that. "No," she said.

McGinn's looked up from his checklist, probably noting her hesitation. She knew her face was red. But he must have decided it was the phrase itself that embarrassed her because he looked back down and checked the box for *no*.

She drove to Ralph's house as soon as she left the station. He and Bobby had just come back sweaty from basketball practice at the middle school. They warmed up some leftover pizza, then Ralph had to go in to the newsroom. Nicole offered to help Bobby with a book report he was writing. Bobby read a lot and, truth be told, she didn't see much difference between his writing and her college students' writing.

While he was finishing up the report, Nicole printed out

a recipe for cabbage pierogi with sausage. It looked a little complicated, but she had time. And it was a Slovak meal, not Italian. Tonight she wanted to make sure Ralph was confident she was nothing like the woman who'd left him.

She had the whole house smelling like cabbage when he came home. "Mmm," Ralph said. Bobby held his nose. But they both ate lots of it.

Ralph had been in his bedroom fussing with something instead of listening to the nightly reading of *Treasure Island*. When Nicole went in, she found him already in bed but awake. She faced him like she'd done before and started undressing, dropping her clothes on the floor. She didn't know if this is the way it worked with all women, but getting him excited got her excited.

"You don't have to drop your clothes on the floor any more." Ralph grinned, gesturing behind her with his chin.

There was a little maple dresser standing next to his with a matching clothes tree rack beside it.

"Ralph, how did these get here?"

"They're not new. Bobby and I brought them over yesterday evening from Beth's house. She's downsizing. They're for you."

"You brought them here last night?"

"Yeah, you said you wouldn't be sleeping here, so—"

"Oh, Ralph." She stepped over her clothes into the bed. "Ralph, you have to believe I'd tell you where I was last night unless I had a really good reason to keep it secret."

At Piskasanet Community College, Chad, whose mother wouldn't let him read *The Scarlet Letter*, was waiting for her in the hall. "I've been home-schooled," he told her. Nicole couldn't tell whether this was an explanation or an apology. "My mom says *Christmas Carol* is OK."

"Good." She started for the door.

"Excuse me. Something else. My mom doesn't want the kids teasing me about it. Would you mind not telling them I'm reading something different?"

"Your secret's safe with me."

Janet, the woman with a perm and a dress, was sitting erect, composition text open to the page assigned for homework. All the others were hunched over their phones, backpacks closed on the floor. Nicole cleared her throat. "Please turn off your phones and put them away." Most of the class did, right away. A few looked at her to make sure she meant it first.

"Let's see what you learned from the chapter on organizing an essay. Would someone read the first sentence of the sample on page 23?"

Janet raised her hand and read. There were sighs and groans as backpacks scraped the floor and thumped up onto desks. A few students looked at her again before they bothered to unzip them to make sure she was really going to make them open their books.

"Question." Blake in the back row was raising his hand. "Are we going to get Presidents' Day off?" The class was on alert, fearing the answer.

"No," Nicole said. A round of grumbling reminded her of something Prof. Shandule had said: "Education is the only business in which the customer is eager to get less for his money."

When they finally opened their books—those who had them—it was clear that most were seeing the chapter for the first time.

"Your next assignment will be to write a draft of a brief essay. Pick one of the suggestions on your course schedule. Now let's examine how the model in your text is done."

There was a general reluctance to look at the book. Instead, there were more questions.

"The introduction has to state the three main points, right? Do you take off if we only have two?"

"How many sentences before you start a new paragraph?"

"Can you start a sentence with *And*?"

"Does *its* have an apostrophe or not? I was told it does."

"A conclusion repeats what you said in the introduction, right? Do you have to repeat everything? Do you take off if something's left out?"

"Ladies and gentlemen," Nicole said, "rules are fine as starting points. But I'm asking you to paint a picture. You're asking me to give you a coloring book to fill in."

Nicole liked teaching here. It was exciting to interact with adults. But she really wished she could go back to teaching in elementary or middle school. That's where she felt she belonged.

After three of these classes, she went back to her house exhausted. She flopped down on her bed. "Too early for dinner, Smokey. Let's just lie here a few minutes." She was drifting off to sleep when Liz called.

"Hey, stranger. Pregnant yet? Heh-heh. You know I'm kidding. Me, though? I'm puking my guts out every morning. I have a new favorite student, your Juan Moreno. He was heartbroken when you quit, but now I'm teaching him how to play basketball. They don't play it much in Nicaragua."

Nicole felt a little pang of jealousy.

"So I have to tell you the latest on Higgy. I hear you brought Juan's mother in to talk to him? Esmeralda? Well, Juan's back in Higgy's good graces now, and all Higgy talks about is Esmeralda."

"You mean—"

"Not romantic. Can you imagine Higgy being romantic? But he's got a new take on 'community relations' now. He got Esmeralda approved as a temporary teacher's aide in Spanish. She'll come in once a week."

Smokey pounced on Nicole's stomach. She slid him off.

"You still there? How do you like teaching the big guys?"

"I like it. Not as much as teaching little kids."

"Maybe you can get back to elementary or middle school some day. Oh—I need to ask you something. My friend Linda? She saw you in TJ Maxx buying a gorgeous black evening gown. So when were you going to tell me what that's all about?"

Keeping Reverend B's soirée a secret weighed on Nicole. She didn't know what to say. She didn't want to lie, and, besides, Liz would see right through it if she did. She didn't answer.

"Nicole, I can't believe you. You don't want to tell me?"

"I can't right now, Liz."

"No?" Liz laughed. "Uh-huh, we'll see how long you can hold it in."

20

Father issues

*They call that govment! A man can't get his rights
in a govment like this. Sometimes I've a mighty
notion to just leave the country for good and all.*
—Mark Twain, *The Adventures of Huckleberry Finn*

Since Nicole had lost her health insurance when she quit her job, she couldn't afford to see a physical therapist as the doctor had suggested. So she Googled exercise and workout websites. There were some routines she could do at home. Some required special equipment. She remembered seeing something in her contract with the college about instructors and students having permission to use exercise equipment and went to check it out.

A rush of stuffy, humid air surged out as she pulled open the door of the physical training room. Exercise bikes whirled, treadmills hummed, and joggers thumped to a low, steady rap beat playing in the background. Nicole had changed into an old T-Shirt, a little more tight-fitting than she remembered, and squeezed into her high school gym shorts. She'd tied her hair back in a mini pony tail. Walking from the locker room, she lowered her eyes, hoping no one would recognize her. Inside the room, she was relieved that nobody even looked up, consumed as they were with flattening their abs, firming their pecs, and trimming their glutes. She found what *workitout. com* had identified as a "calf machine" and climbed unsteadily onto it like a panicky cat balancing on a tree branch. It didn't matter. Nobody knew who she was.

She slipped her feet under the bars. The idea, the website said, was to lift them, but they didn't budge. She tried harder. Nothing.

Grunts and gasps bellowed out behind her. For a moment, she thought people were laughing at her, but when she sneaked a glance, she realized the groans were from a guy lying on a bench press, his legs stretched in her direction. Sticking partly out from his sweat pants on one ankle was a black band of some kind.

"I can do it. No help. Uuugh." His arms quivered as he forced the barbell up inch by inch. Nicole tried not to stare, but he was loud. Others were watching, too. "Yaah," he gasped when he got the bar up all the way. He clanged it back down into its rack. Nicole saw the tattoo of a cross on his forearm.

"Hooah," he shouted. "290 pounds." He slid cautiously from the bench, and Nicole saw he was wearing a neck brace.

She turned away fast, trembling, eyes on her sneakers, and busied herself trying to lift the bars with her legs. Again nothing. She tried a couple more times. She rested, panting from the effort, then heard a guttural "Huh" and looked up. Willard stood stiffly in front of her in a sweat-drenched sleeveless shirt, his bulging arm reaching toward her. She tried to jump from the machine, but her feet were caught.

Willard lifted a heavy disk from one side of the calf machine, then from the other, leaving only a small weight on each side. "Try now."

When she caught her breath, she said, "Oh. I didn't realize—"

"Go ahead."

No way she was going to do leg exercises with Willard standing there watching her.

"Good for your hurt leg," Willard encouraged. "Don't be a pansy—what my dad tells me. Just pressed 290. Nobody calls me a pansy." He jammed his hands together in front of his chest. "Look at that."

Nicole extricated her feet from the machine and said she was through for the day and it was time to go home. Willard knelt and gently closed his hands on one of her sneakers. "Don't quit. Let me help. Put it like this." He placed her feet correctly. Then he pulled at the bars to give her a start. "Kick it up. Kick it up. Way to go. Hooah!"

A gray haired woman walked by. "Lucky you," she commented. "That's what I need. A personal trainer."

Nicole was so embarrassed she wanted to melt. "OK, I got it," she told Willard. To prove it she started more leg lifts. Willard stepped back, studying her legs with a disturbing intensity. "Real nice," he observed. "Looking good."

Nicole closed her eyes and kept it up. A rush of adrenalin flashed through what *workitout.com* called her "core." She wanted to believe it was from the muscle activity and not from Willard's praise.

When she finally stopped, he was still standing there and gave her a thumbs up. "Sorry," he said.

"Beg your pardon?"

"Your leg. Andre says it's my fault." He stepped aside, leaving her a clear path to the door.

Nicole couldn't help asking, "What do *you* think?"

"Guns don't prove you're tough. What Mr. Charles says." He was quoting Emma's husband. That seemed promising. Nicole said she agreed.

"But do I look tough?"

Nicole couldn't believe she was having this conversation but ventured, "You know what would be a tough thing to do? Write a letter to Shahnaz Delpak's family apologizing for the harm you've done to them."

Willard's eyes drifted off towards nowhere in particular. After a moment, he said, "Huh." Nicole hurried off to the women's locker room.

As soon as Nicole got home, she called Liz. Liz was the teacher who'd wrestled Willard to the ground when he came into the board hearing with a gun. "I have a feeling," Nicole told her, "he might be better off separated from his father."

Liz agreed. "I used to talk to Willard sometimes when he was in my gym class. From what he says, his father hates non-whites, non-Christians—anybody not just like himself—and the government that coddles to them."

Nicole chuckled. "He's like Huck Finn's Pap."

Liz didn't seem to hear. "So anyway," she said. "It's a girl."

"What?"

"I had a sonogram. Can you believe it? This is really going to happen."

"Oh, Liz. I'm so happy for you."

"Thanks. Waiting on you now."

Nicole let this go. She wanted to have a baby, Ralph's baby, but she didn't feel like talking about that now. "You still have Juan in your basketball class?"

"He's picking it up fast. Likes playing point guard. Also, that Cultural Alliance Club I was getting started? I couldn't get any student to run it, so I asked Juan, and he agreed. Too bad, though. Some of the kids told their parents about that picture on his phone. Now I'm getting some complaints the school is allowing a pervert to head up a club. Which sent Higgy on a trip to City Hospital. An 'anxiety attack.' That's what Brian wrote in his report."

"Poor Higgy. Hold on, Liz, I have another call I want to take. Talk to you later, OK?" She wanted to talk to Andre while she was in her own house.

Andre sounded mournful. "Willard and I had a little tiff yesterday. It's his father I'm angry at, not him. I need to show

Willard I support him. I'm going to vouch for him at his sentencing."

Anthony and Pari had reported in the *Ledger* that Willard planned to plead guilty. So there wasn't actually going to be a trial. He would be going before a judge, and his lawyer would be trying to show why he deserved a light sentence. Nicole tried to picture Andre making a statement in court in support of leniency. It was hard to imagine one of his erudite disquisitions being helpful.

Putting her doubts aside, she couldn't help asking about the "tiff."

"Children are naturally inclined to overlook or deny physical or mental abuse by a parent. Willard's father constantly finds ways to humiliate him. I was there when he told him he didn't have the guts to be an infantryman but border guard might be more up his alley."

Nicole was disappointed to hear that Andre was still going to Willard's house. Or rather, confused. Andre had already come close to admitting a sexual attraction to Willard. But Andre was her age, 37, and Willard was 18. She wasn't sure whether Andre wanted to be his lover or his father. She wondered if Andre himself was sure. "I guess Willard didn't want to hear that" was all she said.

"No. He actually went for the idea. Then I had to point out you couldn't be either an infantryman or a border guard if you had a felony conviction." Andre let out a frustrated breath between his lips. "His father turned on me. He said he guaran-damn-teed me the President was going to change all that."

21

Tran's America

For where'er the sun does shine,
And where'er the rain does fall,
Babe can never hunger there,
Nor poverty the mind appall.

—William Blake, "Holy Thursday,"
from *Songs of Experience*

Nicole wanted to get some egg rolls for dinner from the Tran's America Restaurant. It was early, and she wasn't sure it was open but went anyway. The door swung into a dusky dining room with a faint fishy smell. It took a while for her eyes to adjust to the dim light. "Anybody here? Am I too early?"

Scraping sounds echoed from the corridor that led out from the kitchen. Tran, a baby hung papoose style on his back, shuffled into the dining room in straw flip flops while simultaneously bobbing up and down, humming a melody she wasn't familiar with. "Sorry. Try to get baby sleep. Up all night. Ah, Missy Ern." He bowed, giving Nicole a view of his daughter, who looked less than a year old.

Nicole was surprised he remembered her name.

"Thieu say she see you at college. She there now, study English. Henry there, too, in college ple-school." Tran pulled a chair out from one of the tables. "Please. I bring tea." He seemed to consider this a social call. They obviously weren't ready for business yet. He poured a cup for both of them and, when she insisted, sat down with her. The baby watched quietly over his shoulder.

She noticed a pencil behind his ear. "Did I interrupt your work?"

Tran scratched his head. She pointed to a tattered little book in his breast pocket, an English to Vietnamese dictionary. He took it out along with a form folded between the pages. "Very hard understand. From rikker board." He spread it out on the table.

"Response to application for liquor license," Nicole read. "The Piskasanet County Liquor Board, after a hearing attended by County Executive Andrew Mauer and with his advice, rejects the application of the Tran's America Restaurant for a license to sell alcoholic beverages."

"Here's the key word." Nicole pointed. "Rejects." She pursed her lips. "It's strange, though. "The liquor board is appointed by the governor and reports to him, not the county executive." As soon as she said it, she realized what must have happened. County Exec Mauer was notoriously against "immigrants coming in here and taking our jobs." He probably knew they weren't taking anybody's jobs, but he clearly knew that's what his voters wanted him to say.

Tran found the word "reject" in his dictionary.

"You could try again," she suggested.

"Try many time. You want to see?" He led her down the corridor and up a flight of rickety steps to the attic. But Nicole saw that it wasn't an attic. There was a lamp, a mattress on the floor, and piles clothes folded neatly beside it. A partly-drawn plastic shower curtain divided the room, and on the other side was a smaller mattress, along with a baseball glove, baseball, some books, a little portable radio, and a pile of clothes stacked more haphazardly than the others.

"Our home," Tran said. "Kitchen, toilet downstair. No more taking bus from Northbrook. Only Thieu and Henry take bus to college. Not far."

The baby on his back was still quiet, nodding off. Tran went to an overturned cardboard box that he'd been using as a desk. "See," he said, picking up three or four rejections from the liquor board.

Nicole looked around Tran's "home." The rough wood ceiling boards sloped low towards the walls. She would only be able to walk halfway in any direction, but for Tran it was less of a problem. The floor boards, where they were visible, were as rough as the ceiling, but the Trans had covered them with pale bamboo mats. Nicole noticed Tran had shed his sandals just inside the doorway and she self-consciously eyed her dirty shoes.

The baby woke and started to cry. Tran began his humming and bobbing again. "Maybe go downstair get milk from flidge," he said. If the bedrooms were spartan, the Trans's kitchen was magnificent. Huge stainless steel stoves and ovens. The refrigerator was five times the size of Nicole's. And there was an even larger freezer standing next to it. Everything was spotless, gleaming in the fluorescent light. Tran took a baby bottle of milk from the fridge, warmed it under steaming hot water from the stainless sink, set it on the counter.

"Want me to take the baby," Nicole offered. She extracted her from the back carrier. "If you're busy, I could—"

Tran handed her the bottle and smiled as Nicole sat holding the baby against her breast and fed her. "Michelle," he said.

"Pardon?"

"Baby's name Michelle."

Nicole felt goosebumps as she cuddled the warm bundle in her arms. Michelle, little Michelle. That sweet, innocent face. Nicole closed her eyes, entering a world of secret longing.

She heard Tran bustling in the kitchen, taking advantage of her help with the baby. He probably had no idea what joy she was feeling. For just a few more moments, she kept her eyes closed, willing all else to disappear.

Little Michelle jerked, coughed, burped. When Nicole opened her eyes, Tran was watching her. Self-conscious but not willing to hand over the baby right away, she stalled. "Tran, if you want to submit the liquor license application again, I'd be glad to help you fill it out. Maybe wait another week or so." She was thinking that Mauer might be in jail by then.

Tran bowed, and she maneuvered Michelle back into the empty carrier still on his back. As Nicole started to leave, Tran said, "Just minute. I give you some egg roll take home. Ready to cook for tonight. You just put in oven."

As Nicole's footsteps echoed on the bare wood floor of Ralph's house, the vision of Tran's living quarters came back. Ralph's quarters were not as empty as Tran's, but the two men had something in common. Both Tran and Ralph were so intent at doing whatever it took to survive that they readily gave up instant gratification. Tran was putting all his effort and money into his business, into the future—immigrant style. And Ralph, the son of an immigrant, was driven to keep the *Shady Park Ledger* financially afloat despite the odds against print media surviving in the current age. Maybe his insecurity about her was partly a general unwillingness to relax and enjoy the here and now because of worry about the future.

Even in making love, Ralph never let down his guard. He always used a condom. Nicole needed somehow to draw him into the present moment. She needed to show him the abandonment to sensual exhilaration she'd felt capable of since waking at the Yaldā vigil, the loving, unworried bliss she'd felt on holding baby Michelle.

22

Trials and tribulations

Secret griefs are more cruel than public calamities.
—Voltaire, *Candide*

Willard's trial was in the historic domed courthouse in Colonial City. Nicole had driven past it often but had never been inside. Along a marble central hallway, men and women in gray suits darted in all directions with yellow folders like mice carrying pieces of cheese, up and down the echoing staircase, along the overhead balcony, towards the elevators. She found Willard's courtroom on the second floor and slid onto a church-like bench next to Emma and her husband Charles.

Willard sat with a lawyer at the front of the room. Since he was pleading guilty, hoping for a light sentence, this wasn't a trial but a sentencing hearing.

Emma whispered, "For some reason Willard expects County Exec Mauer to vouch for his character and argue for leniency. He told me Mauer was a 'straight shooter' who 'had his back.'"

She and Nicole looked around and picked out Pari and Anthony. Also a couple who probably were Willard's parents. And they recognized Shahnaz, the woman Willard had aimed the gun at.

"No sign of the county executive yet," Emma whispered. "Willard's counting on him."

Nicole whispered back, "Guess he's busy preparing for his own trial next week."

"And Andre Smyth said he was going to come." Emma

glanced at Nicole as if she might know why he wasn't there. Nicole shrugged.

The judge came in from a door behind the bench. Willard remained standing, and the prosecutor read the charges. Carrying a firearm in public under the age of 21, taking a gun onto school property, aiming a gun at someone at a school board hearing, and taking a gun onto school property a second time while out on probation before judgment.

"Do you understand all these charges?" the judge asked Willard.

"Sir, yes Sir!"

"How do you plead?"

"Guilty, Sir!"

"Do you have any statement you wish to make before sentencing?"

"Sir, I'm sorry, Sir!"

The judge asked Willard's lawyer if he had anything to add before he passed sentence.

"Your honor, Mr. Scherd has begun a psychological counseling program and has agreed to continue with it." He called Emma's husband, Charles, to the stand. "Mr. Bovant, would you tell us your qualifications as a psychologist."

Charles's face beamed a childlike candor. The question seemed to take him by surprise. "Well," he said. "I have a master's degree in psychology, seven years' experience as a Psycho-Social Interventionalist for Piskasanet County—"

Nicole noticed the judge's eyes glaze over at the term.

"—and considerable experience as a life coach."

"Life coach," Willard's lawyer echoed. "And have you observed any progress since you have been counseling the defendant?"

Charles closed his hazel eyes and took a breath. "Mr. Scherd appears to exhibit a defensive masculinity syndrome in which he conflates religion, aggression, and fear of foreigners with—"

Emma gripped Nicole's arm.

"Excuse me," the lawyer interrupted. "I've asked if there's been any progress, not for a diagnosis."

Charles looked confused by the interruption.

"I repeat," the lawyer said. "Any progress?"

A troubled furrow appeared on Charles's face. "We have made some progress, yes." He leaned towards the microphone. "And more is to be expected."

"Thank you," the lawyer said. "That is all. Your Honor, Mr. Scherd has also begun a course of GED preparation with Piskasanet Community College, which serves incarcerated inmates. And finally …." The lawyer looked around the courtroom. "Your honor, we were hoping to hear from County Executive Andrew Mauer on behalf of Mr. Scherd, but I see he's not present."

Willard shouted out, "He's coming. I'm sure." The judge banged his gavel.

The public prosecutor stood. "Your honor, this morning I received a written statement from County Executive Mauer."

Nicole remembered Mauer sitting on a platform at the school board hearing, face drained white with fear as he looked towards the door where Willard stood aiming his gun at Shahnaz. She remembered Mauer and others fleeing out the back door of the school room when the shot that wounded her rang out.

Willard's lawyer asked to see Mauer's letter. When he'd read it, the judge asked if he had any objection entering it into the record.

"Yes. I do object, your honor."

Willard shouted, "Read it."

His lawyer whispered something privately to him, but Willard stood up. "Read it!"

The judge banged his gavel, then said, "Very well. I am

going to honor the defendant's request."

"Recommendation of Andrew Mauer, County Executive," the prosecutor read. "It is my opinion as a witness to Mr. Scherd's firearm and assault felony that the safety of our community demands Mr. Scherd be incarcerated for the maximum allowable time without the possibility of parole."

Nicole saw Willard turn stiffly in his neck brace towards the prosecutor, his face red, his mouth sagging in a blank, grief-stricken stare. In a movement that seemed painful, his head jerked in a kind of tic. "No," he shouted. "He wouldn't write that."

Another bang of the gavel.

Considering that Mauer himself would soon be tried for graft and misdirection of federal funds for personal gain, Nicole wondered how much effect Mauer's opinion would have on the judge. She didn't have long to wait.

"If there are no more comments, I will pass sentence without further consideration," the judge said. "Mr. Scherd, you are sentenced to the required minimum of three years." Over the low murmuring in the courtroom, the judge added, "With the possibility of parole."

Willard was handcuffed, and as he was being led away, the courtroom door opened, and Andre lumbered in, sleepily rubbing his eyes. It was 1:00 p.m.

Nicole flashed Andre three fingers, sadly mouthing "three years." She couldn't help feeling sorry for Willard. Andre cocked his head as if wondering if he were dreaming. She knew he'd been hoping to speak on Willard's behalf before sentencing. But she couldn't help thinking that might have made things worse.

The courtroom quickly emptied. Anthony and Pari rushed out to the *Ledger* newsroom. Emma gave Shahnaz and her son Jim a hug and walked into the hallway with them. Andre stood in the aisle, a finger on his temple.

"You missed it, Andre. The sentence was mandatory. But the judge emphasized parole was possible."

Andre spoke as if the legal system had betrayed him. "I had something to say before he was sentenced. You would think they'd start trials at a more convenient hour. In Anglo-Saxon times …"

Nicole checked the time on her phone. Ralph would be in the newsroom, waiting to edit Pari and Anthony's report of the trial. She knew they'd stay there late so the article could make it into the morning paper.

"… in Common Law." Andre paused. "Was the county exec here? Willard was expecting him."

Nicole told Andre about Mauer's letter.

Andre blanched. "How did Willard take it?"

"He was shocked."

Andre nodded sadly. "Everybody probably thinks the three years in jail is what's hurting Willard right now. I know it's not. He's grieving over the betrayal of what he thought was a friendship."

Nicole wasn't sure what Andre meant by this. She put her hand on his arm. "Certainly you haven't betrayed his friendship."

"No, not me." He rubbed his eyes. "But I couldn't even say good-bye."

"I know. You can visit him in jail, though. You can help him with his GED work." She walked Andre back to his little blue car with the dented fender.

"I'm feeling a lot of stress," he told her. Nicole had heard from Emma that Andre was into stress avoidance these days. Previously it had been mindfulness and, long before that—but only briefly—organic food. "I feel like I've let Willard down. I should have been here to speak for him." He scraped his shoe across the ground as if trying to erase that from his mind. "And now I'm about to let Natalie down."

"Who's Natalie?"

"A friend of mine who needs a job."

Nicole was getting better at sifting facts from the irrelevant background in Andre's ramblings. She found out he had worked at a church-owned child development center—for about three days—reading stories to little kids. It was the Invokers of Jesus Child Development Center that Bea Doggit had announced was closing. Andre described the pastor who ran the place as a disreputable character. There had been some tension between them—Andre, of course, wasn't specific. The rent on the childcare center was paid up for another month. "After that, Natalie's going to need a job."

"So you're close to Natalie?"

"I worked with her at the center. She's from Guatemala. A close friend of Esmeralda Moreno. She sings—at the Church of the Invokers of Jesus before it shut down, and now Juan Moreno's inviting her to the high school Cultural Alliance Club to sing Spanish songs for the kids."

"My friend Liz said some Northbrook High parents protested against Juan heading the club. Is he OK?"

Andre shrugged. "Juan never complains. I see him when Esmeralda brings him to help his dad out with Old Man Grayson's house construction."

"Let me see. You taught Esmeralda how to drive so she could go to work, and you got Mateo a job building a house for your neighbor, and now you want to find their friend Natalie a job?"

"Well, I'm the Morenos' sponsor, so—"

Nicole allowed a trace of sarcasm in her voice. "Just saying. Did you ever think of getting a job yourself? Or would that be too *stressful*?"

In less than a week, the county executive himself was on trial in the same courtroom. This was a full jury trial. Pari and Anthony offered to take Nicole with them, but she preferred to go alone. She was still trying to keep it secret from Reverend B that she had any connection to "the press," and she thought he might be there.

One member of the jury, a powerfully built brown-skinned man, looked familiar to Nicole. It was Lloyd, the manager of the county warehouse where textbooks were stored. She remembered him reading Anthony and Pari's reports in the *Shady Park Ledger*. That seemed encouraging. Ralph had told her there was considerable doubt that a jury "(1) would understand the charges, and even if they did, (2) would convict the man who promised to defeat gun control, reduce taxes, and keep foreigners out of the county."

It was the same prosecutor who had handled Willard's sentencing, a tall, gangly man with thick glasses and a face squished in from the sides that was hard to look at. He could only have reached his position through unquestionable merit. He brought forth an impressive array of witnesses. The ones who made the deepest impression on Nicole were the fishermen displaced by Bea Doggit's planned Riverside Paradise development, which Mauer had supported in return for a below-market price on a prime house there.

Mr. and Mrs. Grayson testified that Bea's development company had bought and foreclosed on a lien on their property that they weren't aware of, bulldozed their cottage, and built Bea's luxurious villa on the lot. They had been forced to move into a trailer on a relative's lot in the Florida panhandle. Only after the Riverside Paradise scam had been exposed and they were compensated for the loss of their property could the Graysons afford to come back. They still owned a piece of property behind Andre's house, and were staying with friends while building a cottage there.

The Trouts had lived in the house next to Andre's. It had been the one most recently demolished. When the crabbing business dried up and they had difficulty paying their second mortgage, they signed over their home to Bea Doggit with the provision that they could buy it back as long as they kept up with the rent her corporation was charging them to stay there. At first, the rent was lower than the mortgage. But when the rent kept going up, they were no longer able to pay the full amount, and Bea had them evicted.

Bea had already lost the property. Now Mauer was on trial for diverting federal environmental money to build an unapproved sewer line which required a frontage fee that the holdouts in the area wouldn't be able to afford.

The witnesses citing federal, county, and state law gave drier, less emotional testimony. Nicole could see that many jurors still held their eyes on the Graysons and Trouts while these bureaucrats were talking. It was these famlies' personal grief that would convict Mauer, she was sure, not what the witnesses were calling his malfeasance in office.

Because of her classes at the college and the armfuls of papers she had to grade, Nicole could only attend this first day of the trial. As she left the courtroom, she felt a tap on her back. Detective McGinn. He walked out with her.

The air was chilly under low gray clouds. McGinn had something to ask her, and they walked to the city dock instead of to their cars. They sat on a short concrete wall in front of the dark bronze statues of Alex Haley reading to children of different ethnic backgrounds, presumably about how his and their ancestors came to America. "Makes you think," McGinn said. "That Willard ought to be made to sit here and look at this."

"Yeah," Nicole agreed. "His father should, too, from what I hear." She thought for a second and added, "So should a lot of people."

A group of tourists walked by, their children stopping by the statues to toss crackers to the mallards circling in the murky water of the harbor. McGinn turned towards Nicole. "Here's my problem. You got us evidence of kid porno deals being made at the Rectory. That's great. We really appreciate it. But did you notice the Rev never went into the Buy or Sell rooms himself? It wasn't the Rev who gave you the money. We figure his soirées are arranged like that on purpose so he can deny knowledge of the deals."

A cold burst of wind made Nicole fasten the top button of her coat.

"The prosecutor says this case would be a slam dunk if we could catch the Rev doing a deal himself."

This seemed impossible, and Nicole said so.

"We're thinking if you could get him to meet you personally, not at a soirée. Say you tell him you have something very graphic. You don't want anybody else to know you have it."

Nicole was shivering. She felt dirty.

"Once again," McGinn said, "you don't have to do this. It's just that the department is determined to get this guy. That student of yours? Juan Moreno? The Rev is pressuring us to charge him with distributing child pornography. It wouldn't stick, but he could cause a public scandal over it."

Nicole inhaled a stuttered breath. She felt her fingernails scrape against the wall. McGinn must have seen that he had her. "So here's what I think," he said.

The white columns of the Rectory appeared on the little rise in front of Osprey Creek. It had taken Nicole only ten minutes to walk here from the dock after Detective McGinn left. She knew the doorman wouldn't let her in to talk to Reverend Blatchford, even if he was home, so she'd bought a card on Main Street and sealed a note in the envelope. *Rev. Blatchford, I have come across some disturbingly graphic material that I think you should see. It would be too embarrassing for me to turn it over to you in public like the last time. Could you possibly grant me a private interview?*

She had to knock several times. In the daylight, she noticed the muscles of the man who opened the door. He looked more like a bodyguard or bouncer than a doorman. He held the envelope in the flat of his huge hand like a formal message on a tray. "Does Reverend Blatchford know how to reach you?"

"Would you please ask him to leave a message at my college number?"

23

Looking under rocks

Few secrets can escape an investigator who has opportunity and license to undertake such a quest and skill to follow it up.

—Nathaniel Hawthorne, *The Scarlet Letter*

Executive Mauer's trial lasted only three days. Anthony and Pari's *Shady Park Ledger* reports kept Nicole up to date. There were protests each day outside the courthouse calling for Mauer to be found not guilty. TV newscasts constantly dragged up old footage of him defending gun rights, calling for teachers to be armed, complaining that immigrants were sucking the welfare coffers dry, and, of course, promising to reduce taxes.

But the case against Mauer was clear-cut. Thanks possibly in part to warehouse Lloyd's thorough understanding of the case, he was convicted in 24 hours of misconduct in office and sentenced to six months in jail. "A white-collar sentence," Ralph called it when he phoned Nicole.

Mauer was replaced with a big blond woman of the same party with the same values, but Ralph predicted Mauer would be out before six months and easily re-elected the next time around. "You can't keep a bad man down," he quipped. "Not in politics." He said a felony would prevent you from running for office, but not malfeasance. Robo calls were already starting to flood the county urging "all citizens in favor of the American way" to vote for Mauer on the next ballot.

Nicole sat at Ralph's dining room table trying to prepare

for the next day's classes but couldn't concentrate. She opened her laptop and started paging through displays of infant wear for girls. The little outfits were so cute they almost made her cry.

Ralph called again. "We're really busy here reporting on Mauer's sentencing. Want me to bring some Grab 'n Go chicken for dinner?"

Nicole didn't feel like cooking. She wanted to sit and look at baby outfits. "Yes," she said, feeling a little guilty. "Would you?"

"Oaky doaky."

"Ralph?"

"Uh-huh?"

"I love you."

"Oh, uh, yeah, me too."

By the time Bobby got home, Nicole had already ordered $98 worth of clothes for Liz's baby. She'd glanced again at the community college lesson but then started flipping through old photos on her laptop.

Bobby dropped his backpack on the floor beside her. "Looks like pictures from Shady Park Elementary and Middle School. Everybody wants you to come back."

Nicole smiled.

"Well, maybe not *Chal-say*." Bobby pronounced Chelsea Grosbeck's name the way Chelsea did. "She talks to me while I'm waiting for the bus and she's waiting for her mother to pick her up. She says her mother steals her Adderall and uses it. She said her parents might be getting a divorce."

"Oh, that's too bad." Nicole hoped that didn't come out too flat.

"Yeah, I looked up Adderall on Wikipedia. All the symptoms of overuse? Mrs. Grosbeck has them."

"I see. Anything else you've been looking into?"

"Uh-huh. Zillow. You wouldn't believe how much they

say your house is worth. You could sell it and move in here."

Nicole's cheeks warmed.

"I mean, Dad told me he was going to ask you to move in. Did you say *no?*"

Her cheeks aflame, Nicole said he hadn't asked her. What she didn't tell him was she suspected he was having second thoughts after she'd gone to the soirée, stayed out all night, and never offered the explanation he'd probably been waiting for. To hide her embarrassment, she turned on the local news—"the local shootings," as Ralph called it.

"Live. Breaking news. WPSK brings you up-to-date news, weather, and sports." A ruggedly handsome man and a doll-skinned blond woman, her long glistening hair showcased over one shoulder, sat side by side at a desk in front of a background of swirling logos and colorful designs probably meant to attract viewers with short attention spans. "Here with the latest developments are John Rowland and Megyn Drumpfer."

"Burr. Another chilly day, wasn't it, John?"

"Megyn, it sure was. And coming up soon, we'll have Victoria Whitman from the Statewide Weather Service here to tell us just how cold it was."

"That's Dad's boss's daughter," Bobby told her. "She used to be a reporter, but she quit to go on TV. Dad says her new boyfriend's father is in show business or something."

There was no news about Andrew Mauer's sentence.

"They'll read about it in tomorrow morning's *Shady Park Ledger*," Bobby quipped. "Then they'll go and stand outside the courtroom and do a 'live' report on what they read."

Instead of a report on Mauer's sentence, old clips of the ousted County Executive Mauer dominated the "news." There was a clip of him bragging about signing an executive order prohibiting companies that do business in the county from hiring illegal immigrants. "We have to stop criminal immigrants from flooding the county, terrorizing our citizens, taking our jobs, and draining our precious resources."

Megyn's head bobbed. "Well, John, these are important issues for our viewers."

"Yes, Megyn, this is what the polls show."

Later, after Bobby was asleep, Ralph wanted to talk about Reverend B. He'd asked Anthony to dig into his past using the paper's access to public documents. "He flaunts his Doctor of Divinity degree. But that's strictly an honorary degree, I found out. You can actually buy one on the internet. His is from a seminary in Ohio. Cost him $129, including frame. No evidence he's ever been to Ohio."

Nicole was less surprised than Ralph might have expected.

"He has been to West Virginia, though. Grew up there. Alvin Blatchford. Married a 15-year-old, annulled the next year. No details on that yet. Never remarried. Sexual harassment charge—dropped—in Morgantown, where he ran a Bible study school. He shows up in Piskasanet County as the Reverend Augustus Blatchford, Doctor of Divinity, about ten years ago."

"Sexual harassment? You think he might be dangerous?"

"Can't say, Nikki. From now on, though, you should definitely stay away from him. I'm going to have Anthony and Pari see what else they can uncover."

"You're not going to put it in the *Ledger*, are you?"

"What do you mean? Probably. He's on the school board. People should know who he really is."

Nicole squeezed his hand. "I wish you wouldn't put this in the paper."

Ralph drew back a little, frowning a confused *why*.

"I ... because ...." Nicole gave up trying to contrive an explanation and sat in his lap instead. It wasn't hard to distract him.

Ralph got into bed first. Nicole lit a candle on the dresser he'd given her and stood facing it in the dim light, removing her clothes piece by piece and draping them on the clothes rack next to it, studying herself in the mirror. Her stomach was flat, firm to her touch. She had the kind of figure that wouldn't show much if she got pregnant. That's what her mother had told her. Nicole moved her hands over her abdomen. It couldn't be her choice alone. Ralph had to want a baby, too.

From the dresser, she pulled out the raspberry red nightgown she'd been looking for the night Ralph first came to her house. Raising her arms to let it drop in place, she felt her heart beat faster as she recalled how passionately he had desired her then. Slowly, she turned and stepped towards the bed. There was a gentle wheezing sound. Ralph was asleep.

Nicole found a note in her college mailbox the next class day. *Please see Prof. Shandule about a student complaint.*

There was no time to see him before teaching, so of course she fretted about it through all three of her classes. It seemed hard enough getting students to *notice* what she said or did, much less judge it. If Janet the perm student had any objection, it had to be the apathy of the other students rather than anything Nicole did. The only muttering she'd heard from any of the other students was about Presidents' Day not going to be a holiday.

When her last class was over, she walked down the narrow hallway to the open door of Mark Shandule's office. As usual, he was staring so intently at his computer he didn't notice her standing there until she cleared her throat. He leaned forward and shook her hand. "You're doing a great job, Nicole."

She took a cursory peep at the note, now shriveled with sweat in her hand. Yes, it was for her. Her name was on it. "I had a note to see you."

Mark's thoughts were obviously still on his computer. "Ah, that was, oh yes, about a student?"

"A complaint, the note said."

Mark swiveled his chair and rustled through some papers on his desk. He chuckled. "Right. It seems you've been teaching witchcraft."

Nicole's books slipped from her hands onto the floor. She didn't know whether to laugh or cry. She must have been closer to the latter because Mark said, "No. No. Nothing to be upset about." He picked up her books and stacked them on top of his desk. "The complaint is from the mother of a student."

Nicole raked her mind for any possible explanation. Then it came to her. Following Mark's syllabus, she'd asked the students last week to write a definition of what it means to be a hero. One student read from a draft he'd written that used Harry Potter as an example. She told this to Mark, and he nodded with a grin. "Bingo," he said. "There you are."

Mark seemed to think the discussion was over. She wondered if she was being fired. But then, "We have these parents sometimes," he went on.

"So—?"

"No use arguing with them. You just have to learn to ignore them." He studied her face. "Do you know which student's mother might have made the complaint?"

It was probably the Christmas Carol boy's mother, Nicole now assumed, but she didn't want to cause him any more embarrassment. "No," she answered. "I can't be sure."

"Good," Mark said. "We can't hold it against a student that his parents are jerks."

Nicole relaxed in her chair, noticing for the first time the picture of a man on Mark's computer. He saw her staring at it. "Doing a little research," he explained. "Digging up information on a potential candidate to replace me on the board of education."

The man on his computer screen was bald, with a pointy goatee. She leaned forward for a closer look. There was no doubt. It was the man who'd bought the child pornography from her at Reverend B's soirée.

Mark said, "He's a friend of one of the other board members, Reverend Blatchford. Supposed to be close to the county exec, too. But I don't know. This might be a rock I wasn't supposed to look under. According to *peoplesearch.com*, he's had several arrests. Drunk and disorderly conduct, assault."

"You're not going to quit the board, are you, Professor Shandule?" Nicole had attended the meeting when he was narrowly elected to replace Bea Doggit, after which he swung the vote against using her fundamentalist texts in the county schools.

Mark shook his head, reading more from the screen. "Battery, spouse abuse. This man looks dangerous. No, I won't quit to let him take my place. They'll have to somehow make me."

Nicole checked her college voicemail before going home. There was a message from Reverend B's secretary. *The Reverend would like to meet you on the pier behind the Rectory on Friday at two o'clock.*

24

Porn pushing

In the destructive element immerse.
—Joseph Conrad, *Lord Jim*

Three cardboard boxes were on Nicole's doorstep when she got home—the baby clothes she'd ordered for Liz. What could be better to clear her head? She wrapped them and sped up to Liz's house in Northbrook.

"They're so cute. You shouldn't have, Nicole." Liz laid the outfits out on the couch for Alfonse to see when he got home.

Nicole wanted all the news from Northbrook High.

"Remember Trisha in your social studies class? She broke up with the boyfriend she was sending nude pictures to. He didn't take it very well. He started forwarding the pictures to all his friends. 'Revenge porn,' they call it. Now Trisha is the laughing stock of the class."

"What's Higgy doing about it? Anything?"

"You know Higgy. He fears bad publicity more than death. So, no. He met with Reverend B on the board, turned the kids' phones over to him, and they agreed to keep it quiet. I got this all from Brian."

"Are Trisha's parents OK with that? They aren't asking Higgy to suspend the ex-boyfriend?"

"They begged Higgy not to. They don't want it to come out that their daughter was sexting." Liz shrugged. "No, Trisha's life is miserable now, and it looks like it's going to be that way until she graduates. Maybe even after."

Nicole had been thinking of telling Detective McGinn she was too scared to meet Reverend B again. Now Liz's story changed her mind.

In the police station, a busty policewoman took Nicole into a small room with a shelf full of gadgets. "I'm Sergeant Jackson. Detective McGinn said you agreed to wear a miniaturized voice recording device."

Nicole gave her a blank stare.

"A wire. We still call it a wire."

"Oh."

"So, would you unbutton her blouse, please?"

"Oh. OK, I guess."

The sergeant paused. "Better get you to sign this first."

Nicole didn't even read it. There was no turning back now. The sergeant taped what looked like a flattened black earbud with a short wire hanging from it just beneath her breast. Below that she attached and taped a tiny black battery, then said, "Button up, please." She stood back and looked. "All set, then."

Nicole felt anything but all set.

McGinn had her sit down in his office. Three cameras with long lenses were lined up on his desk. We'll be in place with zoom cameras trained on the pier." He met her eyes. "No worries. Worse thing you can do is look nervous or afraid." He took something from his desk drawer and slid it across to her. "The flash drive."

If he knew what she was doing, Ralph would have a heart attack. She filled two bowls with Tuna Florentine and Garden Greens in a Delicate Napolitana Sauce for Smokey and drove her own car to Colonial City. Luckily, she found a spot to park near Osprey Creek. A cold northern breeze made her shudder as she walked down Creek Street towards the Rectory. She turned up her collar and pulled her hands up into the sleeves of her coat.

No one was in the front yard. A flagstone path led around the side of the house, probably to the pier in the back yard. She followed it.

The cold caused her leg to ache. She wondered if it was always going to be like this. She could see the pier now stretching out into the creek. Tied to it was a sleek, glittering red cigarette boat. Nobody was on the pier.

Nicole stopped at the edge, looked back at the house, and checked the time on her phone. 1:55. She took a breath and walked out along the uneven boards, the pier shuddering slightly in the wind. She reached the end and looked down into the dark water. Mallards. They didn't seem to feel the cold.

She heard a door open behind her. Reverend Blatchford, in a long black overcoat, black fedora, and red bow tie stole across the grass eyeing the perimeter, then stepped onto the pier. He extended his hand almost as if he expected her to kiss it. "So good to see you again, Ms. Ernst. How wonderful to have you on our side in the crusade for decency in the schools."

She avoided his hand by folding her arms with an affected shiver. "Yes," she said, "I have a video I would like to turn over to you. Actually, I was hoping you would pay for it."

Reverend B took a step back and signaled towards the house. The door opened, and the goatee man trundled out, his German shepherd following him excitedly onto the pier. "Sit," the man commanded, and with a whimper the dog obeyed.

"I believe you've met Peter Diggs? He handles the crusade's expenses."

The goateed Mr. Diggs held out his hand. At first, Nicole thought it was to shake, but he growled, "The video," fixing

Nicole with vacant, slightly bloodshot eyes. "We'll need to examine it first."

Reverend B pulled Diggs aside and lowered his voice, but Nicole could hear him say, "Skip that. We'll have to trust her. I need the money now that the book deal's off."

She felt an icy chill stream up her back and wondered if she could go through with this. She remembered McGinn's final instruction: *Get the Rev to say clearly he'll pay for a child pornography video.*

"How much are you paying me to turn over this child pornography video?" she asked Reverend B, hoping it didn't sound too stilted. She should have practiced.

"I didn't think you were greedy, Ms. Ernst. We'll pay you the same we paid for the last video." He nodded to his partner.

Diggs pulled a wad of bills from his pocket and held it up as if offering a treat to a dog. He held out his other hand. "The video."

Nicole stuffed the roll of bills into her coat pocket, then unbuttoned the coat and took the flash drive from the breast pocket of her blouse. As she did, Diggs took a step closer and narrowed his eyes. "Not wearing a wire, are you, Missy?" He probed beneath her breast with a stubby finger.

Nicole slapped his hand away, and instantly the German shepherd sprang on her. The force thrust her over the edge of the pier and into the dark, freezing water. Her face and hands, first, then neck and arms lost their feeling. Her wet coat pulled her below the surface. She managed to slip it off, but her whole body was stiff. She started to swim towards the black, muddy bank. Then she blacked out.

III

25

Red squares

Yet in our ashen cold is fire yreken.
—Chaucer, *The Canterbury Tales*

She felt soft, warm hands on her face. Slowly drifting into consciousness, Nicole thought it was her mother. Her eyes unlocked to let in a slit of light. She touched the hand on her cheek.

"*Khodārā shukr.*" It wasn't her mother. Nicole willed her eyes wider open. It was Pari's mother, Mastaneh, beaming down at her. "You're back with us," Mastaneh sang out. "Thank God." She swept a lock of hair from Nicole's face. "You've been sleeping for a while."

Mastaneh was in a white uniform. Nicole remembered she was a nurse. At City Hospital! Is that where she was? A silvery sheet of Mylar like she'd seen covering caged immigrant children on the TV news crinkled as she tried to get up. She reached out to Mastaneh and saw there was an IV tube in her arm.

Mastaneh took her hand. "Lie still a minute, Dear." She peeled patches from each side of Nicole's forehead, hurting her a little. "Sorry," she said. "With hypothermia we have to check for, you know, damage of any kind. Your signs are normal."

Glaring white light flooded the hospital room, but through a far window, Nicole could see it was dark outside. A rotting smell of algae hung around the bed, and when she stirred, she realized it was coming from her. She lifted the edge of the

Mylar and saw she was naked.

"How do you feel?" Mastaneh asked, removing the IV and switching off a monitor beside the bed. "Can you talk to me? Do you remember what happened?"

"I ... I was swimming. It was cold."

Mastaneh put her hand on Nicole's forehead. "Anything else you can remember?"

"Nothing after that."

"And before that?"

It was starting to come back. Nicole slid her hand under the Mylar sheet, ran it over her chest. "Where are my clothes? How did I get here?"

"The paramedics." Mastaneh smiled. "Same man who brought you here before with a gunshot to the leg." She picked up a card from the bedrail shelf. "He said to give you this."

It was his Emergency Medical Technician card. On the back he'd written *We have to stop meeting like this*! Emergency room humor.

Mastaneh cranked up the bed so Nicole could sit holding the silvery sheet to her neck. "He's a nice man, the paramedic," she said. "He wants you to call him when you get better."

The conversation was taking on a surreal tone. Nicole wondered if she were dreaming. She closed her eyes, then opened them to make sure this was real.

"A county policeman followed the ambulance here," Mastaneh said. "He was worried about you, but we couldn't let him come in." She giggled, handing Nicole another card. "Also wants you to call him."

Nicole nodded. "Um, my clothes?"

Mastaneh pointed to a plastic bag on a chair. "Funny. The policeman wanted to look at your clothes. We couldn't let him do that. Hospital rules."

"Could I see them, please?"

"Your phone and keys are there on the shelf. The phone

seems to still work." Mastaneh lifted the bag and dropped it back down with a splat. "The clothes are a soggy mess. But don't worry. I called my daughter Pari. They heard the call to the ambulance on the newsroom radio. Pari, Anthony, and their editor Ralph should be here any minute." Mastaneh took a white robe from a shelf. "Can you stand? Here, you can put this on for now."

When Mastaneh left to give her some privacy, Nicole slid off the bed, slipped on the robe, and opened the bag of clothes. An even stronger algae smell seeped out as she raked through the cold, wet mess, pulling out her blouse. It's pocket was empty. She went through the bag with both hands. No wire.

"Those things are going to need a good washing." Mastaneh seemed puzzled. "Everything there?"

Before Nicole could answer, Ralph, Pari, and Anthony burst into the room. Ralph started to put his arms around her, then hesitated as if afraid he might hurt her. The room resounded with concern. Was she OK? What happened? Nicole's answers were evasive. Mastaneh frowned, noticing, and told them Nicole was still weak, needed to sit down. Which was true.

Anthony had his notebook out. Pari was asking more questions. The ambulance was sent to Osprey Creek—what was she doing there? Why were the police on the scene?

They were Nicole's friends, but they were "the press." After all she'd been through, she didn't want to expose Detective McGinn's operation prematurely. She needed to talk to him before she said anything more.

Ralph put his hands on Pari's shoulders. "Pari, Anthony, I think that's enough for now. I'll call you after Nicole and I have time to talk at home."

Ralph drove down North-South Highway with the heater

on full-blast despite the beads of sweat dotting his forehead. He was quiet, only resting his hand on her knee now and then as if to make sure she was still there. He seemed too occupied with his own thoughts to talk. *Home* had meant where? Nicole saw he was heading for his house—*her* home now, this seemed to imply. And yet they weren't talking like a happy couple.

Bobby was staying at his aunt's. Ralph made her a bowl of Ramen, which she slurped down still wearing Pari's overcoat. He put his hands on her cheeks. "You're warmer now. But you smell like the creek. Want to take a hot shower?"

She stood under the hot water until her fingers turned to prunes. As soon as she turned off the shower, Ralph tapped at the door with a huge red, white, and blue beach towel to wrap her in.

"What's this?" he said, touching a red mark on her chest. Nicole herself hadn't noticed. Now she saw two small red squares just below her breast and two larger ones a few inches below—obviously where the tape holding the wire had been removed. It was odd that Mastaneh hadn't mentioned anything about this.

"Oh, um, must be where they hooked some device up to me in the hospital. My skin's so sensitive."

Ralph seemed mesmerized by the geometrical red shapes as if she might have been abducted by aliens and marked with their sinister designs. "Does it hurt? Should we put some lotion on you or something?"

The marks didn't hurt, but Nicole said, "Yes, that might be nice. There, on the shelf." She held the towel open with both hands for Ralph to perform the application. Of course, this got both of them excited.

Later that night, in Ralph's arms, she fell into the deepest sleep she'd had in a long time.

In the morning, though, Ralph stared into his coffee, stirring and stirring as if looking for the answer to a troubling question. Nicole knew it wasn't only how she ended up being pulled from the bank of Osprey Creek but something deeper than that: why was she keeping it secret from him? In his downcast face, she read a struggle to trust her, to repress a fear that she was not completely his.

Nicole swirled a spoon in her own cup, searching for something she could tell him without spoiling a police investigation into a real threat to children in their neighborhood—and beyond. She knew Ralph well enough by now to realize he wouldn't interrogate her. He'd brood silently, waiting for her to come out and tell him. He'd been doing that since the night before the soirée when she couldn't tell him where she was going.

The more Ralph brooded, the cloudier his eyes became. She knew it was her fault. But he had to hold out a little longer. Maybe she could tell him everything soon. She'd find out today when she talked to McGinn.

Ralph put down his coffee without finishing it. "I'm off to the newsroom. No classes today, right? Any plans? Maybe you should just hang around and take it easy."

"I'm really feeling fine" was all she said.

Ralph pulled on his coat, stuck his glasses into his pocket, bent to Nicole for a kiss.

Her phone rang. Piskasanet Co. Police.

"Oh, sorry, Ralph. I have to take this."

His eyes glazed over. "Sure. OK. Bye."

26

Unwired

"Conflicting duties divide my mind
Like the current of a river
Split by a rock into two courses."
—Kalidasa, *The Recognition of Sakuntala*

Detective McGinn said he'd come to her house, so Nicole had to rush over there. She felt ashamed. She was keeping a secret from the detective as well as from Ralph—because she didn't want McGinn to think she was "in league with the press," cooperating only to get an exclusive story.

McGinn held a bottle of wine. "I don't know if you … I thought after what you've been through—"

"Thank you. The nurse said you followed the ambulance to the hospital."

"I tried to ride along with you, but the paramedic said *no*. We're not family. I wanted to make sure you're OK." McGinn swept his eyes over her as if searching for evidence. "*Are* you OK? I called the hospital this morning. They said your 'recovery was complete.'"

Nicole nodded. "I don't remember anything from the time I fell in until I woke up in the hospital."

"We were watching the whole time, but it happened fast. I radioed for the paramedics, and my buddy and I rushed to the creek. When we pulled you out, I was afraid you were dead."

Standing over dead people probably was something Detective McGinn was accustomed to in his line of work, especially since Piskasanet County bordered the City, which had one of the highest murder rates in the nation. But Nicole imagined him reflecting that hers would have been a corpse he was responsible for.

"You're very brave, Ms. Ernst. I never imagined something like this might happen. The department dragged the creek last night and pulled out your coat. We got the roll of wet bills from the pocket. And the nurse said your phone was still in your jeans, wet but still working."

"Did you arrest Reverend B and his henchman?"

"Not yet. Something I wanted to talk to you about. We got plenty of pictures, but to clinch the case, we need the wire. Matt says it's waterproof, should be fine."

"That's a relief," Nicole said.

"So where is it?"

"What? I thought you had it."

"No. When they pulled the curtain aside in the hospital, after you were in bed and being treated, I asked to look through your clothes, but they wouldn't let me. They knew I was a cop, but they're worried about missing personal belongings. Can't blame them. We take the same precautions at the station."

Nicole was confused. "You didn't take the wire?"

"No. I assume the hospital staff must have taken it off and put it in with your wet clothes."

"But they didn't."

"You're saying—"

"It wasn't there when I looked."

"Wasn't there? Hold on." McGinn called the station and talked for a minute, then told Nicole, "Sergeant Jackson says she taped it on 'real good.' It wouldn't fall off in water."

Nicole thought of the red splotches on her body and agreed. "So where does that leave us?"

McGinn was staring at her. "Mind if I see the bag of wet clothes? Check it again?"

It was at Ralph's house. That would be hard to explain.

"Trust me," she pleaded. "I took everything out, and it wasn't in there." She thought for a minute. "One thing, though." She told him Reverend B's henchman Peter Diggs had poked her to see if she was wearing a wire. "But I think I pushed his hand away before he could tell."

McGinn took out his notebook and a voice recorder. "Would you mind giving me your account of the whole exchange? As step-by-step as you can?"

When she finished, McGinn said, "Anything else you can remember? Anything at all?"

"I heard them talking. I got the idea Reverend B has a financial stake in Bea Doggit's fundamentalist textbook company."

"I don't see—"

"That's got to be why he tried to get Bea's books voted back in."

"You're talking about a board of education meeting you went to?"

"Right. As soon as Bea was kicked off the board for voting to sell the county her own books and the purchase was rescinded, Reverend B asked for an immediate vote, legal this time, to re-adopt Bea's books. It didn't work."

"So it's all about money with this guy."

Nicole gave this some thought. "Maybe. But there was something about the way he laid his hands on the girls when I visited the Wilcox. It gave me a chill."

McGinn tightened his jaw. He turned off the recorder and snapped his notebook shut. "I think I'll go back to the hospital, see if anybody knows anything about the missing wire." He rolled his eyes towards Nicole. "Mind coming with me? You know, give your permission to show me anything of yours they might still have?"

The hospital was in a City district where shootings constantly occurred. McGinn drove. He'd been there many times. Nicole gazed silently through the window at the growing number of liquor stores, auto body repair shops, and fast food places that sprang up along the highway as they neared the City. McGinn was quiet, too.

The low bridge over Harbor Inlet provided a gray, misty view of freighters, barges, and tugs moving so slowly they seemed painted on the leaden water. McGinn maneuvered the one-way streets, lane changes, and traffic jams like a taxi driver. Nicole gripped her armrest, now and then closing her eyes.

"Short cut." McGinn turned into an alley between the chain-link back yard fences of brick row houses, swerving to avoid garbage cans left in the way. They came out on a street filled with people walking towards an old stone church at the end of the block. "Looks like some big rally," McGinn said. The crowded street gave him no choice but to pull over and stop. He opened his door. "Let's see what this is about."

"You sure?"

Taking her arm in his, he weaved through the crowd towards the church. Most of the people were black, more of them women than men, and all were dressed in their Sunday best. "I know the woman up on the church step," McGinn said. "Amanda Winwright."

"Um-hum," the woman next to them said. "That's her."

Nicole recognized Amanda, too. She was a gun control advocate who'd recently replaced Derek Grosbeck as state GOP Central Committee chair when his reputation was tarnished by his fundraising for the Riverside Paradise scheme.

"That's Pastor Holmes with the microphone," the woman beside McGinn told them.

Pastor Holmes had glossy brown cheeks, wore priestly black, and had a distinguished touch of gray at his temples.

"The time is now," he pleaded passionately through the loud-speaker. "The bloodshed must stop. Just last night a child was shot dead by a stray bullet. And our politicians are calling for it to be even easier to buy guns. O Lord, we ask you to help our lawmakers see the light."

Amanda Winwright took the mic, although with her portly stature and booming voice she hardly needed it. "We hear you, Pastor Holmes. One long-time opponent of gun control in our neighboring Piskasanet County has been removed from office. This must only be a first step. We must continue the fight to keep guns out of the hands of the violent, the mentally sick."

McGinn was nodding his approval. "Guess you agree," he said to Nicole, glancing at her leg.

"I'd agree even if I'd never been shot," she said, a little indignant.

"Well, sure. I didn't mean ...." McGinn took one of the flyers being passed around. "Cops have their own reasons for wanting gun control, too."

Nicole also took a flyer. At the top it read *Citizens for Gun Control*.

Whenever Amanda Winwright made a point, the crowd called out, "Uh-huh, uh-huh." When she gave the mic back to Pastor Holmes and he called for a change, they shouted, "Amen!"

"We need to elect politicians brave enough to oppose the gun lobby," Pastor Holmes said. Under her breath, Nicole mouthed, "Amen."

McGinn put his hand on her back. "OK. I think I know how we can get around this demonstration and into the hospital parking garage."

A ramp led from the garage into the emergency waiting room. McGinn showed his badge, and the desk clerk checked the records for the medical staff who'd treated Nicole. Mastaneh and the doctor were paged.

A hysterical scream issued from outside the entryway. "Counseling? Are you crazy? There's nothing wrong with me." Nicole thought the voice sounded familiar.

"I'm sure my husband is behind this. I take a few pills to keep me going, OK?" It was Britney Grosbeck, Nicole was sure. She walked to the swinging door and peeked through the glass to confirm it.

"I'll tell you who needs counseling. Depraved kids in our schools sending pornographic pictures. That's who." It was definitely Britney. "If there are pills that give me the energy I need to find and expose these perverts, that's a good thing. No, no counseling. I'm going home."

Mastaneh tapped the back of Nicole's shoulder. She was with a doctor so young he looked like he'd just been hatched. They'd already talked to Detective McGinn. The doctor said, "Ms. Ernst, I watched the nurse put your wet clothes into the bag. There was a cell phone in your pocket and some keys. Nothing else. I presume those items have been returned."

Nicole involuntarily touched her chest where the wire had been taped. She nodded.

Mastaneh said, "A preacher man came looking for you this morning. Very concerned. He wanted me to ask you to call him if I see you again. He said you have his number."

"A preacher?"

"Yes. Dark suit. Bow tie. Very nice."

"Nice?"

"He thanked me and said, 'God bless you.' Only a nice man would say that."

Nicole made no comment.

The trip back from the hospital was even more silent than the trip there. Detective McGinn was probably mulling over the missing wire. Nicole wondered about that, too, but was mostly worried that McGinn would want her to contact Reverend B again. She dreaded the thought.

McGinn pulled up in front of her house. Before Nicole could get out, he said, "Going to give the Rev a call?"

She gripped the door handle. "How can I be sure he and Diggs didn't suspect I was setting them up the last time?"

"That is a concern." McGinn drummed his fingers on the steering wheel. "Just thinking. What if you called him right now from the car while you're with me? Just see what he says. You can put him on speaker phone and I'll record him."

Nicole let out a sigh. "Detective McGinn, there's another reason it's hard for me to go on with this." She gripped her hands together. "There's something I should tell you. I'm ... seeing somebody. It's Ralph Novich, editor of the *Shady Park Ledger*."

McGinn gave her the sideways look of a dog trying to focus.

"I mean, please don't think I've ever said a word to him about this. I understand any publicity would compromise the investigation."

"It would. The whole case against the Rev and now this Peter Diggs guy would fold if word got out before we can make an arrest."

Nicole fingered her house keys. "It's hard. I never gave Ralph any explanation for being pulled from Osprey Creek. None at all. The secrecy is causing problems between us. I don't know if you can understand."

"No? Believe me, Ms. Ernst. I understand." He looked away. "Good thing you're not a cop." A dull cast clouded his eyes as he stared through the windshield, and Nicole saw the detective in a new light. He was probably used to making personal sacrifices in order to bring criminals to justice. "I'll call him," she decided.

McGinn brightened. "Tell you what. If you can just find

out when his next soirée is, that might be good enough. I'm assuming we'll turn up the wire. If we do, my guys will raid the Rectory and arrest him that night."

"And if the wire can't be found?"

McGinn shifted his eyes towards her without turning his head. "We might have to ask you to go in and make another sale."

Nicole's hands were shaking when she dialed. Reverend B himself answered, all solicitous. "What a terrifying accident, Ms. Ernst. We were worried to death. Thank the Lord you survived."

"Yes, I've completely recovered. I must have slipped. I know I've caused everybody a lot of trouble."

"Not at all, Ms. Ernst. And, I must say, we are extremely pleased with the material we received from you."

Nicole took this as her cue. "I may be able to get more. Would you let me know when you're having a soirée again?"

"Definitely, Ms. Ernst. I'll give you a call. I have your number now."

Nicole ended the call. McGinn shut off his recorder. "And you have *my* number, Ms. Ernst. We'll wait. If we can find the wire and keep this investigation under cover until the next soirée, we might be able to catch these scumbags."

27

Mother issues

"Soma distribution!" shouted a loud voice.
"In good order, please. Hurry up, there."
—Aldous Huxley, *Brave New World*

Nicole picked up that morning's paper from her front yard. In the Police Blotter section was a brief note: "At 6:00 p.m. yesterday a woman was rescued from Osprey Creek and taken to City Hospital to be treated for hypothermia." That was it. Ralph had kept his promise to clamp a lid on the story, but the *Shady Park Ledger* couldn't completely abdicate its duty to report on every local news event. This was Ralph's compromise. If anybody read the notice, there was no way they'd imagine she was that woman. Not Liz, not her mother—nobody. Bobby was confused that the *Ledger* didn't have a story about her being fished out of the creek, but he promised not to mention it at school.

She bought some chick peas, cauliflower, and spices to make vegetarian curry at Ralph's with a recipe Liz had given her. Ralph was quiet the whole evening. She could tell Bobby didn't like the curry, but he ate it all and told her it was good. After dinner, Ralph went into the kitchen to wash the dishes, and Bobby went to his desk to do homework, rolling the basketball on the floor between his feet. Nicole heard him shut his book and sigh.

"Need any help, Bobby?"

He shook his head.

"Your dad says Aunt Beth is going to Pittsburgh to visit

relatives in a couple days. When she does, I'll be here when you get home from school."

"Awesome." He stood up and started dribbling the ball in front of his desk, the thumps reverberating in the nearly empty room. Then he stopped. "Our school trip to the Air and Space Museum was canceled. The principal said, "No more *te-rips* until we find out who's sending *lew-id* texts. One of our *in-felu-ential* parents is going to take this up with the board of education if we don't find the *cul-perit* by the next meeting."

"I see why you're upset."

"It's Mrs. Grosbeck, he's talking about. She's the influential parent. She's always coming to our school." Bobby twirled the basketball between two fingers. "*Now* do you think I should tell who the girl is? I'm letting everybody down."

"If you tell, the girl might be expelled. So—"

"I know. She's silly, kind of stupid, but I can't see getting her kicked out of school for that."

From the kitchen she heard Ralph talking on his phone. She couldn't hear well, but she caught the words "appointment with the principal."

"Did you tell your dad about the canceled trip, Bobby?"

"Not yet." Bobby had a conspiratorial grin. "He's talking about something else."

"With your principal? What is it?"

"No. Not with him. He asked me not to tell."

Things had changed between her and Ralph. Nicole couldn't deny it. She was being forced to hide something from him—and now this secret of his. At night, things hadn't changed much. They still made love. But sometimes Nicole worried she was the one initiating it. She'd read that sexual desire decreases with age, but the opposite seemed to be happening with her now that she was with Ralph. Maybe she was a "late bloomer." That's what her mother would say. Maybe

Liz would say it was her biological clock racing towards a shutdown. But what it felt like was love, maybe with a tinge of insecurity.

After classes at the college, in which the discussion of *The Scarlet Letter* showed neither that the students appreciated the story nor that they objected to it but that most of them had not read it, she drove to her house. The morning *Ledger* had landed on a yellowed azalea when the delivery boy's mom threw it out her car window. Next to the trellis above the entry path to her cottage was a post supporting a wooden mailbox, shedding its white paint. She drew out an official looking envelope. From Starkezahn, Starkezahn, and Starkezahn.

The name brought a sour taste to her mouth. She never thought she'd have to encounter Derek Grosbeck's lawyer again. She recalled the dapper figure of Mr. Starkezahn in his gabardine suit last spring questioning her claim that Chelsea Grosbeck had plagiarized her paper.

She was struck by the nerve of Grosbeck. He and his wife Britney had humiliated her, used their influence to get their daughter Chelsea's grade changed, and then seen to it that Nicole was transferred out of the school she loved.

Nicole sat in the kitchen, forcing herself to focus on the letter. It was short, the letterhead taking up more room than the message. The law firm of S, S, and S had been requested by Mr. Derek Grosbeck to arrange a "settlement interview" as per the attached document. The attached document was a note by Derek asking if she would agree to meet at his house. He was needed at home these days to help his wife, who was recovering from a medical problem.

Nicole poured a glass of the Shiraz Detective McGinn had brought her and called Liz.

"I can't believe you're actually thinking of going to meet

that guy, Nicole. Derek's the man who shot you in the leg. Remember?"

"By accident, though."

"So what? He shouldn't have been carrying a gun on school property. He's lucky he had enough money and influence to keep himself out of jail, which is where they put Willard Scherd."

Nicole said she was thinking of going anyway. "Mostly out of curiosity."

"What does Ralph say?"

"He'd probably discourage me, too. I haven't called him yet."

She hung up, swallowed a second glass of wine, and found herself starting to giggle at the thought of Britney's "medical problem." Bobby and her friend Emma had both told her Britney was overdosing on Adderall—stealing pills from Chelsea and using Chelsea's prescription to get more.

It was Britney herself who'd plagiarized the paper for her daughter, then dragged in her husband and their lawyer to intimidate her. Actually, it was Britney and the lawyer who'd done all the talking. She didn't remember Derek saying anything at all, only that he'd made a feeble, absurd effort to shake her hand as Britney stomped out of the school room.

She poured out a little more wine and made her decision.

Nicole had never been inside one of the McMansions in Nottingham Estates, the wealthy (*executive* in real estate parlance) neighborhood of homes that looked like they'd been air-lifted from the Loire Valley or the shore of Lake Como— except that they were brand new. The Estates lay on the east side of North-South Highway, which separated it from old Shady Park on the west. Nicole had driven down the winding road through the Estates a few times and grinned at the gilded concrete lions that stood guard at the entrance of some of the driveways. She'd talked to parents on the porticos outside of their houses. But she'd never been invited inside.

The housemaid opened the door to the two-story entrance hall. She spoke softly. "Must quiet. Ms. Gros, she upstair, need sleep."

A door off the hall opened, and a smiling Mr. Starkezahn appeared, now in a dark gray worsted suit. Still the same gold glasses and embroidered pocket square. He gave Nicole his soft, flaccid hand.

Derek appeared in jeans, flannel shirt, and disheveled hair, a bluetooth receiver flashing in his ear. He shook her hand with a firmer grip.

He said, "Maria, take the lady's coat."

Britney appeared at the top of the stairs in a mint green satin bathrobe, calling out "Maria, I need you up here."

"Go on up to Mrs. Britney," Derek told the housemaid.

Maria whimpered, "Jes, but Miss Chelsea, she need me do her Spanish homework. And also Mr. Chip, his Spanish homework."

The lawyer shot Nicole a glance. Cheating at schoolwork is what had initiated his first meeting with her. Nicole was sure Starkezahn knew Chelsea had been in the wrong then. Or, really, her mother Britney was to blame since she was the one who'd downloaded the review from the internet. But money could buy loyalty, obviously. She found herself staring at him, and he looked away.

Derek repeated, "Go up, Maria. She's not going to hurt you, for goodness sake. Don't give her any pills, though."

His arm on her back, Derek ushered Nicole into what looked like a walnut paneled conference room where she, Starkezahn, and Derek faced each other across a table elaborately inlaid with woods of dark and pale colors in a geometrical pattern. Derek kept adjusting his blinking blue earpiece.

Britney's voice rumbled through the thick closed door.

Derek cracked it open and stuck out his head. "Please, Dear. This is a very important meeting. —Maria, see if she wants some wine or something."

Last spring, Nicole had been too timid to look Starkezahn in the eye. Now it was Starkezahn who fiddled with his gold Cross pen and avoided her gaze. The reason was simple. Nicole had grounds to file a civil suit against his client.

Derek had illegally brought a gun onto school grounds—for self-defense he claimed—and when Willard Scherd stood at the door with a gun in his hand, Derek tried to pull his own from his pocket and it went off and hit Nicole in the leg. Derek had used his influence and possibly his money to get off with a slap on the wrist for the criminal offense, but he was still liable for civil penalties for injuring Nicole.

Derek leaned forward, palms flat on the table. He stopped Starkezahn before he could speak. "Ms. Ernst, I first want to say I'm very, very sorry about your injury. I think of it constantly. I've had trouble sleeping at night, what with that and some other things going on in my life. Wounding an innocent person is the last thing I ever imagined myself doing. I regret ever thinking that carrying a gun was a sensible defense against violence."

Nicole hadn't expected him to begin like this. His sad eyes looked sincere.

"Of course," Derek went on, "you are entitled to compensation for the injury. It won't undo the harm to your leg, but I hope—"

Starkezahn interrupted. "I've inquired about medical bills, the amount of insurance the school system provides you, and we can assure you that you will come out of this with no financial loss whatsoever."

"I'm no longer employed in the school system," Nicole clarified.

Derek put his hand on Starkezahn's arm and added, "So

forget the school insurance. We'll cover all the bills. Not only that, of course. We will offer you a generous amount for your pain and suffering. I'm a business man, Ms. Ernst, so pardon me if I'm blunt. I'd like to settle this out of court for $100,000. I'd offer more, but I've had some business losses recently. Maybe you've read about them in the paper."

He was referring to the Riverside Paradise scheme, of course. Pari and Anthony had exposed his connection as an investor.

Nicole studied Derek. Somehow she cared more about whether he was truly sorry than about what seemed the fantastic amount of money he was offering.

Starkezahn pushed a sheaf of papers across the table. "It's all here, Ms. Ernst. You understand, the $100,000 is in addition to any medical expenses you might have until doctors declare you rehabilitated to the to full extent possible."

Derek spoke up. "Ms. Ernst, I sincerely apologize for hurting you and," he coughed, "for my participation in the Riverside Paradise venture. I don't know how much you know about it, but I'm no longer associated with the realtor Bea Doggit or the fundraiser Pastor Mitchell Rainey, who's fled to Nevada, I understand."

"Without admitting any guilt in Mr. Grosbeck's former association with them," Starkezahn added.

"You can take the papers home with you," Derek said, "and take your time deciding whether to accept the offer. It might be advisable to hire a lawyer yourself to get advice." He asked for her phone number and gave her his.

Maybe she was being gullible, but Nicole was pleased to hear Derek dissociate himself from the other Riverside Paradise conspirators. She believed he meant it. It was probably his eyes. She had years of experience judging whether a student was telling the truth or not, and Derek seemed to be speaking honestly.

Nicole picked up the sheaf of papers. "I do want to show this to somebody before I sign, Mr. Grosbeck." She rested her finger on the $100,000 figure. "You say you've had business losses. Are you sure you can afford this?"

Derek's eyes met Starkezahn's. When she sat silent waiting for an answer, Derek said, "Yes, well, those losses are behind me. I have new investors now. We're going to make sure our next project conforms to—"

"Enough about that," Starkezahn interrupted. "Mr. Grosbeck can afford the compensation he's offering. That's really all you need be concerned with."

A loud voice rang out from the top of the stairway. "Maria, get Chelsea."

Derek opened the office door.

"I'm right here, Mom." Chelsea shuffled zombie-like into the hallway, cell phone in front of her face. She wore a long-sleeved pink blouse riddled with white ruffles that gave her the appearance of an airy confection. When she stopped under the hall chandelier, two long strands of purple glittered in her hair.

Nicole gasped. There was no doubt about it. That was the hair in the Headless Nude Reclining photo. Chelsea was the Shady Park sexter, the girl who'd been sending the nude pictures to Juan, the girl who'd flashed a nude picture of her breast to Bobby.

Britney made her way down the stairs, holding shakily onto the bannister. Her face was paler and thinner than Nicole remembered. "Look at you, Chelsea," she croaked. "You look like a tramp."

Chelsea stomped back into the living room, one hand over her mouth, choking back a sob.

"*Deeerek*," Britney screamed. "My pills! I need my pills."

At the outburst, the housemaid dashed into the hallway, coat on, bag in her hand. She spoke to Derek. "Very sorry,

Mr. Gros. Is so much trouble in this house. I must quit." She gave a kind of curtsey and left. They heard a car come to pick her up.

Britney huffed indignantly, then recognized Nicole. "Oh no. In my house? Derek, what is that woman doing in my house?"

Derek lost his composure. "Enough, Britney. Enough." He turned to Nicole. "Sorry, Ms. Ernst. If we're finished for now, I have another settlement to draw up." He went back into his office with Starkezahn and closed the door.

Britney glared at Nicole. "What does my husband need to talk to a lawyer about? Maybe you can tell me?"

Nicole was surprised she didn't know. "There were some papers he—"

"I'll tell you what he should get that lawyer to do. Sue the principal of Shady Park Elementary/Middle for allowing kids to send indecent pictures to each other in his school. I'm not going to stop until I find out which kids are doing this." Britney had a one-track mind. It seemed protecting her kids from exposure to public school riffraff was all she thought about.

This gave Nicole an idea. "You know, Mrs. Grosbeck, the police have phones with some of these pictures on them. You could ask the police to show them to Principal Prosterner, see if he recognizes anybody. Just a thought."

Britney tried to open the door to Derek's office. The knob didn't turn. "Derek," she yelled. "Why is this door locked? Where are my pills? I need them. I have an important call to make."

Nicole made a quick exit.

Ralph thought Nicole should hold off signing Derek's agreement until he had a chance to talk to the *Ledger*'s lawyer. "He might have an idea what a typical settlement should be."

Nicole was thrilled just to be talking to Ralph about it. At least there was no need to keep *this* secret. They talked about whether Derek was sincere, and then she kept the conversation going with plans for spending the money. She said they could save some for Bobby's college, she could start paying half of Ralph's mortgage, they could go on a long vacation. The Galapagos Islands—what did he think of going to the Galapagos Islands?

She didn't mention moving in. She wanted Ralph to think of that.

"And a physical therapist," Ralph said. "You could hire one like your doctor suggested."

"The college gym is good enough, really." Nicole stretched out her leg. "It doesn't even feel stiff any more." She wiggled her toes, lips pursed. "I don't know."

"What, Nikki?"

"It doesn't seem right, to tell the truth. Derek didn't mean to shoot me." She twisted her jaw. "And he seems to be having lots of problems with that wife of his. It feels mean to be punishing him."

Ralph shrugged and pulled her onto his lap. "Forget it, then. We don't need the money." He kissed her. "And don't worry. We can still go to Galapagos."

28

Just sign here

And thus I'll curb her mad and headstrong humor.
— Shakespeare, *The Taming of the Shrew*

Bobby studied the spaghetti he was swirling around his plate. "A police detective was at our school. So were a couple of *Ledger* reporters."

Ralph didn't look surprised. "Um-hum. Anthony and Pari got a tip from Britney Grosbeck he was coming."

"Yeah, Mrs. Grosbeck followed the detective into Principal Prosterner's office. Then there was a middle school assembly in the gym. The principal and detective walked along the stands looking at us. It was weird. Like a lineup. Then we all went back to class. Nobody told us what was going on."

Ralph's eyebrows arched. "Here's what Britney Grosbeck told Pari. The police had a nude picture on one of the phones they confiscated. They wanted to see if they could recognize the girl who sent it."

Bobby scoffed. "Recognize her boobs?"

Ralph's cheeks bulged to keep from spitting out his spaghetti. "Uh, I think the police told Britney you could see part of the girl's hair in one of the pictures. Let's not talk about it any more during dinner."

Bobby usually gulped down his dinner, yet he hadn't taken a bite. "See her hair?"

"That's what I understand."

Bobby put down his fork. "Mrs. Grosbeck fell down. There were cameramen outside after school. You think it's on TV?"

They tuned in the local news on their little television. Megyn Drumpfer of WPSK TV stood pointing to a vacant Shady Park Elementary/Middle School. "John," she said, "I'm standing at the SCENE of a terrible tragedy that HAPPENED earlier today. Community activist Britney Grosbeck collapsed while bringing her daughter out of school in the COMPANY of a police detective. John."

"Megyn, can you tell us anything more?"

"John, when Mrs. Grosbeck first ARRIVED with the detective, witnesses report she was determined to IDENTIFY a student who had been sending sexually explicit messages and PICTURES to classmates and friends."

"Unbelievable," Bobby said. "It sounds like Mrs. Grosbeck herself called in the police."

"John," Megyn continued, "the TRAGEDY occurred AFTERWARDS when Mrs. Grosbeck came out of school WITH her daughter. We have a clip." The news report switched to a video showing Britney pulling Chelsea by the wrist behind Detective McGinn towards her white SUV, which she'd parked on the sidewalk. Megyn Drumpfer approached Britney with a mic, but Britney's knees bent. She slumped to the ground.

"That was when school let out," Bobby said. "We all saw it."

"John," Megyn said. "We were TOLD by the paramedics that Britney Grosbeck was TAKEN to City Hospital."

"Megyn, do we have any further word on Mrs. Grosbeck's condition?"

"No, John. Not at this time."

"Thank you so much, Megyn. We'll keep our viewers informed of all the latest developments."

Ralph chuckled. "Right. As soon as they learn them from Anthony's *Ledger* report tomorrow morning."

"I heard them ask Mrs. Grosbeck if she took drugs,"

Bobby said. "Her answer was 'Arrrrgh.' They slid her onto a stretcher and rolled her away, just like on TV. Do you think they'll give her a tox screen?"

Nicole managed not to laugh.

Ralph used a fatherly tone. "It's good you know the consequences of taking drugs, Bobby. Yeah, likely they will test her."

"What's going to happen to Chelsea?"

"Chelsea?" Ralph frowned. "What do you mean?"

"It looks like her mom found out."

Ralph's eyes widened as the truth seemed to dawn upon him. "You're saying—?"

"Chelsea Grosbeck is the sexter."

When Nicole called Derek Grosbeck back, he wanted to meet in her house. He came without his lawyer and stood on the fluffy rug in her living room looking around. "You live here? We pay tons of taxes for education. I guess not much trickles down to the teachers." He shifted his eyes as if searching for a place to sit. "Now, see, if I were you, I'd look into some other line of work."

If Nicole told him how little she was being paid to teach classes at the community college, Derek would think she was lying. He ran his eyes over the walls and ceiling. "Guess you could put on a second story. If you need a zoning exception, I still have some influence." He snorted out a laugh. "Not with the county exec any more. But with some people still in office."

Nicole led him to the kitchen table, where he dropped down a legal-sized document, presumably the final version of the draft Nicole had shown to Ralph. "So what do you think?"

"I guess I'd need to read it over first."

"About the second story, I mean. I know a couple of architects. I could get them to dash off some sketches."

Nicole told him she'd lost her job and at the moment couldn't—

"Not because of your disability, was it? Because Starkezahn could make sure the school board—"

"No. My leg's fine. Pretty much back to normal. It wasn't related to that."

"Tell me. Because Starkezahn—"

"Thanks, Mr. Grosbeck, but it's something I'd rather not talk about."

Derek rubbed his forehead. "Not that plagiarism thing again, is it? I'll tell you the truth, Ms. Ernst, I knew we shouldn't have—"

"No. Not that."

Derek's eyes clouded. He seemed to be looking at Nicole without seeing her. Finally, he said, "You're not married, are you, Ms. Ernst? Good for you."

Nicole shifted in her chair, hands clutched in her lap, as Derek lamented, cautiously at first, then with more abandon, the humiliations Britney had caused him. He'd taken her side in all the disputes she had with teachers, coaches, neighbors. He'd entered into shady partnerships to afford her the privileged life she expected. He'd even started to raise money to build an exclusive private school she believed her children deserved to be in.

"That project came to an unceremonious halt," Derek sighed. "When Bea Doggit and Pastor Rainey barely escaped going to jail, and the exec did go to jail, the rest of the Evergreen Academy investors withdrew."

Nicole offered him some coffee, but he didn't seem to hear.

"And now this thing with Chelsea."

Nicole bit her lip.

Derek had seemed to be talking to himself, but now his eyes focused on Nicole. "She's suspended from school. I don't even want to tell you why. If my wife hadn't been so ... I don't know."

"Your daughter must be upset."

"I guess. It's my wife who's really out of her mind over this."

The legal document lay open in stiff accordion folds on the table. Twin red lines marked the left margin and a single red line the left. Nicole used both hands to flatten it on the table. She read "NOW, THEREFORE, in consideration of" while Derek muttered particulars of Britney's mental decline.

"And housekeepers, for crying out loud." Derek breathed in through his teeth. "First she fires Esmeralda, the best house-keeper anybody could ask for. Then she makes the new girl's life a living hell until she quits."

Uncomfortable listening to a man complaining about his wife, Nicole busied herself trying to make sense of the agreement. She understood she was not to sue Derek or his wife or family or business or legal representatives for being shot in the leg.

Derek cleared his throat. "Sorry. You didn't need to hear all that." He narrowed his eyes over the slight crook of his nose—his business mien, Nicole assumed—and said, "The offer's the same."

"Are you sure this is what you want to do? It's a lot of money. Because I know you never meant to hurt—"

"Sign it, Ms. Ernst. Maybe you've heard rumors. Britney and I are getting a divorce. Believe me, I'd rather you get it than her."

"Oh. Oh, I mean, will the kids be OK?"

"The mother always gets the kids. And the house. But I'll be fighting for joint custody."

"And Britney. She'll manage on her own?"

"Got that covered. I called in help—her mother in Arizona. She's coming back and moving in." Derek couldn't hide his amusement. "If anybody can tame Britney and keep her in line, that woman can. The kids call her the Wicked Witch of the West." He stroked his square chin. "There's a facial resemblance, maybe, but Hortense doesn't cackle." He smiled. "It's more like a scowl."

Nicole covered her mouth. Derek was opening his personal life to her. He seemed to have forgotten why he'd come.

"Of course, I need a decent place if I'm going to get half-time custody. I lucked out there. An investor friend of mine who lives right here in the Estates 'found it advisable to relocate abroad for some time.' Won't tell even me where. Anyway, I'll be his house sitter, keep the place in good shape. I'll have to get a housekeeper."

Smokey jumped onto the table as Derek fidgeted with his Bluetooth earpiece. He sat up, raising a fascinated paw. "You know the first thing I'm going to do when I move out, Ms. Ernst? Get a cat. Always wanted one."

"**I** signed. We're getting the money."

Before Ralph could push his glasses up on his head, there was a loud knock on the door.

"Goodwill pickup."

"Over there," Nicole directed the two Latino men. Ralph squinted, scratched his head, but moved aside so the men could pick up the red Victorian couch. They had to tilt it to get it through the door. Ralph helped. He stood in the open doorway watching them carry it across the porch and down the front steps. When he turned around, Nicole saw he was grinning.

She showed him an insert from the *Ledger* advertising a long, low, brown leather, L-shaped couch. "Half price," she giggled. "The *Ledger* wouldn't allow false advertising, would they? What do you think?"

29

Bank pollution

However gross a man may be, the minute he
expresses a strong and genuine affection,
some inner secretion alters his features,
animates his gestures, and colors his voice.

—Honore de Balzac, *Père Goriot*

It was time to call Liz. Nicole felt guilty. She'd worn a wire, tried to trap Reverend B, almost drowned—and hadn't been able to tell Liz even a word about any of it. But she could tell her about the money she was getting from Derek. She had a baby furniture website open on her laptop when she called.

Liz's voice rose about two registers above normal. "Sure there's not some trick to it?"

"Meeting him at the bank tomorrow." Nicole chuckled. "So I'm wondering about a crib. You said you didn't have one the last time we talked. We should go shopping."

Liz moaned about staying home these days whenever she wasn't in school "sprinting from the gym to the locker room to puke." She made it sound bad, but Nicole could tell she loved being pregnant. Nicole would have traded her own good news for Liz's morning sickness in a second.

"We'll go when my stomach stops throwing tantrums," Liz promised. "Maybe by then there'll be some news about you and Ralph. None yet, I take it?"

Nicole told her about the couch-switch.

"That's something, I guess." Liz made a sound like "uumpf-uumpf," then said, "False alarm. Just a burp. The

214

kids imitate me when I do that in class. By the way, Juan? He won some kind of prize for a carbon-dating demo he did in our science fair. He thanked you when they gave him the certificate."

"He did?" Nicole swallowed. "Well, I have an update for you. The mysterious sexter who almost got Juan kicked out of school has been identified. It's a 13-year-old girl at Shady Park Middle. I'm pretty sure her sexting days are over."

Nicole was glad Liz didn't ask who it was. She changed the subject. "Is Natalie still volunteering to teach Spanish songs to the Cultural Alliance kids?"

"Sure is. The kids love her. Too bad, though. The child care center where she works is shutting down and she's desperately looking for any job she can find."

Nicole thought about Derek needing a maid but wanted to check with him before mentioning it.

"Oh," Liz said, "Something else. You know Brian takes notes at the board of ed's closed-door meetings, right? He told me a cabal of parents are pressuring the board to replace Professor Shandule with somebody Reverend B promises will 'end promiscuity in the schools.' Brian said a mother in Shady Park has gathered pages of signatures in support."

"Did you get the name of the anti-promiscuity guy?"

"Last name is Diggs. That's all I know. The board chair, Dr. Bland, opposes ousting Professor Shandule. But you know Reggie Bland. He always votes with the majority."

Nicole shivered at the thought of this pervert getting on the board of education but couldn't say anything about him to Liz because Detective McGinn's operation was still a secret.

"I'm rounding up teacher support for Professor Shandule," Liz said. "Best we can do."

Nicole said she'd help and was about to hang up when Liz said, "Oh, one last thing. Remember that good-looking paramedic who took you to the hospital when you got shot last spring? He stopped by the school looking for you. He wanted your number. I told him to give me his and you'd call him if you wanted."

"I have it already. He left me his card."

Liz whistled softly. "Nicole, he's way too young for you. You can't be—"

Nicole just laughed.

There was only one bank in Shady Park, and you could walk to it from Nicole's house. This hadn't always been the case. Back when she was in high school, in the dot-com boom, banks were springing up everywhere, offshoots of investment banks in Delaware with names to suggest they were local. "Bank pollution," her father called it. Banks supplanted a book store, a carpet store, a lighting shop. Others appeared as new brick buildings in parking lots—one of them no bigger than a toll booth set with its drive-through lane protruding into the road through the lot. You had swerve to avoid stopping at its window to deposit your check.

By the time Nicole was in college, the dot-com bubble had burst, and the banks quickly vanished. The book store never came back—the Shady Park Citizens Bank was bulldozed for more parking. Free State Savings and Loan morphed back into Carpet World. Piskasanet Equity Investments had previously been a Chinese carry-out but was refried into a burrito stand when the bank disappeared. The Park Bank became a Blockbuster video rental, which lasted until Nicole got her first teaching job, then vanished when Blockbuster folded and turned into a mattress store. As for the brick booth with the drive-through lane, Gibraltar Trust, it was easily turned into a film drop off. And then film died.

Derek was one of the dot-com investors who'd gotten out in time, according to Ralph. Nicole didn't see him in the bank lobby until she noticed a boy at the counter pulling at his mother's jacket, pointing to a man on a couch in the waiting area. It was Derek, blue light blinking in his ear as if beaming in nonstop investment tips.

There were eight teller stations, but often only one of them was staffed, with a line of customers winding left and right inside the roped waiting lanes. There was only one bank now. No competition—you had to wait. Derek shook Nicole's hand and led her to a desk behind a gray fabric partition. A young man in a buttoned-up suit stood with a smile etched on his face. "Mr. Grosbeck. A pleasure to see you again. Miss. Have a seat. May I get you some—?"

"I'll need a cashier's check," Derek said.

The nameplate on the young man's desk said *Bank Manager* in gold letters. For a moment, he seemed confused, looking towards the teller as if that's the place you went to get a cashier's check. "Ah," he said, "wouldn't want to make you wait." He went behind the counter himself and brought back a form.

Nicole tried to act uninterested as she noted the figure out of the corner of her eye. The bank manager took the form back behind the counter, calling in a second teller from somewhere in the back to cut the check. It would have taken Nicole half an hour to cash her paycheck, but it only took five minutes to get Derek's check, cash it, and have the bank manager deposit $100,000 into her account.

"Coffee?" Derek asked as they left. "Little local place right across the street."

The Bean Brew was between an old-fashioned barber shop and a dry cleaners. Nicole had never been inside. If she wanted coffee, she made it at home instead of paying three or four dollars to have someone else make it for her. Maybe the shop wasn't for people like her but for people like Derek who probably needed a place to get away from their families or offices now and then.

Of course, the barista there knew him. He took an envelope from a thin leather case he was carrying and put it on the table in front of Nicole. She gave him a cautious look and opened it. "What's this?"

"Couple of different plans for the second story of your house."

Nicole paged through the plans without much comprehension.

"I've asked my guy for drawings to help make sense of these plans. Should be hearing from him soon." He pressed his earpiece in tighter and stirred his coffee.

Nicole had never given a thought to expanding her house. If Derek knew how little she stayed there these days—

"I know what you're thinking," he said. "It's a neighborhood of picturesque cottages. You wouldn't want to build something that clashes." He tapped one of the plans. "We allowed for that. See? It'll still look pretty much the same from the street, only it'll actually be twice as big. See here? The front view."

"Thank you, Mr. Grosbeck" was all Nicole could come up with. It was strange. She'd always thought of Derek as unattractive—angular chin, crooked nose, stupid blue light always flashing in his ear—but as soon as he did something kind, these defects melted away.

"Derek," he insisted.

"Right. Thank you, Derek. If I actually ever decide to build an addition, I'll definitely use one of these plans."

Derek smiled. "Tell you the truth, I like your street. Great location. I'm tired of Nottingham Estates. If I hadn't agreed to house sit for my friend in the Estates, I'd buy a house on your street and renovate it. Living there ought to change Chelsea and Chip's attitude for the better. Take them down a peg or two."

"How is Chelsea? Chelsea and Chip, I mean."

"Chelsea, she's a problem. You're not at the school any more, so you probably haven't heard. She's suspended for doing something stupid to try to attract a boy. Now if it was just me, I'd let it go. Try to get her interested in ballet or softball or something. I can't see what good it does to scream at her."

Nicole nodded agreement.

"Britney wants me to pull strings to revoke her 10-day suspension. I'm not going to get her out of trouble this time. And I'm not going to lean on the principal to get her into the gifted and talented program, either." Derek scoffed. "You realize one in six students in the state are now being called gifted and talented?"

Nicole nodded again. It was one of her pet peeves, but she didn't want to go into it now.

"Anyway, Britney's mother arrives in a few days. As soon as she does, I'm moving out. Starkezahn's sure I can get joint custody. And when her mother finds out what kind of settlement I'm offering, she'll beg Britney to take it."

Nicole folded and unfolded her paper napkin. "You said—I was just wondering. If you'll be needing a housekeeper, I know somebody who needs a job. Her name's Natalie."

Derek sipped his coffee. "I knew somebody named Natalie who worked in Pastor Mitch Rainey's daycare center. Everybody liked her."

"I think that's her."

"You're kidding? Can I get her phone number?"

As he entered it into his phone, Nicole had another thought. She was nervous—her napkin was tattered from her damp fingers—but she forced herself to speak up. "Some parents want to replace Professor Shandule on the school board with a man they say will rid the schools of promiscuity. That sounds good, I guess, but—"

Derek set his cup down with a clank. "Sounds like Reverend B wants to put a disciple on the board. That's what it sounds like to me. Personally, I don't think the board should get tangled up in eliminating promiscuity. Focus on teaching, that's their job. And I'm not just saying that because of Chelsea."

"No, of course not." Nicole was so happy to have him on her side she could have hugged him.

"Professor Shandule, you say? Sensible guy. I like him. I'll see what I can do."

30

Contraband Power Bars

"If the law supposes that," said Mr. Bumble,
squeezing his hat emphatically in both hands,
"the law is a ass—a idiot."

—Charles Dickens, *Oliver Twist*

Nicole had found Pastor Holmes and Amanda Win-wright's rally in the City quite moving. The nonprofit Citizens for Gun Control flyer still lay on her kitchen table. She checked it on the internet. It seemed to be legitimate, so she wrote them a check for $1,000. Nicole, the wealthy benefactor.

Next, Natalie. Nicole thought it best to contact her before Derek did. She remembered Andre said she worked at a childcare center in the Church of the Invokers of Jesus in Northbrook. She knew the church and had often wondered about it. Supposedly it was the outreach branch of the megachurch the Horsey Invokers attended in Bay Hills. She and Liz had heard Bea Doggit announce in Bay Hills that the outreach branch was closing and the Invokers' pastor had moved (fled?) to Nevada.

Occupying a former hardware store, the church had pictures of Biblical scenes taped to the display windows on each side of the door. Attached to the roof was a wooden cross. Nicole found a parking space on the busy street right in front of the door.

The building didn't look open, but she tried the door. It swung open. A musty odor invaded her sinuses as she waited for her eyes to adjust to the dim light. A short Latino man came into view stacking metal folding chairs onto a wheeled dolly. He turned, startled. "Not open," he said. "Church closed."

Nicole read *Temp Rentals* stitched on the back of his jacket. "I'm looking for the Church of the Invokers of Jesus Child Development Center."

"In back." The man pointed towards the front door and waved his hand.

Red graffiti marred the rusty back door. *Free Mauer. America First.* The door screeched open only after Nicole pulled at it with both hands. The room pulsed with fluorescent light. A toddler sleeping on a thick rug sat up and rubbed his eyes. Two dark-haired little boys were crashing plastic airplanes into each other. At the far end of the room a full-bodied, attractive woman sitting at a desk looked up, startled. "Center is closed."

"Natalie?"

"Yes. But I am very sorry. Center is no longer operating. Not assepting new children." She dabbed at her eyes with a tissue. It looked like she'd been crying.

"I'm Nicole Ernst. A friend of Andre Smyth's."

"Oh, Ms. Ernst." Natalie stood, reached out and took her hand. "You are Juan Moreno's teacher, yes? His mother Esmeralda has told me much about you. I'm sorry. I thought you were an inspector."

"I heard from Andre the center's been struggling since the pastor left and stopped paying the rent. I wanted to see how you're doing." Nicole was thinking she had some money now. Maybe she could help.

Natalie handed Nicole a form from the desk. "Mr. Andre does not yet know this." The title read "Daycare Operator's License."

"I don't understand."

"Is in Mrs. Rainey's name. Pastor's wife. She has gone to Nevada with the pastor." Natalie plopped back down in her chair, pressing both hands to her head. "Mr. Andre says he can pay rent for another month or two. But I find out we have bigger problem. No license to operate. We must close down."

Nicole glanced at the three toddlers on the rug. All three were smashing their airplanes together now. "These children," she said. "I guess their mothers work?"

"Yes. I will keep them until the end of the month. After that, I do not want to break the law any longer. I am afraid inspectors will come. I am U.S. citizen but born in Guatemala. These days, no one can feel safe."

"Then what will happen to the children?"

"Me, Esmeralda, plenty of friends from my country living at Northbrook Apartments. We will take turns babysitting while their mothers work."

"That's good. You couldn't be making any money here now anyway with only three children."

"You are right. I do not charge. And beside, Pastor Mitch Rainey, he was not a good man. He owed me two months' pay when he left."

When Natalie picked up another tissue to dab her eyes, Nicole summoned her courage and said, "Natalie, I'm wondering, this is nothing like being in charge of a childcare center, but if you need to get some kind of job quickly, I know a man who's going to need somebody to take care of his house for him."

Natalie blinked. For a moment, Nicole thought she was insulted. Then Natalie reached across the desk and took both of her hands. "Ms. Ernst, you would do this for me?"

"The job should start in a few days. It's Mr. Derek Grosbeck."

Natalie's mouth dropped. "Oh, Ms. Ernst, no." Her face paled. "I know this man and Mrs. Britney. My friend Esmeralda, she worked for Mrs. Britney, worked very hard and got fired for nothing. Esmeralda told me about Mrs. Britney. I cannot work for her. I am sorry."

Nicole explained that the job would be strictly working for Derek, not Britney. She told Natalie about the coming divorce.

"He will divorce her?" Natalie covered a sniffle with a tissue. "Is too bad. But I think I can understand."

Nicole added what Derek said about trying to change Chelsea and Chip's attitude.

"This is good, I think. Esmeralda also told me about those kids."

"I think you'd be a big help, Natalie. You should think about it."

"Thank you, Ms. Ernst. If he calls me, I will try it. Esmeralda only said bad about Mrs. Britney. She says she feels sorry for Mr. Derek."

One of the little boys on the rug started crying when another took away his airplane. Nicole went over, picked up a book, sat on the floor, and started reading. Immediately, the boys dropped their toys and gathered around to listen.

"Ms. Ernst, it is just like with Mr. Andre. They love to hear you read." Natalie was beaming. She held her hands to her breast. "Mr. Andre loves the children. He gave a science award party for Juan at his house. Lots of donuts."

The party was news to Nicole. She felt a little hurt. But it was probably her own fault she hadn't been invited. She'd been rather snippy with Andre the last time she spoke to him, suggesting he might find getting a job too *stressful*.

"Mr. Andre said he called to invite you but your phone was dead."

It was silly, but this came as a relief. Andre must have called when she was in the hospital. She slipped her phone out of her pocket and checked Recent Calls. There it was.

Two unanswered calls, in fact.

"I am worry about Mr. Andre. Maybe you know he has become friends with Willard Scherd?" Natalie's scowl showed that, like everybody in the Northbrook Apartments, she knew Willard had aimed a gun at Shahnaz Delpak and sprayed hate slogans on her door. "Andre says he can make Willard a better man. I hope so."

Nicole agreed and got up to leave, reluctantly saying good-bye to the boys before the book was finished.

"And now more worry," Natalie said. "I should not say, but Mr. Andre, he is breaking the law."

Nicole stopped buttoning her coat.

"Yes, he is taking *contrabando* into the detention center."

"What!"

"For Willard. Yes, he sneaks in many Power Bars for him to eat."

Before Nicole got to her car, Detective McGinn called. "I have something to ask you, Ms. Ernst. Any chance that wire came off when the dog pushed you off the pier? Maybe came off and dropped on the pier before you fell in?"

Nicole said she didn't think so. A lot of that night was still a blank, but she did remember falling into the water.

"Because that's the only explanation I can think of. It fell off and the Rev and Diggs have it."

"I just think I'd remember that. It was taped on really tight."

"Yet nobody knows where it is. Here's the thing. Without that wire, the prosecutor doesn't want to pursue the case. If the Rev and Diggs have it, that means they know we're after them. Our tech guy Matt says they could have wiped all their computers clean by now. We could put you on the stand, but it would be your word against theirs."

Nicole definitely didn't relish that scenario.

McGinn asked if Reverend B had got back to her yet. "Because if he doesn't, it would look like he knows we're onto him. But if he invites you to another of his soirées—"

"What?" Nicole stood shivering by her car, the phone to her ear.

"I might ask you to wire up again and go in to make another sale."

31

Pillow talk

If I can stop one heart from breaking,
I shall not live in vain.

—Emily Dickinson, *Poems*

"**H**ow do you like teaching in college, Nikki? Now that you've had some time to give it a try?"

"I like it. I've never had to say, 'Quiet, please' or 'You two stop fighting.' But—"

"But you like teaching little kids better. I can tell losing the Shady Park job broke your heart."

"Sort of." She told him about reading to the toddlers at the childcare center where Natalie worked. "Kids' minds are so open to new ideas."

"What would it take to get your Shady Park job back?"

Since she'd quit, she'd have to apply all over again, she told him. "I'd have lots of experience to put on my résumé, of course. But I'd need a recommendation from Principal Higgenbottom. I'm afraid he would mention that picture he saw on my phone."

Light was creeping through the window, casting a roguish sparkle in Ralph's eyes. "What if Higgenbottom writes a letter and doesn't mention the picture?"

"The only reason he'd do that is if he thought mentioning it would bring even more scandal to his school."

"So the threat of scandal at Northbrook High is your friend?" Ralph grinned. "Yesterday, a father called the *Ledger* with a tip that a girl at Northbrook High's been caught sending indecent pictures on her phone. Trisha something. We don't print that kind of story. But I sent Anthony there to check it out anyway. All Anthony promised the jumpy North-brook High principal was not to use the student's name if we did the article."

"Ralph, you're going to give Higgy another one of his panic attacks."

Ralph laughed out loud. "I'll let you know. I have an appointment to talk to him."

Now that Nicole had some money of her own to contribute, she wanted even more to move in permanently with Ralph. It had looked like he was going to ask her—Bobby said so—but then she'd obviously given him doubts when she started keeping secrets from him. Part of the reason she hadn't told Ralph was because she didn't want him to be frightened for her safety. He wasn't the type to tell her not to go, but he might have followed her and somehow messed up the police operation. Another reason was that he was so devoted to reporting the news—church dinners and store openings and golf tournaments, yes, but he was also driven to expose the bad guys. That was his job, too, which he was always afraid of losing as his father had if the paper failed.

But now Nicole felt she had to do something. She had to tell Ralph what was going on with the police and Reverend B, no matter what she promised Detective McGinn. She had to put an end to the aching doubt that surfaced on Ralph's face from time to time. McGinn didn't know Ralph like she did. She was sure he would keep the story quiet if she asked him to.

First she'd let McGinn know she was going to tell Ralph, assure him it would be OK. Just as she picked up her phone to call him, it rang.

"Ms. Ernst, it's Reverend Blatchford. I'm hosting another

soirée that I'd be honored to have you attend. I believe you said you might have some new material for me?"

She could just say no, no new material. She'd be off the hook. McGinn wouldn't even have to know about Reverend B's call.

"Ms. Ernst?"

But then Reverend B and Peter Diggs could carry on with their business as usual. She thought of Trisha's pictures now stashed in the Rev's database. Eventually he might even try to blackmail her to give him more.

"It's fine if you don't have anything for us at this time, Ms. Ernst. You can just call me when you do."

Nicole took a deep breath. "No, I do."

"Wonderful. It's this Friday at 8:00. I'll be expecting you."

When she hung up, Nicole tapped Detective McGinn's number, then ended the call before he answered. She called Ralph instead. Her call rolled over to the *Shady Park Ledger* main line, and Anthony answered. "Hi, Ms. Ernst. Ralph's not in. He went to interview the principal at Northbrook High."

Nicole hadn't realized he meant to go so soon. "You guys aren't going to write a report on that revenge porn incident, are you? I worry that could cast a pall over those kids' future."

"We wouldn't want to ruin any kids' lives. That's why Ralph went to talk to the principal. Ralph'll be the one to decide. Even if we did a story on the new phenomenon of revenge porn in high school, it'd be general, no names given."

The call waiting beep sounded, and Nicole hung up and answered. "Ms. Ernst, McGinn here. I see you tried to call me."

Ever since the pier incident, Nicole had been trying to recall exactly what happened when the dog jumped up and pushed her in. Diggs's finger did touch her. That she was sure of. She shuddered at the thought of him poking her. What she couldn't be sure of is whether he'd felt something beneath her loose blouse. It all happened so fast. If he'd felt the wire, or even thought he did, going to the Rectory again would be insane. Reverend B's invitation would be a set up.

She said, "I'm scared, but Reverend B called and I said I'd go."

McGinn seemed to be writing this down.

"But what if, I mean you said they might have the wire. It might have come off before I fell in the creek."

"I understand, Ms. Ernst. I never expected we wouldn't have located the wire by now. But I can get a search warrant using your testimony and the pictures we still have. If you agree to go in, we could raid the soirée after you come out, or maybe while you're still in there if something goes wrong."

"Like if that doorman or bouncer or whatever searches me and roughs me up?"

"I can't say that's not a risk. But if we let these guys go, the Rev's porn ring will keep expanding."

"I know. I told Reverend B that I'd go. I'll stick to it." She bit her lip. "But, Detective, I really have to tell Ralph Novich about this. We're together, as I told you. It's not fair to keep him in the dark."

After a pause, the detective said, "Please don't tell him yet. What if we have to postpone the operation for some reason? If our suspicions of the Rev were made public—"

"You think Ralph would print something before you told him it's OK?"

"He has his job, and I have mine."

Nicole rushed back to her house to feed Smokey and gather up some student essays to take to the college. She slid open the closet door to get a clean blouse. The formal black dress she'd bought for the soirée hung there, sequins glittering in the overhead light. Even though there were more important things to worry about, the thought of wearing the same dress to the next soirée is what came to mind. Besides, the bodice was tight. It would be hard to conceal a wire and battery under it. Would some kind of elegant loose blouse be formal enough? But would that be a clue to Reverend B and his men that she might be wearing a wire? She'd have to worry about all that later.

She made it to the college just in time for her classes. It was the day for her to return their essays. The students quickly flipped to the end of her comments to see the grade, then shoved the papers into their backpacks. Except for Janet, they showed no interest in her suggestions or even the simple corrections. None of the papers had used the apostrophe correctly. A few featured an apostrophe everywhere there was a final *s*, randomly in front of or behind it, as if apostrophes were something to sprinkle on like pepper to season the writing to the English-teacher taste. Others had no apostrophes at all. "If you like apostrophes," they seemed to say, "put them in yourself."

After class she usually went back to her own house. She used her own kitchen table for school work. It was comforting to have Smokey sidling between her legs, purring. Besides, in Ralph's house it was awkward sharing Bobby's desk. But this was the day she needed to be with Bobby after school because his aunt was going to visit relatives. She drove to Ralph's.

The screech of school bus brakes sounded out front, kids' voices rang out, and Nicole ran to the front door to see Bobby springing up the walkway. It was the first time Nicole had been on the receiving end of a school bus. Up to now, she'd seen the kids onto the bus and gone home alone. It was a thrill to stand on the porch waiting for Bobby as he bounced up the stairs. She gave him a hug, and he turned to face 10-year-old catcalls from the sidewalk. "It's Ms. Ernst." "Yeah, it is." "Woo-hoo! Bobby, is she your mother now?"

Bobby threw his backpack on his desk, picked up his basketball, and dribbled it into the living room. It bounced up onto the new couch. "Sorry."

"Don't be sorry, Bobby. *This* couch is meant to be *used*." She gave a demonstration by pouncing on it and stretching out her legs over the cushions. "Think of it as a bean bag big enough for more than one person."

"If you say so." Bobby grabbed the ball, dribbled, and took a set shot up and onto the corner of the couch. He looked at her as if to double check she wasn't annoyed. "It's great you've been coming to my games, Ms. Ernst. Want to go out and shoot some hoops?"

"Sure, but you have to start calling me Nicole."

Bobby slid his lower jaw to the side. "I'll try."

There was an old brown cedar shake garage in the back yard with a bare hoop nailed over the door. A gravel path led to it, but in front was a new-looking concrete pad.

"We didn't have enough cement to make it any bigger. Catch, Ms. Ernst. I mean Nicole. Take a shot."

Nicole had never been good at any sports, but she had spent a lot of gym classes and recesses shooting a basketball. She wasn't any good at getting it in the basket, but she knew she could throw it all the way up there. Besides, this basket hung a little low. She took a shot. It bounced off the rim. She grabbed the ball and took another shot. It went in. She gave Bobby a satisfied side-glance.

"You know how to play HORSE?" Bobby held the ball under his arm at his waist like a referee.

At first, Nicole's goal was simply not to make a fool of herself. But she was taller than Bobby, the basket was lower than regulation height, and before long they were tied at HORS. Now she wanted to win. She stepped back farther than either of them had done before, breathed in, and shot. It went in.

"No problem." Bobby stood at the same spot. And missed.

"That's E for you. Game over, Ace."

Nicole was exhausted, but Ralph wanted to talk. He slid his pillow closer to hers. "Not asleep, are you? Wanted to tell you, I talked to the principal at Northbrook High today. I see what you mean about panic attacks. He almost had one when I gave him my card." The light from the window gave his eyes a playful glow. "You get the idea he'd do anything to keep the revenge porn story out of the newspaper."

Nicole was interested but had to hide a yawn.

"Don't worry, Nikki. We wouldn't damage that girl's reputation. Besides, we have bigger fish to fry. Maybe you've seen the signs and flyers everywhere supporting Andrew Mauer? And all the TV pundits saying how great a county executive he was? Well, we found out he's getting an early release—one month instead of six. And that month was reduced by the time he was in house-arrest before the trial. That'll give him plenty of time to plan his next campaign."

"Campaign for what?"

"Not for county exec. That election's a couple years away. But there's a vacancy on the state legislature. A lot of pols say he's a shoe-in for that. After that he'll probably run for the U.S. Congress."

"Ugh."

"Yeah."

Nicole was wide awake now. Ralph's eyes were sparkling. Although the conversation quickly trailed off, it was a while before they went to sleep.

32

A vehicular tryst

Ask me no questions, and I'll tell you no fibs.
—Oliver Goldsmith, *She Stoops to Conquer*

The baby blue car with dented fender must be Andre's. Nicole parked beside it, got out, and observed him through the Tastee Donuts window. With an unopened book on his table, he was staring abstractedly into a cup of tea. He'd said he had a lot to tell her.

Almost all of the customers were men, talking in low voices, scribbling on forms, or reading the Sports section of the *Ledger*. For Andre and those men, Tastee Donuts was a workplace. Andre half-stood politely, and the other men gawked as Nicole sat across from him. There was a donut on the table beside the book. A woman behind the orange, pink, and white counter called out, "Another tea, Hon?"

"No. Coffee." Andre remembered what she liked. Well, the choice of coffee or tea must take on singular prominence in the jobless Andre's life. He began:

"Thank you so much for helping Natalie. I drove her to that absurd McMansion Derek Grosbeck's living in now. At first she was afraid to walk through the door. I have to say, my impression of the man as a wheeler-dealer developer had prejudiced me against him. Funny, though. Seems like the divorce humbled him." Andre breathed in. "Ever since divorce became legally possible—"

"Sorry, Andre, you were saying about Natalie?"

"What? Oh, she actually seems to like Derek. He needs

her full time, so she's going to live in, taking care of the children when it's his turn to house them—"

"You mean when they're staying with him?"

Andre frowned. "Isn't that what I said? Anyway, she has her own modest room up on the third floor. Juan and I helped her move her things from the Northbrook apartment." He reached around to rub his lower back, twisted his head from side to side. Nicole got the inference: he was suffering from the physical exertion. She'd learned from her friend Emma that Andre lived on disability payments for a lower back condition that rarely seemed to bother him.

He tapped the cover of *Child Care and Development*. "Natalie and I were hoping to keep the childcare center going. Turns out you need a license. And all the workers need certificates. I talked Derek into letting Natalie take a class two nights a week at the community college. I'm going to take it along with her. I'll pick her up and drive her to class."

"How long has Natalie been at Derek's?"

"Hm? I don't know. What day is today? Anyway, she's been there about a week, I guess."

"Helping take care of Chelsea and Chip?"

"Who?"

"Derek's kids."

"Ah, the post-millennials. The generation Z kids. Natalie says they assumed her job was to do their Spanish homework for them. When she refused, the girl said, 'Who's going to do it for us, then? As if *Grandma* knows any Spanish!' Natalie offered to help them do it themselves, and the girl complained, 'Do you know how much *time* that would take? As if we wanted to talk like *foreigners* anyway!'"

Nicole shook her head. She knew Chip, and she'd taught Chelsea at Shady Park Middle School. "It might be good for them to get away from their mother now and then."

Andre agreed. "Last summer the boy—Chet, Chad, Chip,

whatever—liked to go up to the Northbrook field to play baseball with Juan and the kids up there. His mother wouldn't let him. No associating with children who don't come from her own privileged world."

"Let's hope Derek lets—"

"Derek's already promised he could go up there next summer. From what Natalie says, Derek's trying to turn things around." Andre meticulously added two dollops of honey to his tea. Tastee Donuts didn't provide honey, apparently. He'd brought his own in a repurposed herbal supplement bottle.

Nicole was enjoying the silence while he concentrated, but she reminded him he had "a couple" of things to tell her.

"What? Oh, it started probably some time in the 1950s or '60s. People stopped reading books and watched television instead. Nowadays lots of people never learn to read books. Whatever's on TV, that's what they know."

"This is what you wanted to tell me?"

He broke his donut into four even pieces and offered her one. "Of course, you can learn more from watching TV than from playing video games all day, shooting at animations of bad guys and—"

"Andre, you didn't call me here to tell me this."

He bit a piece from one of the quarter-donuts, swallowed some tea, eyed Nicole with a cocked head. "Pardon? Jail is what I'm talking about. They have the TV on all day, mostly local stations. Willard never watched a news broadcast in his life, but now he doesn't have a choice. Whatever's broadcast on TV, that's what he knows. I think the oversimplification of the issues appeals to him."

"Natalie told me you visit Willard in jail."

"He's doing better. My friend Charles Bovant visits to counsel him. A community college adjunct comes to work with him in a prep class for the Graduate Equivalency Degree."

"And you sneak him Power Bars."

Andre's face reddened. He sipped some tea. "So with the TV, Willard knows what's going on. He's furious that Mauer's getting out early and running for office again."

"That's understandable, considering what Mauer did to him."

"Willard says he's sure Mauer will never be elected again."

"Why?"

Andre dipped a piece of donut into his tea. His only response was a mysterious grin.

It was a first. Ralph had invited Nicole to his office at the *Shady Park Ledger*. She didn't know what to expect. Had he already told everybody about them? And what would she wear?

In a gray pants suit and white blouse, "low-key professional attire" according to *dressforsuccess.com*, she pulled open the heavy glass door of the old brick structure that had been converted from a fire station into the *Shady Park Ledger* building at the end of the Second World War. In a huge room with a ceiling high enough to accommodate a fire truck, a woman with a gray bun and a younger woman sat at desks facing each other. As soon as they saw Nicole, they burst into simultaneous smiles. They knew.

"Ms. Ernst?" the gray haired woman said. "So nice to meet you. I'm Nora. And this is Sharise." Nora and Sharise led Nicole to a stairway. When Nicole paused for a second, Nora offered to take her up.

The worn wooden stairs might have led to firemen's sleeping quarters back when this was a fire station. Now the second floor was an open area with several carrels and monitors along the wall. Nobody was sitting at any of them.

"Ralph's office is off this hall." Nora took Nicole's arm. They could hear voices before they reached the open door to

the bare, beige room. "Everybody, this is Ms. Nicole Ernst."
Nicole was surprised Nora knew her first name.

Reading glasses flipped up on his head, Ralph rose from a
worn gray chair. He was with Anthony and Pari. This seemed
to be some kind of a meeting.

Ralph cleared his throat. "I asked Nicole to meet me
here." He checked his watch. "We're going to lunch. But I'd
like to finish this business first."

A gust of cigar smoke rolled into the room, and a bulky
man in a rumpled tweed jacket stepped through the doorway
with a broad smile.

"Pop, this is Nicole Ernst." Ralph introduced her to the
paper's publisher and editor-in-chief, Harold Whitman.

Pop shook her hand. "Anybody watch television lately?"
He searched their faces one after the other. "No? Well, check
out WPSK-TV tonight. My little Victoria is making it into the
big time. She's featured in a new skin cream commercial."
Pop sucked on his cigar and blew out a triumphant puff.

Pari said that was great; they only picked the most beauti-
ful girls for those ads. Nicole knew Anthony had briefly been
Victoria's boyfriend before he met Pari. He smiled and said,
"Way to go, Vicky." As for Ralph, he managed a nod and a
"Hmm."

"Next step, the movies. Hollywood. That's what her new
boyfriend Tim Hathaway tells her." Pop sucked at his cigar
but it was out. "Truth is, I'll be sad when she leaves, but a
little relieved, too." He relit, puffed out some smoke, snapped
his Zippo shut, and left.

Pari waved her hand in front of her face, coughing. There
was a moment of silence. Finally, Ralph got back to business.
He put his hand on Nicole's shoulder. "Nicole and I are …
close." He looked at each of them. "You can be sure she'll
keep anything she hears in strictest confidence."

Anthony spoke up. "I'm sure you will, Ms. Ernst. We're

discussing a story—something I got from a contact of mine at the police station. We can't put it in the paper yet."

"Pop's orders," Ralph said. "I was just explaining to everybody."

"I guess you've told Ms. Ernst about it?" Anthony asked.

Ralph looked embarrassed. "No. Maybe you can give her the short version."

"So, last fall," Anthony told her, "a lady working in a high building looks out her window down onto the Colonial City parking lot, sees two naked people in a car, calls the police. Interesting thing: it's a county car. The police come but make no arrest. The names are on record with the police, though. My friend at the police station tells me one of them was Andrew Mauer."

"Why no arrest?" Nicole couldn't help asking.

"The police chief says no law was violated. Their report doesn't say the people were naked."

Ralph added, "Anthony has lots of details from the woman who witnessed it, but the police report contradicts her. We plan to print her story if we can get a second witness saying Mauer's into that kind of stuff."

Nicole didn't ask what kind of stuff that was.

33

More fun with wires

When tears of confession run down the sinner's cheek,
The sword of punishment is blunted.

—Dante Alighieri, *Purgatorio*

Friday afternoon she had to tell Bobby she couldn't make it to his game. She tried to make up for it by shooting hoops with him longer than usual. When Ralph got home, she could barely look him in the eye. She had to tell him, too. All through dinner she wondered if Bobby would mention it. He didn't. When Bobby was in the other room doing his homework, Nicole took Ralph aside. "I'm going out tonight. I'll come back here. But it'll be late."

Ralph's face did a slow-motion change almost like a child trying to hold back tears. Nicole actually felt her own eyes get watery. She couldn't take this any more. McGinn's investigation be damned.

She took Ralph's hand. "I'm helping the police. That's what this has all been about. That first night I stayed out? Then when I fell into the creek? The detective insisted I tell no one." She squeezed his hand. "Especially the press. It would ruin the operation. He's trying to break up a child pornography ring headed by Reverend Blatchford."

Ralph was breathing hard. "Nicole, you almost drowned in that creek. That detective is going to get you killed. It sounds like he's already asked enough of you."

"Yes, but ...." Nicole told him this was absolutely the last time. The wire she'd worn on the pier was lost. The prosecutor wouldn't bring charges without a recording. McGinn and two other cops would be watching the Rectory, ready to rush in if there was any trouble. "As soon as this is over, I'll tell you everything, Ralph. Really."

Ralph gripped her hand. "What do you mean *any trouble*? Is Reverend Blatchford dangerous?"

"No. I'll be backed up by the police. That's all I meant."

"Reverend Blatchford's running a child porn ring? You kept this from me?"

Nicole had recently seen that Ralph and the *Shady Park Ledger* could keep a developing story quiet when they had to. She felt ashamed for not trusting him from the start despite what Detective McGinn said.

Ralph's feelings were hurt, obviously, but he wasn't the kind of man who tries to tell women what to do—one of the things she loved about him. He stared at the floor, slowly releasing her hands.

Wired, in a loose silk blouse this time, Nicole got out of her car near the Reverend's Rectory. The coat she'd worn in the pier incident was ruined, but she still had the gray cape she'd bought for the first soirée. She pulled the flaps up to her chin to keep out the icy wind. She didn't see the well-dressed soirée attenders she'd expected on the sidewalk. Her heels clacked on the flagstone steps up to the door.

The doorman in the white jacket stepped in front of her. "Open your coat, please." He took a cursory look, almost as if to see if she was armed, and without checking any list for her name this time, rapped his mahogany stick on the door. In the huge hallway, another man in a white jacket took her cape. No music or voices sounded from the parlor, and she wasn't shown in. Instead, Reverend Blatchford came into the hallway.

"Ms. Ernst, a pleasure. You're the first guest to arrive.

Perhaps we could go to the Presentation room before the others get here." He hooked her arm under his, a little roughly, it seemed.

"You said 8:00, I thought. It's after that."

"Yes, yes." He opened the door to the room and drew her in. There were no computers on the tables now. They were stacked alongside of some large cardboard boxes. The return address on the box nearest the door read *RES-RECT Publishing*. Its shipping label was a school board somewhere in Georgia.

Reverend B ushered her to where Diggs stood, his German shepherd sprawled sleeping at his feet. Nicole felt in her pants pocket for the Mace that Detective McGinn had given her. His warnings and instructions on how to use it made her tremble. From the other pocket she took a flash drive and a few photographs which the detective had advised her not to look at beforehand. She held these out to Diggs, still without looking at the pictures herself. She didn't want disgust added to the dread she already felt.

Following McGinn's script, she said, "Mr. Diggs, Reverend Blatchford, here is the child pornography you agreed to buy from me. These pictures will give you an idea of what's on the drive."

Diggs's mouth dropped as he shuffled through the pictures. The Reverend also took a look but said, "Pornography? We don't know what you mean, Ms. Ernst. Why would you bring us pictures like these?"

"I told you on the phone I had child pornography to sell, Reverend Blatchford, and you asked me to bring it here tonight."

"You seem nervous, Ms. Ernst. You're not making any sense. Neither of us knows what you're talking about."

Diggs made a signal to Blatchford. He pointed silently to the pictures, nodding vigorously, mouthing "good," then shoved them into his pocket along with the flash drive. He stepped close to Nicole. "We'll have to search you first."

Blatchford was still holding her arm. She couldn't back up. Diggs placed two stubby thumbs below her breast, probing, then slowly slid them lower. "Gotcha."

Nicole screamed as loud as she could, yanked Diggs's beard, kneed him in his flabby stomach. The dog jerked up from his sleep, growling. Nicole aimed the Mace, fired. When the dog let out an ear-shattering howl, Diggs and Blatchford released her. She ran down the hall and out the front door without her cape.

Detective McGinn and two uniformed cops were running up the steps. McGinn motioned the cops to go in and held Nicole in his arms. "Are you hurt? Come get in my car."

McGinn turned the heater up full blast and draped his topcoat over her. She couldn't stop her tears. "They knew I was wired," she sobbed. "They were careful not to say anything that would incriminate them."

"But you're OK? Dog didn't get you? I smell Mace. What happened?"

As soon as she finished telling him, he radioed to the cops in the Rectory. "Find any weapons?"

"Negative."

"Search for evidence of kid porn. If you find it, write them up for possession. Otherwise, just for failure to control a dangerous animal, and disturbing the peace." McGinn rubbed his forehead, seemed to be thinking.

Nicole was thinking, too. "I guess my fingerprints are on the pictures and flash drive, huh? It could be explained, but then—"

Right away McGinn clicked on his radio. "Do NOT, repeat NOT write them up for *possession*. Understood?"

"Yes, sir. Failure to control and disturbing the peace. Only that."

McGinn touched Nicole's hand. "Still cold?" He picked up the radio again. "And bring out the lady's coat right away."

"I still have the wire and battery on, Detective." She touched it under her blouse. "There's nothing usable on it." She turned her back towards him. "Can I take—?"

"Wait." McGinn's voice was husky. "Sorry. Protocol. The van should be here soon. Sergeant Jackson will take it off. The same woman who wired you up."

Just then a white utility van pulled up next to them, PO-LICE in iridescent blue letters on its side. McGinn led Nicole to the double doors at the back and banged hard. "Open. It's cold out here."

Inside the van was dark. Nicole saw Sergeant Jackson's eyes before she could make out her face. The van doors slammed behind her. She wondered if this was the same van that was used to take prisoners to jail. Everything she touched was cold.

Sergeant Jackson beamed a flashlight briefly at her face, then at a metal bench. "Sit down there, Hon." The cold shot up into Nicole's body.

"You're shivering. We'll get this over in a minute. Unbutton your blouse, please." The sergeant's fingers were like icicles on her skin. Nicole's body twitched involuntarily.

"Hold on, now. This might hurt a bit." She ripped one piece of tape off.

"Ow!" Ashamed she'd cried out, Nicole steeled herself for the remaining rips—and succeeded for two out of three. In the cold air, her chest was burning.

"OK, then. Go ahead and button your blouse back up. Where's your coat, Hon?"

Somebody thumped on the van door. Sergeant Jackson pushed it open, and Detective McGinn stood there holding Nicole's cape. Helping her on with it, he gave her a hint of a hug. "You're a hero, Ms. Ernst. The department is grateful to you." He walked her to her car and asked her to come to the station in the morning for a debriefing.

"Detective, would you mind ... I'm staying with Ralph Novich. I told you, he's worried about where I've been going. Could you follow me home and explain everything to him? I mean, it's a shame, but it seems like you can't charge Reverend Blatchford and Diggs now. And secretly recording him after this will be out of the question. So there's nothing for the press to report anyway."

McGinn looked at his watch. Nicole reminded herself that he had a family, too. She said, "I mean, it's near my house. If he could hear just a few words from you—"

"Sure, Ms. Ernst. No problem."

Ralph was standing in the hall when Nicole and Detective McGinn creaked across the porch and she shoved the door open with her hip. He threw his arms around her. "Nikki, you look half dead." He frowned at McGinn. "What happened? Tell me."

"Long story. You should be proud of Ms. Ernst." McGinn explained the whole sting operation, citing Nicole as the only person the police knew that Reverend Blatchford trusted.

"So it looks like the operation failed if you can't charge them with anything," Ralph said. "That's a shame." He told McGinn what he'd found out about Blatchford's real name, criminal record, and deceptive "Reverend" title.

"Yeah, we know all that." McGinn shished out a breath through his teeth. "We did our best. Now we need to guard against any charge of slander. The police aren't going to make any claims we can't prove, meaning the whole child porn thing. We'll keep an eye on him, but it's a hard thing to prove. Ms. Ernst says the wire she wore tonight will suggest he's innocent, not guilty."

Ralph smoothed his moustache with a finger, a sign he

was taking this all in.

"So," McGinn went on, "the press can say the police entered his house when they heard screams for help. Better check with us to make sure the animal-control thing and the disturbing the peace charges stick. Not sure they will." He looked at his watch.

Nicole stood up and thanked him. "It's late, Detective McGinn. I'm sure you want to get home."

When McGinn left, Ralph pulled Nicole close and kissed her. "I don't know what to say, Nikki. Do you think I was a fool for worrying?"

"Not about the danger. But, Ralph, I just want you to know. I'll always be faithful to you. I hope you'll stop worrying about that."

She took a hot shower before going to bed. The tape marks on her chest were redder than the ones before. She asked Ralph to come in. "It felt much better when you put that lotion on them the last time."

"Oaky doaky, then. Here we go."

34

Tea party

*"Take some more tea," the March Hare said to Alice,
very earnestly.*
*"I've had nothing yet," Alice replied in an offended
tone: "so I can't take more."*

—Lewis Carroll, *Alice's Adventures in Wonderland*

Instant oatmeal for breakfast, one of Ralph and Bobby's favorites. Nicole? Not so much.

Bobby showed Nicole the article Sam had written in the *Ledger* late last night about his game. "We won, Nicole. I made two baskets."

Ralph looked startled. "What's this 'Nicole'? Is that what you call Ms. Ernst now?"

"I asked him to, Ralph. You don't mind, do you?" Nicole swished her oatmeal around the bowl. Her mind was reliving last night. Ralph had shocked her. Before making love, almost as if making an editorial decision, he'd said, "What if I don't use a condom? What do you think?"

She'd said, "You know what that means.

"I know what *I* think it means."

"It means I might get pregnant."

"Um-hmm."

She'd paused, then given a tremulous *OK*.

"Oatmeal still too hot, Nikki?" Ralph seemed to be claiming the nickname, at least, for himself.

"Oh, no. It's delicious."

Ralph wasn't going in this Saturday until the evening, an

hour or so before the Sunday paper deadline. Nicole said she wanted to do some shopping. Ralph's eyebrows showed he knew she meant go to the police station. He and Bobby went out to shoot hoops.

The glow of last night with Ralph faded as she drove up North-South Highway. This wasn't her idea of how to spend a Saturday. She knew everything she would tell Detective Mc-Ginn would make prosecuting Reverend B and Peter Diggs impossible.

"I've run what we already know by the prosecutor." McGinn shook his head. "Not enough. From what you're telling me, I guess we could charge both of them with assault—holding your arm, pawing you—but then we'd have to explain what you were doing there. See what I mean? And there was no witness. So—"

"No. Let it go. Please, I couldn't—"

"Don't worry. That's not going to happen." McGinn shrugged. "So he gets away with it. The Reverend Blatchford keeps exploiting school kids and selling kid porn."

"It's even worse, Detective."

"How's that?"

"Bea Doggit owns the company that recently sold books to the county schools. They've been rejected, but all she needs is one more vote on the school board to bring them back. The contract is worth millions of dollars."

"I don't see the connection to Blatchford."

"I heard him talking to Diggs when I met them at the pier. I'm pretty sure Blatchford and Bea are partners in the book company."

"So Bea and the Rev stand to make a lot of money if the books are voted back in?"

"Right. And I've heard they're working to get Peter Diggs onto the board to make that happen."

McGinn stared down at his desk. "What can I say? We've

both done our best."

Before she left, Detective McGinn went over what he thought she, and the *Ledger*, could say. "If it comes out, you say yes, you went to a couple of the Rev's soirées. You say they're private parties, you'd rather not discuss them. If you're identified as the woman who was rescued from the creek, you could say the Rev was showing you his boat and you fell in. Something like that." He looked her in the eye. "Anything that does come out won't be from the police."

Nicole called Liz from her car. "Your morning sickness letting up? You have any free time today?"

Liz was on her way to Shady Park to get some winter pansies at Nielsen's open-air market. "Meet me there?"

Nicole bought some pansies, too. Then she couldn't decide whether to plant them in her yard or Ralph's. "Anyway, Smokey needs to be fed. "Let's go to my house."

"That girl Trisha?" Liz said. "She shaved her head."

"No!"

"She's going nuts. The boys keep teasing her, saying things like 'You look better with your clothes off.' She told me in gym class she wants to change schools."

Nicole still felt she had to keep the whole Reverend B operation from Liz, but she did say, "Rev. Blatchford has her phone. Let's hope he doesn't do anything creepy with her pictures."

Liz only groaned. "By the way, a *Ledger* reporter was at Northbrook High talking to Higgy. The next day, so was your Ralph. I haven't gotten the scoop from Brian yet on what it was all about."

Nicole said she wasn't sure, either. "He told me he went there. He was mysterious about it. But you can be sure Ralph won't let Trisha's name appear in the *Shady Park Ledger*."

Nicole's phone rang. Andre. She turned the phone so Liz could see the screen.

"You still hanging out with that blue-eyed hunk?"

With a shrug, Nicole answered. Andre wanted to invite her to a "tea" at his house.

"A tea? When?"

"Uh, right now. I'm working at getting certified in child-care. I'd like to get some ideas from you."

Nicole said she was with Liz.

"Great. Another teacher. You can bring her, too."

The snow along River Road had melted long ago, leaving patches of exposed dirt which had turned to mud. She and Liz walked on planks laid out to mark the way to Andre's back door—an improvement over the previous time she'd been there. Nicole suspected it was Esmeralda's husband Mateo who'd put them down.

"Reminds me of the cabin at girl scout camp." Liz chuck-led as they made their way around the sagging bungalow.

Andre pulled open the kitchen door with a pleased grin. "Ladies, welcome. Tea, we'll have some tea."

There were three chairs at the kitchen table already set with three mugs and a baby blue teapot, all empty. Nicole noticed a book. *Child Development: A Scandinavian Perspective.*

Andre began a rather lengthy explanation of his own thoughts on teaching children. Prominent in his disquisition were Ogden Nash's poetry, *Winnie the Pooh*, and *Alice in Wonderland*. Although he'd said he wanted ideas from teachers, the "tea" was turning out to be basically expounding his own thoughts. "You can't start them questioning our whole socio-economic construct too early. In Sweden—"

Liz cut him off. "Hold on, Andre. These are kids like Christopher Robin and Alice, right? Seems to me they already question pretty much everything. Can't you just let them go at it?"

Andre nodded. "Yes, and let them figure out the absurdities of the adult world for themselves."

The strident horn blast of a 1970s American car rattled Andre's windows. Doors opened and slammed. Nicole recognized Juan's voice.

"Mr. Andre!" That was Esmeralda, clumping along the boards to the kitchen. "We come to bring you vegetable. Too much donut and pizza no good." She, Mateo, and Juan peeped through the kitchen door window. "Oh. You have company. Maybe we come back later."

Nicole wanted to talk to Juan. She pulled open the door. Andre beamed as they came in, and he ran to get blankets for the living room floor. The pot bellied stove needed stoking, and Liz found a poker. It was another Andre-style pow-wow. Juan sat at the edge of the circle, avoiding Nicole's gaze.

"One thing's missing at this tea party," Nicole said. "Tea. I'll go make some. Juan, want to give me a hand?"

As she suspected, Juan had heard Chelsea was exposed as the girl sending him nude photos. "I never told," he insisted. "It wasn't me."

"I know. Juan, she's a 13-year-old girl at Shady Park Middle School. You live in Northbrook. It still puzzles me that she even knew you."

"Mrs. Emma's son Todd likes to come up to Northbrook to play baseball. When my mother was sent back to Guatemala, I stayed at Todd's house for a while. A couple of times Mrs. Grosbeck brought Chelsea to their house when I was there."

Andre called out, "There's instant coffee next to the tea, Nicole. I know some people prefer that." Sometimes Nicole wished her world could be as simple as Andre's. She had to admit some of the things she worried about were what Andre called first-world problems.

She noticed another book on the kitchen counter and

picked it up—a dog-eared copy of *Honoring Our Heritage*, the fundamentalist social studies textbook she'd previously been required to use in her class. *RES-RECT Publishing*, the title page read.

The book was so filthy Nicole hated to touch it, but she brought it back to the tea circle and put it down beside Liz with a sideways glance. Esmeralda was talking about her friend Natalie. "She loves working for Mr. Grosbeck. Very happy. He likes her, too."

"It won't be long before she gets her certificate to run a childcare center," Andre told them. "They're allowing her to count her previous time at the Invokers of Jesus center as her 50 hours of internship."

Nicole said she might be able to contribute some money if Natalie and Andre eventually started their own center.

"You might not have to," Andre remarked. "Derek Grosbeck seems interested in the project himself."

Nicole and Liz stayed until after Juan's family left. Liz held *Honoring Our Heritage* between two fingers and plunked it onto the kitchen table. "Hope you're not getting any ideas about education from this, Andre?"

Andre gave a squint-eyed smirk, pulled another textbook from behind the toaster, and opened it beside Bea Doggit's text. "Whole chapters have been taken word for word from this book that the state of Texas finally got rid of. Pari's brother in Syracuse has been looking into fundamentalist textbooks and sent her this."

Nicole couldn't believe her eyes. "But how did you get hold of *Honoring Our Heritage*?"

"It was Willard's book. He probably should have returned it to the school, but some other things came up."

Nicole smiled. "I wonder if all of Bea's books are plagiarized." She gave Andre the address of the county warehouse where all her remaining books were stored. She gave him

Lloyd's name and suggested he ask to take a look at them.

Before Nicole dropped her off, all Liz wanted to talk about was her swelling stomach—and Nicole's lack of one. She was consumed with dreams of having a baby, yet Nicole, her mind still lingering on the previous night with Ralph, thought more about what leads up to having one. No promises had been made. There'd been no discussion—which somehow made it more exciting.

When she got home, Ralph was more restless than passionate. "I have something to show you." He led her to the vast, empty room where he and Bobby each had a green metal desk. He'd set up a new desk beside theirs for her. To Nicole, it seemed a kind of statement. There are three of us now.

Ralph started rummaging in the hall closet, pulled out a lamp, and set it up on Nicole's desk. He put one of the four dining room chairs in front of it. "I think there's a bookcase in the attic. Let me get it."

"Slow down, Dad," Bobby laughed. "Don't hurt yourself." He ran up after Ralph. The two of them came back down in a cloud of dust, carrying a little bookcase, coughing but grinning.

"Thanks to you, Nikki, that damned couch is gone. I'm going to get more furniture, get some rugs, strip off the old wallpaper, patch the walls."

"I'll believe that when I see it," Bobby teased. "But if you do, can I paint them?" He told Nicole he'd painted his own room himself. She'd wondered about the choice of alternating blue and gold walls.

In the bedroom that night, Nicole felt her heart beating under her nightgown. Ralph was excited in a different way. He brought her some clippings from the top dresser drawer. "I can cook more than lasagna, Nikki. Look. Recipes I've been collecting lately. Here's one Pari gave me. Khoresht.

Kind of an eggplant stew. She says Anthony loves it."

"That's nice." She wasn't really in the mood to discuss recipes.

"Nicole, why don't you—"

"Do this?" She touched him. He took a sharp breath, stopped talking.

They eventually fell asleep in each other's arms. When she awoke in the morning, Ralph had already left for work. There was a note on the dresser: *What I meant to say is why don't you move in with me?*

35

Pleasure before business

To get his sweet revenge
And punish in one day a thousand offenses,
Love stealthily takes up his bow,
Like a hunter awaiting his chance to strike.

—Francis Petrarch, *Sonnet II*

Feed the cat. Check the Sunday paper. There it was, tucked away in the Police Blotter section. "Police responded to a disturbance at the residence of the Reverend Augustus Blatchford on Creek Street in Colonial City at 8:45 p.m. Friday night. No arrests were made." That was all. Her name wasn't mentioned. Thank you, Ralph.

She was about to toss the paper into the recycle basket when a glossy insert fell into her lap. Restaurant ads for Valentine's Day dinner. The ads pictured twenty-something women in sexy dresses toasting men who smiled significantly in suits or tuxes. Nicole had never been on a Valentine's Day dinner date. A friend of Liz's had asked her once, but she'd refused, concerned over the implication.

One ad was for the Tran's America Restaurant. *Valentine's Day Special. Free Champagne. Vietnamese, French, and American food. Romantic Atmosphere.*

Free Champagne? So they got their liquor license. Nicole had helped Tran fill out the latest application—after Mauer was convicted—and he'd wondered why a cover sheet wasn't required this time. He showed her a copy of the previous cover sheet. Along with numerous personal details, it asked for

"Ethnicity" and "Country of Birth." Nicole had called the liquor board office, and the clerk simply said, "That is no longer required."

Ralph took the hint and invited her to go. With the article Anthony had written about the Tran's America opening, along with this newspaper advertisement, and possibly because other restaurants were booked up with Valentine's reservations, Tran's restaurant was crowded. In the candlelight, a heady bouquet of exotic food merged with the melody of vintage French chansons. Tran's wife Thieu met them at the door in a tight, ankle-length dress slit partly on the side. "Welcome, Teacher. And Mister. It is such a pleasure to make your acquaintance." The last sentence, Nicole was sure, came directly from the textbook Thieu used in her college classes.

Grinning in the black tux Thieu had made for him, holding a cloth-wrapped bottle of Champagne, Tran made his way towards Nicole and Ralph's table, bowing. "Ms. Ernst. Mister. Thanks to you, I am happy to serve you Champagne." He filled their glasses and stood by.

"To our future together." Ralph clinked Nicole's glass.

Tran told them business was "very booming" since they'd received the liquor license. "American very much like drink. Big profit margin." Nicole was surprised at the phrase. He was obviously assimilating into American culture.

"Just a moment, please. I will present you Thieu's sister." Tran hurried to the kitchen and brought back a taller and heavier version of Thieu in an apron with a wide-eyed look as if astonished at everything around her. And perhaps she was, Nicole thought. She'd recently arrived from Vietnam.

"Enchantée." Thieu's sister Lan introduced herself as the restaurant's "chef de partie." With a bow she hurried back to the kitchen.

Ralph puzzled over the menu. Tran leaned forwards as if to tell him a secret. "Have American food now. Fly chicken. I remember you like."

"That'll be fine, yes." With a relieved sigh, Ralph lifted his eyes to Nicole—waiting for her to order, yet it seemed more than that. His lips mouthed "Beautiful," and the words on Nicole's menu blurred. "Um, uh, I don't—"

"Fish good tonight," Tran suggested. "Very fresh. Lan cook."

"Perfect."

All of the tables were taken. The flickering light of the candles, the low murmur, and the clinking of glasses made Nicole feel part of something bigger than herself, almost as if she were taking part in a ritual or ceremony dedicated to love. She met Ralph's admiring eyes and felt a sensual chill.

She thought she recognized the couple a few tables away and squinted in the dim light. It was Derek Grosbeck. And that was Natalie with him.

"Somebody you recognize, Nikki?"

"Don't turn around. It's Derek with his housekeeper. This is intriguing."

Natalie and Derek drank a toast. As he refilled her glass, Natalie smiled at him with her deep brown, candle-lit eyes. She tapped her ear. Even in the low light, Nicole could see Derek's face flush. He pulled the Bluetooth receiver from his ear and pocketed it.

Nicole stifled a snicker. Maybe Britney never cared whether Derek looked ridiculous or not, as long as he brought in the money, but Natalie did. Derek reached across the table and took Natalie's hand. This was definitely a date. They held hands so long Nicole felt she should turn away.

"How's the fish, Nikki?" Ralph was teasing. She'd been gawking at Derek and Natalie and hadn't touched her food yet. She nibbled some fish, still sneaking looks at the other table. Tran had set an enormous amount of food on it, all arranged in little plates. Natalie bowed her head, probably in a little silent prayer before meals.

"It's good, Ralph. I'm glad my very first Valentine's Day date is with you."

"Right back at you, Kid."

She wondered what he meant by that. "You're saying you never—"

"Nah, the restaurants are always too crowded." He reached over and took her hand. "Besides, I never felt like it before."

"You mean even—"

He shrugged. "It didn't come up."

Nicole tried not to think of Ralph's ex-wife spending Valentine's Day with her cousin, the man she really loved. She bent and gave Ralph's hand a little kiss.

A chair at Derek's table scraped the floor. Nicole looked and saw him take a portfolio from the floor. He opened it, slid some of the little dishes aside with his arm to make room, and spread some papers on the table. He seemed happy and excited.

Nicole couldn't hear what Natalie said, but the look on her face said, *Maybe business later?* In any case, he obligingly scooped up the papers and put them back. Derek the hard-driving businessman, the cold capitalist developer, had been conquered by ... what? It could only be Love. Cupid's relentless arrow had gotten revenge at last for Derek's ignoring him all those years.

Ralph and Nicole ordered a coffee and coconut jelly dessert, but Tran also brought them cake, cream puffs, and some kind of sweet dumplings. "You please take home to Bobby." He gave them a white paper bag with red lettering that declared *Tran's America Restaurant, Good Food, Good Enjoytime.*

Their table was now completely covered by wine glasses, silverware, and desserts. Ralph poked at his brown, green, and white jelly square. He wasn't the experimental type in the food department. After a bite, he nodded. "Good." He put down his fork, took some papers from his coat pocket, and cleared some room on the table to spread them out.

"What's that?"

"Bobby printed out these house estimates from Zillow. I don't know if you got my note."

"I did, Ralph. Of course, I want to move in with you. There are some things we'll have to work out first."

Ralph ran his finger down a list. "See how much you could probably sell your house for? Of course, the realtor would take maybe five percent. The average cost of selling is listed here. I don't know what repairs you'd have to make first. That would reduce your yield."

Did Ralph really think this was a good time and place to go over a printout of house statistics? Nicole took her cue from Natalie. "Let's finish our Valentine's dinner, Ralph. Maybe talk business later. That song playing now—can you understand the French? Something like *Speak to me of love*."

Ralph wasn't good at speaking of love. But Ralph was good at making love. Her anticipation triggered a catch in her voice as she read Bobby the last chapters of *Treasure Island*.

Ralph had stayed downstairs until his sister went home. When he came up, he said, "Beth took half the cake and some cream puffs. She loves sweets."

"Uh-huh. Bobby's asleep."

"You look so beautiful tonight. That dress. Don't think I've seen it before."

It was the dress she'd bought for the first soirée.

Ralph took out his camera. "Let me take a picture."

She straightened her hair. "What are you going to do with it?"

He snapped the shot. "Just look at it from time to time.

One more shot. Could you turn sideways a little?"

Nicole smoothed the front of her dress. This was embarrassing but also exciting. No man had ever asked to take pictures of her before. First, a Valentine's Day dinner, now this. Ralph showed her the pictures. She did look good. This excited her even more.

Ralph took off his coat, slipping the list of house statistics from the pocket. He gave her a look.

"Not now, Ralph." She was trembling. "Please. Pleasure before business."

36

Leftover pineapple pizza

It is the bungled crime that brings remorse.
—P.G. Wodehouse, *Love Among the Chickens*

After her classes at the college, Nicole went to Prof. Shandule's office. Mark was hunched over his computer as usual and didn't notice her at the door until she tapped on the wall.

"Ah. Thanks for stopping by, Ms. Ernst. I wanted to talk to you. Yesterday Pari brought in this fellow Andre." The gleam in Mark's blue eyes seemed to say he was waiting for her reaction.

Nicole shifted in her chair.

"Anyway, Andre brought in an armload of the recently rejected fundamentalist textbooks for grades 1 through 12. Pari brought in another bunch of books that her brother in Syracuse had mailed her—fundamentalist texts formerly used in Texas. All of them are social studies and science textbooks."

Nicole saw two stacks of books on Mark's office floor. She knew his vote had been instrumental in getting the Piskasanet County School Board to vote out Bea's Bible-based books.

Mark pushed a fluffy tuft of white hair from his eyes. "Anyway—strange thing. Andre went through the first chapter of the books for every grade. Here, look." Mark picked up one of Bea's books from the top of the pile. "Andre underlined every passage in Bea's first chapter that was taken from the Texas book's first chapter."

Every word in Bea's chapter was underlined. Mark picked up another of Bea's books. Same thing. "Every one of her books is plagiarized." Mark eyed Nicole teacher to teacher, it seemed. She returned his look of disgust.

"Here's the thing," he said. "Andre only did the first chapters. It must have taken some time." Mark smiled. "But, then, Pari says he has lots of free time."

Nicole bit her lip.

"We'd like to expose Bea. But Pari and her friend Anthony worry she could claim it's only the first chapters that are copied. It would be best to check other chapters, too."

"How many?"

"Anthony suggests checking a few random chapters in each of the 12 science books from each publisher and in each of the 12 social studies books from each publisher."

"That sounds like a big job even for somebody like Andre without a lot to do."

Mark's eyes lifted towards hers. His face turned pink.

Nicole understood. "I'll help Andre."

"Great. I'll set up the books in a workroom the college isn't using now."

Andre didn't seem to mind—at least there was no heavy lifting. He brought tea, coffee, and donuts into the workroom for both of them. Before he even finished his donut, Nicole had realized the chapter arrangement of Bea's books matched that of the corresponding Texas books perfectly, with only some minimal changes in Bea's chapter titles. This made the job relatively easy. Simply thumbing through the books showed that the content inside the chapters was the same— exactly the same. After a while, Andre had finished his donut and tea, brought his disquisition on plagiarism to an end, and started to help her go through the remaining books.

Nicole photocopied enough to show that Bea's books were the same as the Texas books, with changed chapter titles probably designed to make them look different at a cursory glance. She wrote up a report confirming the plagiarism.

Pari posted the report, anonymously, on her *Searchlight* blog as soon as Nicole brought it to her in the *Ledger* newsroom. Pari and Anthony immediately began a more comprehensive article for the newspaper, asking Nicole to give them anecdotes from her experience teaching with Bea's texts. Nicole asked to be referred to as "one teacher."

While Anthony was typing the article at his carrel, Ralph emerged from his office, winked at Nicole, flipped his reading glasses down from his head, and peered over Anthony's shoulder. "Good work. Better say '*appear* to be completely plagiarized.' Be on the safe side."

The phone on Pari's carrel rang. A frantic voice on the line bawled so loud Pari had to hold the receiver away from her ear. Ralph signaled for her to put it on speakerphone. It was Bea Doggit. She'd just read Pari's blog.

"You better take those ungodly lies off that website of yours, young lady, if you don't want a libel suit on your hands."

Nicole held her breath. It was her report that Bea was calling libelous. Ralph, Anthony, and Pari were calm, unperturbed, but this kind of attack was new to Nicole.

"Thank the Lord Jesus a friend from the Bay Hills congregation saw what you wrote and called right away to warn me."

Pari answered, "My blog simply lists the facts, Ms. Doggit. You say 'lies.' Are you denying the books are plagiarized?"

"Let me talk to your superior."

"I'm here, Ms. Doggit." Ralph stepped closer to the phone. "We're working on a story for the *Ledger*. Can we say you don't deny the books are plagiarized?"

"This is outrageous. Piskasanet County won't use the books, so I'm going to sell them elsewhere. Some have already been sold and shipped to a God-fearing school board in Georgia. If they read your fake news report and send them back, I'll sue your newspaper for damages."

Nicole glanced at Ralph, knowing how he worried about the *Ledger* ever going out of business. Ralph, however, was calm. He seemed hardened to this kind of harassment—something that she hadn't realized must be required in his line of work. She watched with admiration as he simply asked again if Bea denied her books were plagiarized from books previously published in Texas.

"As Jesus is my Lord and Savior, you'll regret it if you print that in your paper." Bea hung up.

Ralph said, "Let's hear what the county school superintendent has to say before we go with the story."

Anthony was already holding the phone and held up a finger. "Superintendent Wilson, please. This is Anthony Mansfield from the *Shady Park Ledger*. We're doing a story— Hello, Mr. Wilson."

Ralph pointed to the speakerphone button.

"We're writing a report that the science and social studies textbooks which the county purchased and briefly used in the schools have been unlawfully plagiarized from books previously used by a school system in Texas."

Superintendent Wilson's voice was gravelly. "We no longer use those books, you understand?"

"Yes. I wondered if you were aware of the plagiarism."

"Certainly not. This is a shock."

Ralph made a sign like counting money.

"I presume the county paid for the books?" Anthony asked.

Wilson didn't answer at once. They heard a muffled discussion with someone in his office. After a few minutes he said, "Apparently the accounting office is still waiting for my approval before releasing the payment. I had no idea."

Ralph stepped forward. "Superintendent Wilson? Ralph

Novich here. The paper's editor. The books clearly violate copyright laws. The sale was fraudulent. It seems to me the county has grounds to refuse payment. If you want to talk to the school board's lawyer to see if he agrees, we can wait to hear back from you before we print the story. Then we could add that the county discovered the books were plagiarized and canceled the purchase. We could wait, say, 24 hours?"

Nicole's mouth hung open. This was a Ralph she'd never seen before, a guy who knew how to take charge and run a newspaper. Ralph-the-editor showed no trace of the insecurity he admitted feeling in ... well, in love.

Nicole went to see Mark Shandule again in his office. He was reading the online version of Anthony and Pari's *Ledger* story. "Thanks for your help, Nicole." He pointed to the computer screen. "The county refused to pay for the books, I see. Plus, now everybody knows they're useless. It looks bad for Bea. Can't say I feel sorry for her. Selling those books to the county was a crime."

Nicole said, "According to Pari and Andre, the school board warehouse is still piled high with Bea's textbooks."

Mark shoved some white hair out of his eyes as if trying to see what she was getting at.

"I found out there's a regulation saying only county material could be stored in the warehouse. I wonder if you or somebody else on the board could get the superintendent of schools to direct the warehouse to remove Bea's books?"

Mark's eyes widened. "I guess I could. Sure. There's 126 county schools, so probably five or six thousand books. We don't need to be storing them for Bea."

Late Wednesday evening, Nicole got a text from Pari. *Dad says tell you the superintendent will send the directive tomorrow.* ☺

No classes Thursday. Nicole drove to the warehouse.

Lloyd stood outside the galvanized roll-up door, one foot braced back against the wall, reading the *Shady Park Ledger* as before. "Ms. Ernst, right? I met an interesting friend of yours. Andre Smyth." Lloyd let out a low half-chuckle. "Come on in. It's warmer inside."

Skids of books were piled high with cardboard boxes and shrink wrapped stacks of textbooks everywhere she looked. "What are you going to do with all of the returned plagiarized books?"

"Don't know. We got a memo from the superintendent this morning saying they can't be kept here. Take them back to the publisher." He picked up one of Bea's books. "RES-RECT's the publisher. I couldn't get a number for them. But the printer's address is listed. I called them. No return policy. The books are out of their hands."

"I know where the publisher is located."

"No kidding?"

She gave him the address of Bea's Executive Homes office on North-South Highway.

"You sure that's the place?"

"It's a big building. Used to be a bowling alley. Now it's Beatrice Doggit's real estate office. Ownership of RES-RECT property passed to her when it folded. You could call and see if she wants the books." Nicole knew Bea didn't want them delivered to her. Until she found some way to sell them, she probably assumed the county would store them for her indefinitely.

Lloyd called. Nicole heard Bea's voice through the receiver. "I certainly do want to keep those books."

"Because, Ma'am, the *Shady Park Ledger* says they're plagiarized. Seems to mean they're worthless. I could just take them to the landfill, if you want. Destroy them."

"Those books are my property now. As the Lord is my witness, if you destroy them, I'll have you arrested."

"Ma'am, the school superintendent says they can't be kept in the county warehouse any longer. I could deliver them—"

Bea hung up.

"Not a very pleasant woman," Lloyd observed. "Kind of a bitch, if you pardon my French." He cast his eyes back on the stacks of books. "I didn't even mention her books reek with lies."

Lloyd had developed a dislike for Bea after this brief exchange. Nicole's aversion had even deeper roots. Her friend Emma told her how Bea had once lured her husband Charles to New York so he couldn't advise Andre not the sell his house to her Riverside Paradise project. And Pari said Bea had tried to blackmail Anthony with a spurious charge—too terrible for Pari to mention—if he printed reports of how Riverside Paradise had cheated Andre's neighbors out of their property.

Nicole pursed her lips. "You know where the place is?" She was nervous but determined.

"Sure. I used to go bowling there." He twisted his mouth. "Even when it was a bowling alley I'm not sure all those books would fit in it. And now it's an office?" He picked up the superintendent's memo from his desk.

Nicole just looked at him.

Lloyd very slowly broke into a smile. "I think I see what you're up to." He read the memo. "It says as soon as possible."

Nicole shrugged.

Lloyd grinned. "I'm on it."

Nobody driving on North-South Highway through Shady Park could miss the imposing Executive Homes building with its high-pitched fake roof over the entrance and its enormous red, white, and blue sign. *EXECUTIVE HOMES—FOR THOSE WHO DESERVE THE EXECUTIVE LIFESTYLE.* Nicole had heard that Derek Grosbeck helped finance the ultramodern remodeling of the Old Tyme Bowling Alley. That was when he was a silent partner in Bea's Riverside Paradise project, before Anthony exposed its illegal dealings and Derek withdrew his support.

Smokey fed, Nicole called Executive Homes to ask for an appointment with Bea. "This is Jane Hawkins," Nicole said. Her burner phone didn't send out caller ID. "I live nearby. I'm hoping Ms. Doggit would like to list my house for sale. I see on her sign she's a Gold Tier Agent."

"Certainly," Bea's receptionist replied. "Let me see. Would one o'clock be OK?"

It was just the time Nicole was hoping for.

The *Visitor Only* spaces in front of the building were empty. Executive Homes had probably lost a lot of business since Anthony's articles were printed. Bea'd been lucky she avoided losing her license. She did lose the Riverside Paradise properties, including the extravagant villa she'd built there for herself, when her project declared bankruptcy.

Nicole parked farther away from the entrance, leaving a good bit of space in front of the building. She'd never been inside. Beyond the glass entry doors was a long, wide hallway. Along one side were doors marked *Financing* and *Insurance* and *Titling* and *Settlement*. Bea had her finger in all aspects of the deal.

On the other side of the hallway, behind a floor-to-ceiling glass door, a heavily made-up fiftyish receptionist, glasses hanging from her neck by a gold chain, sat at a desk behind a computer monitor. Other tables held fax machines, printers, and a huge copy machine in what must be the nucleus of Bea's Executive Homes empire.

"You're a bit early, Ms. Hawkins," the receptionist grumbled. "Would you please wait over there."

Nicole sat in a black leather chair facing the hallway and checked the time. A tall, thin man in a gray suit, long graying hair streaming from under a black fedora, peered through the glass door and entered. He placed a small bundle of books on the receptionist's desk and handed her an official-looking paper. Nicole recognized Trevor Steinborn, the school board attorney.

"The Piskasanet County School Board will need a signature for book delivery to Ms. Beatrice Doggit." The attorney pointed to the place for the signature.

Flustered, the receptionist hit her intercom button. "Ms. Doggit, there's a man here who needs a signature for a delivery."

Bea's voice squawked through the intercom. "I'm on a business call now, Kimberly. Just sign it yourself."

Kimberly signed, then looked at the package on her desk. "It says this is for a large number of books."

"They're coming," the attorney said. He folded the receipt into his coat pocket and left.

Tractor trailer brakes hissed outside in the *Visitor Only* area, followed by a loud clanking and banging. Men were shouting. The hydraulic whine of a truck lift-gate made Kimberly hold her ears. She jumped up, frowned at Nicole. "What in the world is that?"

Through the glass door they saw Lloyd lead tan-uniformed men wheeling stacks of books into the hallway. Others followed with boxes. Nicole saw Lloyd knock on the door of the *Financing* room, then open it up. "Fill this room up first, guys. Use a step ladder to pile them up to the ceiling." He opened the doors to the other rooms. "Then fill these up."

Kimberly clutched her breast. "Stop," she yelled weakly through the glass door. But dollies of books kept moving in. She opened a door into a larger paneled room. Behind an enormous mahogany desk, Bea sat fixing her makeup. "Ms. Doggit, Ms. Doggit" was all Kimberly managed to get out.

Bea dropped a tube of red lipstick onto her desk. The

screeching of the dollies and shouts of the men were getting louder. "That room full up," a man called out in a Spanish accent. Lloyd shouted back. "Move on to the other rooms. I'll clear out some space in here." He came through the glass door and faced an outraged Bea Doggit.

"In the name of Jesus, what do you think you're doing? This is private property."

Lloyd handed her his card, took a paper from his shirt pocket. "Instructions from the school superintendent to return these books to the publisher. The board's attorney says your receptionist signed for delivery stating you are the owner?"

"Get out. As the Lord is my witness, I will have you people arrested."

Ignoring this, Lloyd looked around. "You might want to remove your personal items. We're going to need all these rooms." For the first time, he noticed Nicole and gave her a wink.

A cry came through the glass doors. "Room number two fill up to ceiling."

"OK," Lloyd called out. "When the other two are filled, start bringing them in here. Leave the hallway for last."

Bea backed up to the glass doors, scarlet lipstick smeared at one corner of her mouth and her breasts half exposed in the fashion she seemed to favor. She spread out her arms. "So help me God, nobody comes in here. This is a private office. Kimberly, call the police."

"I'm afraid, Ms. Doggit. I did sign the delivery paper. And the books *are yours*."

Lloyd said. "Files, laptops, any important documents, whatever you might need until you decide what to do with these books." He walked into Bea's office, eying up the space.

"This is trespassing," Bea shrieked. "You can't—"

"Not sure all the books will fit inside the building even after we fill these offices up. There's a loading platform behind the building. We can stack up the rest there, but they won't be protected from the weather. You might want to rent a storage unit. You'll have to act fast, though. The workers are only contracted for today."

Bea jumped when one of the men tapped behind her on the door. "Last room filling up. Ready we come in here?"

"Ladies?" Lloyd raised his eyebrows. "The county's paying by the hour for this delivery, so ...."

Kimberly swept some things from her desktop and drawer into her handbag and ran out in tears. A man guided a dolly through the glass doors. "Coming in." Bea rushed back into her office. Nicole watched her stuff her makeup, some papers, and a laptop into a straw bag.

Two men struggled at wheeling the dolly across the ludicrously thick white carpet. Others followed with cardboard boxes of books.

"Can I help you turn everything off?" Nicole offered.

Turning her back on Nicole, Bea punched a number on her phone. "Augustus Blatchford, may the Lord punish you. You swore to me that if the content of these books was godly, Jesus wouldn't care where we got it. Without having to pay writers, you said, our profit would be tremendous. I'm sorry I ever went into this with you."

Boxes and shrink-wrapped ceiling-high stacks of books covered the floor and the floral chenille chairs, leaving only a passage from Bea's desk to the door. "Please be sure to take the key when you leave the building," Lloyd told Bea.

Bea stomped out. Nicole lagged behind with Lloyd. He lifted his hand, gave her a high-five, and said, "At home the other day it felt good to finally trash a leftover pineapple pizza nobody wanted to eat that was taking up room in my fridge. Know what I mean?"

Nicole nodded. When she left, she heard him yell, "Start

filling the hallway now, guys. But leave a path to the door. Don't want to create a fire hazard."

37

Physical intimacy

Spirits when they please
Can either sex assume, or both.
—John Milton, *Paradise Lost*

Executive Homes Declares Bankruptcy

Anthony's article said Bea had broken her lease on the Executive Homes building, abandoned it still filled with lightly used but useless textbooks, and relocated to Nevada. According to Kimberly Johnson, her former receptionist, Bea planned to join her previous colleague Pastor Mitchell Rainey in his cable TV broadcast "Giving to Jesus."

Nicole folded the newspaper on her kitchen table and spread out the list Ralph had given her of house values in her neighborhood. She'd been to a real estate office now and hadn't exactly left with a good impression. Maybe she could sell her house herself, before moving in with Ralph. She didn't have a full-time job, and the money she had from Derek wouldn't last forever.

Andre called. He'd read the article about Bea's departure for Nevada. He sounded a new note of confidence that she'd given up trying to get his house away from him, that Riverside Paradise was definitely dead.

"Even more good news," Andre said. "Natalie brought Derek to see the childcare center. I was there. She'd brought in about ten kids so Derek would see what the place was like. The kids thought the center was opening up again. Some cried when they found out it wasn't. Natalie shed a few tears, too. I don't know if Derek was moved by the kids' tears, but he definitely was by Natalie's. He asked how much it would cost to keep the center going."

"It really wouldn't be that much, would it?"

"Maybe not. But Derek kept scowling at the sign on the door: CHURCH OF THE INVOKERS OF JESUS CHILD DEVELOPMENT CENTER. 'That name has to go,' he insisted. 'And the whole building will have to be redesigned. It still looks more like an empty hardware store than a church or childcare center.' He said he was going to get in touch with some architects he knows."

"So he's really going to take it over?"

"And put Natalie and me in charge. He even started talking about paying me a salary. Of course, I said I wouldn't need to be paid."

"No, of course not." Nicole knew it was a matter of pride for Andre that his contempt for "capitalistic greed" allowed him live on nothing but Social Security disability payments.

"Derek said he's going to buy the building. It should be ready by the time Natalie gets her certificate."

"Sounds like he and Natalie are a thing now."

Andre didn't seem familiar with the phrase. "Pardon? The overuse of abstract terms like 'thing' often contributes to—"

"Lovers."

"Ah. Yes. Derek and Britney are flying to Las Vegas next week to get a divorce. Then, who knows? The first-world tendency to switch marriage partners—"

"Hold on, Andre. I have another call." She didn't have another call, but she didn't want to hear Andre's analysis of contemporary mores.

"I'll call you later," he said, "to tell you about the villa."

"Bea's Riverside Paradise villa? Oh, darn, my caller hung up. What about the villa?"

"Derek got the bank to let him take over the loan. The villa's his now. Natalie said she doesn't know what he plans to do with it yet."

"He's not going to build more villas along the river, is he? I know you'd hate that."

"Natalie says definitely not. Something else."

Mauer Gets Early Release, One Month House Arrest

Anthony's *Shady Park Ledger* article reported on the county executive's release from jail and his immediate campaign for the vacant legislator's seat. Bea wasn't around to promote him, but the Horsey Invokers were galloping through the district with flyers and posters. Telephone poles, lamp posts, windows of car dealership and banks, the entrances to gated communities—all were plastered with signs urging voters to *Send Mauer to the State House* and *Keep Our Jobs—Keep Our Guns—Keep Our Freedom*. Mauer's supporters didn't stop at that. They started staging made-for-TV rallies.

Mauer appeared in endless WPSK TV ads promising to revive legislation requiring teachers to be armed. He also touted his support of a resolution requiring county and state police to check every detainee's immigration status and report anyone suspected of being here illegally to the U.S. Immigration and Customs Enforcement.

Nicole remembered what had happened to Tran. Emma had told her it was at Mauer's instigation that ICE had raided the Northbrook Apartments and arrested Tran's whole family—unlawfully, since Tran and his wife were legal permanent residents and their two children were both American citizens. Nicole shuddered to think of Mauer now getting statewide power.

But as much as Nicole and her friends feared Mauer, they found themselves outnumbered. Shortly before the election, the *Ledger* published the results of a Piskasanet Community College survey showing Andrew Mauer with a 45% lead over his opponent. It looked like Mauer couldn't be stopped. Ralph stopped talking much at dinner.

Nicole was at her house when she heard a horn honk outside. Andre.

"You still have that cat?" he called from the car window.

Not bothering to answer, she pulled on her coat and got in beside him. In the small front seat, their arms touched on the center console. Her cheeks warmed at the memory of her earliest encounters with Andre. She'd thought of him at first as handsome, a little odd, a man she might possibly be interested in since she couldn't get Ralph. She still found him handsome, but now quite odd, and still interesting, although not in the way she'd originally meant. It was simple, really. She thought of him as a friend.

Andre held a paper on his lap. "You asked me once how I met Willard. I never said." He gazed blankly through the windshield into a cloudy sky as if peering into the past. "It was after Johan left me. I felt empty. I needed physical intimacy."

Nicole slid her arm off the console, folded her hands in her lap.

"I heard about a street in Colonial City you could go to. A place where you could meet … people. The first time I went, a guy tapped on my window and I took him to a nearby parking lot—too excited to wait. After that, I would drive them to my house or we went to theirs. They were guys in their late 20s. Then one day a younger man knocked on my car window. Intense, striking looks, troubled."

"Willard."

"I wanted to talk to him more than do anything. I wanted to hug him, make him feel he was OK. I don't know if you can understand that."

Nicole remembered feeling sort of like that about Andre himself that snowy day she'd first gone to his house.

Andre seemed to read her mind. "Sorry. Of course you can."

The windows in the little car were steaming up. Andre handed Nicole a letter. "From Willard to Andrew Mauer. A copy."

Nicole held the letter close. "Willard didn't write this."

"He dictated it to me over the course of a couple of prison visits—he's not much with grammar or spelling. But that's his letter. He mailed it before his sentencing, but he never received an answer."

The letter wished Mauer luck in his own approaching trial. "You're a good man," Willard told him. "You're like a father to me. I'll never forget the night we met. The love we shared in your car changed me. It was my first time. Even though we never met again, whenever I go by the Colonial Parking lot, I feel your touch. I was scared when the police came, but you handled them."

A sour taste rose in Nicole's mouth. "I don't feel like I should be reading this."

Andre took the letter. "He tells Mauer it was their talk that night about dangerous terrorists pouring across the southern border that made him go to the board of education hearing the next night with a gun. And then he asks why Mauer didn't come to speak on his behalf at his sentencing. 'It hurt me, and I don't understand,' Willard wrote."

"Now I see why he was so sure Mauer would show up."

Andre folded the letter and gazed through the windshield at the clouds. "When Willard rapped on my window in Colonial City the first time, I think he was hoping I was Mauer."

A strong taste of cigar smoke seeped from under Pop's office door. Nicole had brought Andre to the *Ledger* newsroom with Willard's letter. They stood in the hallway with Ralph, Anthony, and Pari.

"Before we go in," Ralph cautioned, "I need to explain something. This is going to be tricky for Pop. He's had some connections with Mauer in the past. He never liked the man personally, but when Mauer said he could convince the county to sell him that Piskasanet River island, he went along."

Nicole knew, but Andre cocked his head with a frown.

Anthony spoke up. "Of course, Pop turned against Mauer as soon as his part in the Riverside Paradise scam came out."

Pari nodded agreement. She and Anthony seemed not to want the visitors to get the wrong idea about their boss. The whole newspaper staff respected Pop.

Ralph knocked on the door and they went in. Plaques on the paneled walls proclaimed Pop a member of the Lions Club, the Rotary, the local Chamber of Commerce. Nicole was surprised to see a double-barreled shotgun hanging behind his desk until she remembered hearing Pop was a duck hunter. The silver sailing trophies announced he was a sailor, as well. The *Shady Park Ledger* publisher was a dynamic member of his community.

Pop shot out a spurt of smoke. "What's this, Ralph? You summoned a posse?" He held up his hands. "Don't shoot. I'll go quietly."

Nicole lagged behind in the doorway until Pop said, "Come in, young lady. Ralph's beloved Nicola, I remember."

"Nicole."

"Pardon? Yes, right. Ralph says you're the love of his life."

Nicole shot a quick glance at Ralph's red face. Pop set his cigar into a brass ashtray. "Well, not in those exact words, maybe." He leaned back against the edge of his desk. "I only have a few minutes. Just got off the phone with Andrew Mauer. He's furious the *Ledger*'s not going to endorse him in the election. He's coming in. Wants to talk to me in private. Says he has something that might change my mind."

Ralph gave his moustache a nervous touch.

"Don't worry. I'd never endorse that sleazebag."

Ralph had told Nicole that Mauer helped Pop buy the island. But Ralph didn't know what kind of help that was. "Anyway," Ralph had said, "Mauer was convicted of malfeasance in office. Nothing related to the island sale."

Andre had been standing silent for what he must have considered an inordinate amount of time without speaking. He breathed in and began an oration on the persistence of bribery through the ages until Pop cut him off. "Andy, isn't it? Ralph says you have something interesting to show us."

"Andre."

"Right." Pop looked at his watch. "Let's get on with it, then."

Andre handed him the copy of Willard's letter. Pop was the only one who didn't already know what it said. Together they searched his face as he read.

Pop retrieved his cigar. "Very interesting. Looks like this is the smoking gun you were waiting for, Anthony. Corroboration of the Two Naked Men in a Parked Car report." Pop waved the letter in his hand. "And this is the man I once ...." He relit his cigar and sent out narrow stream of smoke through his lips. "He told me he had a legal way of getting around land preservation regulations. Got the county to trade off preservation of the island for preservation of some woods somewhere. I assume it was legal. But, still, with people now looking into everything this man did, it's a damn good thing I told the county to cancel the island purchase. The money's already been returned. I should be in the clear."

Anthony and Pari exchanged glances. They were anxious to print the Naked Parkers story, Nicole knew. Not to embarrass Mauer but to prevent this corrupt official from entering the state legislature. Ralph turned to Andre. "This is a copy of the exact letter Willard Scherd sent Mauer? He signed it?"

"And there's more." Andre handed Ralph a blue legal pad filled with cramped script. "Notes I took of what Willard told me during my prison visits."

Glasses flipped down from his head, Ralph turned over page after page. It wasn't long before he flipped his glasses back up. "This is ... these details ... descriptions of physical intimacy, private bodily areas ...." He narrowed his eyes. "Anthony, it looks like we have the additional corroboration we wanted."

The intercom on Pop's desk squawked. "Mr. Mauer is here to see you. Uh, should I tell him ...?" Sharise's voice. Nicole realized she must know more about Pop's political entanglements than you'd expect of the paper's advertisement manager. Anthony had told her Sharise often sailed with Pop.

"Well, go ahead. Bring him up."

Sharise's eyes rolled across the crowd standing in Pop's office. Mauer hesitated at the doorway.

"Andrew, come in. We're expecting you. Show him in, Sharise. Close the door behind you, please."

Mauer held a brown leather briefcase. He still wore the kitschy checked sports coat Nicole remembered from that board of education hearing. As he sized up the unexpected company for this meeting, his face turned as pale as when he'd heard that gunshot. He backed up against the door, clutching the briefcase under his arm.

"We have a copy of a letter sent to you, Andrew. Mind if I read part of it?"

"Letter? What's going on?" Mauer's voice was squeaky.

"It's from a friend of yours, a Mr. Willard Scherd."

Ralph posted beside Mauer so the door couldn't be opened. Pop quoted a few salacious phrases before focusing on the date, time, and place of the parking lot tryst.

Mauer cursed. "That criminal—he's trying to slander me. He obviously got those details from the Police Blotter report in your own paper, which, by the way, didn't mention me."

Anthony spoke up. "Those details weren't published until *after* Scherd wrote the letter."

Mauer eyed his briefcase. "What does he want, money?"

Andre stepped forward and scoffed. "Friendship. Support. That's what Willard wants." He recapped the letter's heartfelt assertions of admiration for Mauer and attraction to him.

"Lies. All lies. You believe a felon like that?"

Ralph pointed out that Willard had given Andre "certain details about your physiognomy that could only be known by—"

"Enough! What do you want?"

Everyone waited for Pop to speak. He seemed to be making up his mind. Slowly, he re-lit the stubby end of his cigar. "It's news," he finally said. "Verified beyond a doubt. And we're a newspaper."

"How much?"

"Now hold on, Andrew. Here's the thing. The state can't have a legislator like you. That's my main concern. Your scandalous behavior isn't what I want to report on. I want to report that you've decided not to run for office. That you're retiring permanently to private life."

Mauer's head sagged. Sweat from his hands smeared his briefcase. "You can't be serious?"

Pop stared him down.

Ralph cleared his throat. He read from Andre's notes, "… and on his penis—"

"Stop!" Mauer slid to the floor, his back against the door. "This can't get out. Think of my service to the county, my reputation."

No one spoke.

"I don't run and you won't print it?"

Pop pulled him up by the arm. "We all think it's time you retire. I hear Florida's nice. Or maybe Nevada. You have some former colleagues there."

"My wife. She can't know about this."

"No one needs to know." Pop told Anthony to make a recording on his phone. "Andrew Mauer's formal and permanent withdrawal from the election and from public life. Go ahead, Andrew."

When his halting, high-pitched announcement was finished and Anthony shut off his phone, Mauer looked around the room. "I need to be sure that everybody will keep this quiet."

Andre put a finger to his temple. "I need one more thing. You have to apologize privately to Willard Scherd and promise to plead for him at his first parole hearing."

Pop gave a slow nod. "Seems reasonable to expect."

Mauer's knees were giving out. Pop held him up. "So. Everybody agreed?"

When Mauer reached for the doorknob, Pop put a hand on his shoulder. "Oh, and since you've been released from jail and retired from public life, I'll see if I can get my wife to invite your Arlene back into her ladies golf group. Or show her how to set up a new one in another state."

At the mention of his wife, Mauer gripped his head. The briefcase slid to the floor and cracked open.

Pop picked it up, gave him a squinty grin. "What the hell you got in here? Cash, it looks like. You need to be careful carrying around a lot of money like that."

Nicole was sure she wasn't the only one to assume it was bribe money he'd brought to secure the *Shady Park Ledger*'s endorsement.

Pop chuckled and snapped the briefcase shut. "Here. You can put it towards a vacation in Disneyland or Las Vegas."

38

Sartorial relapse

Without you, why should I care for my appearance?
I no longer think to take my comb from its case.

—"A Girl from Harima," from the *Manyoshu*

Nicole noticed other signs throughout Piskasanet County along the road to the childcare center in Northbrook. *Clean Up Our Schools. Diggs for School Board. Peter Diggs—Andrew Mauer's Choice.* She wondered if that last one would be changed after Mauer's followers learned he was dropping out of politics. Probably not. For his base, he was more than a candidate. He represented an attitude towards life.

Andre wanted to show her the improvements in the center. A placard reading *Happy Times Childcare* stood where the cross had been. A yellow bulldozer prevented parking in the front. Nicole drove around to a wide lot in the back. A crane was lifting a blue dumpster onto a flatbed truck. She saw an old *Re-elect Mauer* sign sticking out the top. A backhoe was digging up the asphalt in the area nearest the back door—for a garden, Nicole hoped. The parents whose children came to this center mostly didn't have cars. They walked, or brought their kids by bus.

Men in white hardhats were hauling away the rusty back door as she approached. Andre stood in the doorway, grinning. Most people said *Hi*. Andre just looked at you and grinned.

"Looks like a major renovation, Andre."

"Apparently Derek Grosbeck thinks big. Come look inside."

A short, dark haired man she didn't know was scraping up tiles from the floor while a pretty dark haired woman packed up children's toys into cardboard boxes. It was Esmeralda.

"Ms. Ernst. So happy to see you. I come on my day off to help get ready the new chil-care center." She had big news. "My son Juan took a national test, I don't know—PS something—and now colleges sending him letters. Same for his friend Jim Delpak. We must thank you for good teaching."

"He's not talking about dropping out of school any more, I hope?"

"No. Now hoping to play baseball for State."

Banging sounded behind the inner wall. "That's my husband, Mateo. Working for Mr. Derek now. Mr. Derek say Mateo does good work. Now Mateo hiring other people." She indicated the man working on the floor. "Also Juan and his friend help sometimes after school."

There was a crash. A gap opened in the wall between the daycare area and what had been Pastor Rainey's private office. Mateo peered through the hole, smiling, his face white with plaster. "Ms. Ernst, happy to see you. We are espanding the place where children can play."

A sheet of drywall creaked, shifted, then crumbled into a pile of dust. Juan stood there beside his friend Jim—both of their faces powdery white. "Ms. Ernst!"

Nicole wanted to give them a congratulatory hug but held back. Both were covered with plaster dust, only their dark eyes showing, like twin albino raccoons.

Car doors slammed in the parking lot. Derek Grosbeck strode in, Natalie on one side and his daughter Chelsea on the other. Chelsea was a mess—baggy jeans, faded State sweatshirt hanging almost to her knees, and hair that looked like rats might be nesting in it. Natalie took her hand. "Remember. You promise."

Chelsea wiggled her hand free. "What? He's not even here."

"There." Natalie pointed to the two raccoons.

Chelsea's hand was over her mouth.

"Go ahead. You promise."

Head down, studying her feet, Chelsea made her way up to a raccoon. "I'm sorry, Juan. I shouldn't have sent you those pictures. I'm sorry I got you in trouble. I promise I'll never do it again."

"Um, I'm Jim. That's Juan over there."

Chelsea tugged at her hair, her face blood red.

Juan held out his hand. "Yeah sure, Chelsea. All's forgiven." She shook his hand, giggling now, and wiped the white dust on her jeans. Her father came and wrapped his arms around her. She was crying and laughing at the same time.

Andre and Natalie went through the opening Mateo and the boys had cut into the wall. Nicole followed. "Pastor's office was here," Natalie told her. "Gone now. But we're keeping this stage. For the kids to perform. Maybe put some desks in this big worship room, make it a study room for older kids."

The grin Andre had greeted her with was still on his face. "We might hire my friend Johan to teach here."

"What do you mean? I thought you said—"

"He came back." Andre led her away from the stage, lowered his voice. "Turns out he tried one of those Gay-Be-Gone camps. I could have told him it wouldn't work. I tried one myself last summer. The psycho-physical basis for even thinking something like this would—"

"Andre, I'm so happy for you."

"Johan used up all his money trying to de-gay. He's living with me. I might get Mateo to 'espand' my house as soon as he's finished with all the projects Derek Grosbeck's giving him."

"Other projects?"

"I've been talking to Derek. He lost money with the failure of Riverside Paradise. I suggested looking into special Housing and Urban Development grants. His lawyer Starkezahn came up with a way to get a low-cost HUD load to buy up all the bankrupt Riverside Paradise property and build houses for low income renters and buyers."

"Not monstrosities like Bea's villa, I hope?"

"No. The Esmeraldas and Mateos and displaced fishermen wouldn't be able to afford them. He plans cottages like mine." Andre cocked his head. "Maybe a little newer and nicer. Same basic style as the originals that were torn down. The Trouts and others who were forced out will be able to come back."

"What about that empty villa?"

"He doesn't say. He seems to have a plan for it but I don't know what it is."

Esmeralda and Natalie were talking in Spanish. It seemed to be about decorating. They asked Juan to measure the windows. Jim helped, and Chelsea wrote down what they called out.

Derek took Nicole aside. She noticed he wasn't wearing the bluetooth earpiece any more.

"What do you think?" He reached up to adjust the nonexistent bluetooth receiver. "I mean about Chelsea."

"Her apology? It was sweet. And I'm sure sincere."

Derek's face brightened. "We're trying."

The "we" must mean Derek and Natalie.

"Chelsea doesn't waste all her time deciding what to wear these days."

Nicole had suspected as much.

"Another thing. This guy Peter Diggs you told me about? I had Starkezahn check him out. Diggs has two previous arrests for indecent exposure. One for failure to pay child support. Doesn't sound like the ideal guy for a board of education slot."

The thought of Diggs directing children's education choked Nicole up.

"Ms. Ernst?"

"Oh, thanks, Derek. Would you ask Mr. Starkezahn to send his report to the *Ledger*?"

Bobby was in rare form, not just because Ralph had cooked his favorite lasagna for dinner. The Air and Space Museum trip was back on. "I am *ex-ter-emely* pleased to announce that our school *com-yuu-nity* is no longer *pe-lagued* with disgusting *lew-id* texts and so the *te-rip* to Washington, D.C., has been rescheduled."

"Great, Bobby. You'll love it." Ralph filled Nicole's glass with Chianti. "And now let's drink to a Mauer-free legislature."

"What?" Bobby mocked. "Teachers won't be toting guns? Boooring. Science books will be stuffed with science? Dark-skinned kids like Carlos won't be deported?"

"At least for a while."

"That's just un-American."

"Do your homework, Bobby."

Nicole saved her own good news for when they were in bed. "The *Ledger*'s going to get an interesting background report on Peter Diggs from Derek Grosbeck's lawyer. If you guys print it, that should be the end of his scheme to replace Pari's dad and vote the fundamentalist textbooks back in. One more scoundrel out of the picture."

She started playing with the hair scattered across Ralph's taut chest, but he sat up. "I forgot. I have some news that's not so good. Anthony got a call from his friend Rob at the police station. Reverend B is threatening to send one of the Northbrook High girls to the Wilcox Center."

Nicole was surprised Liz hadn't told her.

"The principal, staff, teachers—nobody was informed. All they know is the girl dropped out of school. Trisha Smith. I understand she was in your class."

"I can't believe it. Trisha's such a kind, gentle, girl. What did she do?"

"According to Anthony, a guy in her class, Brett, drew a naked picture of her. She tried to take it from him, he grabbed her wrist, she pushed him in the face. His nose started bleeding."

"That's all? So maybe they both get suspended for a few days. That's what should happen at worst."

"Except Anthony's friend says Reverend Blatchford came to the police station and raised a ruckus. Filed a complaint against Trisha—assault. Insisted she be held at the Wilcox until trial."

"Why would they do that?"

"Turns out she had a prior arrest. Smoking pot in a car with her boyfriend. Her parents couldn't come up with the bail right away. While they're working on it, the girl's stuck in the Wilcox."

Nicole's libido had evaporated. She lay beside Ralph picturing the Rev putting his hands on Trisha at the Wilcox.

39

No-contact prayer

For every guilty deed
Holds in itself the seed
Of retribution and undying pain.

—Henry Wadsworth Longfellow,
The Masque of Pandora

When Nicole pulled up, an ambulance was parked in front of her house. Her first thought was *Smokey!* After her heart slowed down, she felt silly. It must be a neighbor. Most of the residents on her street were old. She looked around. No sign of trouble. Then a paramedic in a blue uniform got out of the ambulance. It was the same young man who'd taken her to the hospital when she was shot and, apparently, when she almost drowned in Osprey Creek.

She'd laughed at the note on the card he left her—*We have to stop meeting like this.* When he'd gone looking for her at Northbrook High School, Liz seemed to like him. But it was weird that he was looking for her, and she'd thought it better not to call. He wasn't much older than her students at the college. She tried to remember his name but couldn't.

"I found you." He was tall, with shiny brown hair and hazel eyes. Good-looking, Liz had called him. Nicole hadn't had time to notice at either of the two times they'd "met." She stopped at the trellis.

"Finally. How are you, by the way? Recovered from … everything?" He was holding something wrapped in brown paper.

Nicole gripped her keys.

The paramedic flashed her his identity badge. "Alan Rodgers. Of course, you don't remember me." When Nicole started looking up and down the street, he said, "Don't worry. I'm not here on business."

Nicole felt for her house key.

"I have something for you."

She didn't take the little package he held out.

"I know. Maybe it's better you opened it in private."

Nicole stepped back.

"I took it off you in the ambulance when we removed your wet clothes. I didn't know whether you were the police—which I doubted, since I knew you were a teacher—or maybe it was a private matter. In either case, I assumed you wanted to keep it secret, not have people asking questions about it at the hospital."

"You mean—"

"A wire. I guess that's what they call it."

Nicole took the package, pressed with her fingers to see if it really could be the missing wire, tore open a corner. It was.

The wire. She had the wire. As soon as Detective McGinn got this, the Reverend's days on the loose would be numbered. The young paramedic, Alan something, couldn't realize how important this was. "Thank you. Thank you so much."

"Sure. Glad I finally tracked you down."

It would only be polite to ask him in for a cup of coffee. And she would have, of course. But she couldn't shake from her head the picture of him removing her wet clothes.

The *Ledger* lay open on McGinn's desk. "Did you see the article on Peter Diggs's past arrests, Detective?"

"Not only that, Ms. Ernst. We ran a check and he's wanted on another charge in West Virginia. Hold on." He picked up his phone and listened. "Good news. He's already been arrested. He'll be extradited."

"I have more good news." She put the wire on his desk. After he was able to close his mouth, he called in his techie Matt to examine the device, then insisted on recording Nicole's explanation. The minute she finished, he called the hospital ambulance department. "I believe you, Ms. Ernst, but we have to verify the chain of evidence." He was put through to Alan Rodgers, who confirmed Nicole's story.

Matt came in with the wire, beaming. The recording of Nicole's sale on the pier to the Reverend and Peter Diggs was intact. McGinn leaned back in his chair, hands behind his head. "With this recording and the pictures we took of that transaction, we'll get an arrest warrant." He smiled at Nicole. "Coffee, Ms. Ernst? Donut?"

The warm March day instantly produced purple and white crocuses along Nicole's front walk. She let Smokey out into the yard to sniff around and called Liz. Finally, she could talk about her encounters with Reverend Blatchford. "The detective said they'd drop the charges on Trisha as soon as they get a warrant for Reverend's B's arrest."

"Poor girl. There's no school today. We should go visit her."

They drove beside the high chain link fence towards the Wilcox parking lot. In the unseasonably warm air, the asphalt playground was noisy with girls playing outside, the youngest at hopscotch and the older ones pumping a basketball through a bare rim. A few came to gawk as Liz and Nicole walked towards the windowless brick building.

"Ms. Ernst! Ms. Costello!" It was Trisha peering through the fence, gripping the links with long, delicate fingers. Her cheeks were hollow and her head fuzzy with fine, blond hair that had started to grow back. The faded blue detention center jumper hid her shape, but it was clear she'd lost weight.

She had to keep pushing the straps back over her thin shoulders.

Nicole swallowed and couldn't speak. She touched her fingers to Trisha's through the chain links.

Liz encouraged the girl. "You're going to get out of here, Trisha. Hold on a little longer."

There were tears in Trisha's eyes. "The girls say you have to let him touch you, or you'll be punished."

Liz kicked the fence. The rattle made some other girls look over to see what was going on, but none came over. It didn't seem Trisha had made any friends yet.

"My mother came to see me yesterday. I told her about the Reverend touching us. She said she was going to report it to the police."

Nicole and Liz said they'd report it as well. If the girls were questioned and stuck to their story, it looked like there would be charges against the Rev beyond trafficking in child pornography.

On the way back, Nicole got a call from Detective Mc-Ginn. "Wanted to give you a heads up. The arrest will be tomorrow morning, 10:00 a.m. at the Wilcox Center. You can tell the *Ledger*—no problem reporting it. Matter of fact, Trisha Smith's mother already notified WPSK TV and the City TV station."

Nicole couldn't wait to tell Ralph. But he wasn't home when she got to his house. Bobby's aunt had made dinner. "Ralph's going to be late. He said he has some business at Northbrook High with the principal."

When Ralph got home, he looked tired and distracted, but she grabbed his hands. "It's over, Ralph. Reverend B's going to jail. Tomorrow."

Ralph pulled out his phone. "What time, Nicole?" He dialed Anthony. "The police say 10:00 at the Wilcox. But they wouldn't want a media circus to alarm the Rev when he shows up for work. I'm sure they'll already be waiting for him inside. We should get there early. Right, drop everything else tomorrow, and would you call Pari? I'm bringing Nicole."

Nicole was so excited she forgot to ask him what business he had with Higgy. It wasn't until late that night when she was lying drowsily beside him that she remembered. But Ralph was already asleep.

Vans with dish antennas on their roofs pulled up near the steps to the Wilcox Center. Men in jeans jockeyed for position, some with huge cameras on their shoulders, others setting up lights or recording equipment. Megyn Drumpfer combed her hair at a mirror hung on the open door of the WPSK TV van and refreshed her lipstick. An assistant handed her a plastic cup of water. "Hem, hem," Megyn practiced, "this morning the Piskasanet—this morning—hem, hem, this MORNING ...."

As Ralph had predicted, Detective McGinn and two uniformed policemen were already in the building. Anthony held firmly to a spot at the bottom step next to his rival of sorts from the *City Paper*. Pari aimed the *Ledger*'s camera from her perch atop Anthony's car. Ralph, Nicole, and Liz made their way towards the fenced playground, back from the crowd of local residents who'd followed the news vans, Ralph taking his own notes.

A blare of excited cries erupted, and a mob of girls in blue jumpers poured out onto the playground and ran up to peer through the links of the fence at the film crews. Nicole recognized Yolanda, the Wilcox administrator standing apart from them, letting them enjoy the spectacle, it seemed. Then she saw Trisha on her knees clinging to the fence, shivering.

"Camera!" someone yelled. "Megyn, the mic. Clear the way, please." The front door was opening. "It's Reverend Blatchford," a woman in the crowd yelled.

Reverend B's black overcoat was draped over the shoulders of his dark pinstriped suit. His hands were cuffed in front of him, a uniformed cop holding each arm. Blatchford's hair was immaculately parted, his yellow bow tie perfectly tied. He paused on the top step, his patent leather shoes gleaming.

"Sir ... Sir," Anthony called out, "will you be pleading guilty to trafficking in child pornography?"

"You've got the wrong man," someone shouted. "That's Reverend Blatchford." But a high-pitched scream followed. "Pervert! How dare you touch my daughter?" Liz nudged Nicole. "Trisha's mom."

The girls behind the chain link fence started yelling. "You creep. Keep your hands off us."

Yolanda, her yellow hair blowing over her tawny skin, held up a hand to stop an approaching guard. She folded her arms and stood watching the girls vent their rage. Nicole had assumed Yolanda knew nothing of what Reverend B was up to, but apparently she did—and had been waiting for a moment like this.

Megyn Drumpfer took up a position in front of the camera. "I'm here at the Wilcox CENTER as Pissa—Cut! I'm here at the Wilcox CENTER as Piskasanet County police are taking Reverend Blatchford into custody. Officer! Can you tell us what the charge is?"

"Kiddie porn!" a man in the crowd called out. "My daughter will testify."

"So will mine," Trisha's mother shouted.

"Impossible," another bellowed. "That's Reverend Blatchford. He's crusading to *end* lechery in our schools."

The cops took Reverend B down the steps, weaved through the crowd, and drove him away in a police car. Reverend B hadn't said a word.

Pari slid off the car roof and went to interview the man who said his daughter would testify against Reverend B. Anthony ran to question Trisha's mother. Then Nicole saw Detective McGinn come to the Wilcox Center door and wave Trisha's parents to come inside. Another guard came onto the playground and spoke to Yolanda, who helped Trisha off her knees and took her inside. It looked like Trisha was being released. Nicole gripped Liz's hand.

Ralph asked Nicole if she knew who that woman with the yellow hair was, then went to speak to Yolanda through the fence. "He prayed for them," Yolanda told him, "but I always thought he could pray without touching."

40

Not blackmail

A snake was never called by its name at night,
because it would hear. It was called a string.

—Chinua Achebe, *Things Fall Apart*

Recently Nicole's attention to her classes at Piskasanet
Community College had taken a back seat to her preoccu-
pation with crime and punishment. She had essays to grade,
texts to read, lessons to prepare. She sat at the little desk
Ralph had given her and got to work.

Chad wrote, "Scrooges suppose to become a good man
but, its not relly the spirit of Christmas, Christmas is about
Jesus but, Jesus isnt' ever mentioned in the story."

Nicole corrected the misspellings and punctuation errors
without making other comments.

Gordy wrote, "Hester is too blame she should of controlled her urges, I dont fill sorry for her."

Same response from Nicole. She knew her corrections
and points taken off were going to be wrongly interpreted
as disagreement with the content. She'd have to spend time
showing that wasn't true. It was like trying to change their
view of human nature—nearly impossible, but she enjoyed
the challenge.

After her classes, she often met Emma for lunch in the
cafeteria. Emma's husband Charles was still counseling Willard in jail. He reported great progress. For one thing, he said
Willard was "more verbal." Willard had joined Citizens for
Gun Control despite his father's mockery, and he was teach-

ing a group of inmates how to use a computer. "I visited him with Charles once," Emma said, "and it's clear Willard's also working out a lot in the prison weight room. Charles thinks his chances for an early parole are good."

Nicole unwrapped her peanut butter and jelly sandwich.

"So," Emma said. "You going to sign up to teach classes again next semester?"

"I'd like to. I think I'm starting to get better at it. But I do miss the security of a full time job."

"A lot of that going around."

Nicole laughed. "Bobby calculated I could make twice as much at McDonald's working the same amount of time I spend here on paper grading, lesson preparation, and teaching the classes."

"And I know you like teaching young kids better."

"I do. Anyway, yeah, I think I'll put my name on the list to see if the college has any classes for me next semester."

Nicole was cooking a recipe she got from Thieu. In case Ralph and Bobby didn't like Dum Phum Do, she had some fried chicken from the Grab 'n Go as backup.

Ralph came in grinning like the Cheshire cat. "Nikki, you're going to get your teaching job back."

Bobby gave Nicole a high-five. "Woo-hoo! I can't believe it. Way to go, Dad."

"This is your doing, Ralph? You knew about this, Bobby?"

"Bobby just knew I was trying to get your job back. I didn't want to get your hopes up."

"But—"

"Long story, Nikki. I told Higgenbottom the *Ledger* thought now that Reverend B has been arrested and Trisha's back in school, this might be a good time to report on sexting at Northbrook High."

"You were really planning to do that?"

"No, Anthony's full report on Reverend Blatchford, Peter Diggs, and sexting in general won't mention any specific schools or, of course, students. But I wanted Higgenbottom to think I might focus on Northbrook. I said I was aware of the potential embarrassment for lots of people. I pointed out that Ms. Ernst's quietly resigning had *so far* kept a lid on a lot of details that would have to come out."

"Ralph, you didn't!" Nicole held her burning cheeks.

"Then when your 'Higgy' looked like he was about to have one of his panic attacks, I put my hand on his shoulder. I said we might not have to name his school. Maybe we could keep the lid on what went on specifically at Northbrook—including your story. I suggested he write you a letter of recommendation."

"Dad, isn't that black—"

"It's not blackmail. It's 'coming to a mutual understanding.' That's what Principal Higgenbottom called it."

"Gosh, Dad."

"Gosh, Ralph."

Mr. Prosterner, the Shady Park school principal, phoned. "Ms. Ernst, I had a call from Superintendent Wilson praising you. The police told him about your help in putting a corrupt school board member behind bars."

It was mousy Mr. Prosterner who'd been intimidated into making Nicole change Chelsea Grosbeck's grade. Derek had apologized to her for his part in that. She wondered if Prosterner would mention it.

"The superintendent says you'll be coming back to Shady Park. That's good news."

"Really?" She allowed a note of sarcasm into her own voice. Prosterner said nothing. "I mean, Mr. Prosterner, if you think I can be trusted to give fair grades."

A bluster of *um*s and *well*s and *of course*s was all Prosterner could manage. The call ended with Nicole agreeing to start back at the end of August when the teachers prepared for the next school year.

41

Garden and agora

And the Spring arose on the garden fair,
Like the Spirit of Love felt everywhere;
And each flower and herb on Earth's dark breast
Rose from the dreams of its wintry rest.

—Percy Bysshe Shelley, "The Sensitive Plant"

When she went back to her house to feed Smokey, the daffodils were in bloom. No matter how harsh the winter, they always surged back in the spring. She missed Smokey and her flowers a little when she was at Ralph's. When she was here, she missed Ralph and Bobby—a lot.

She knew Ralph wanted her to move in with him. He'd actually written a note asking her to. And he had asked her again last night. She could bring Smokey and plant flowers in Ralph's bare front yard. But she needed time. She had to decide what to do with her own house.

She slid a couple of leftover spring rolls into the microwave and poured out a little soy sauce, then added a drop of fish oil that Thieu had given her. Too bad the Tran family couldn't live here instead of over the restaurant. It would be walking distance to work. And even nearer to the bus stop.

Maybe they could. Andre had told her Derek knew of special-rate mortgages with the Department of Housing and Urban Development for low income builders. HUD probably had something for low income buyers, as well. She picked up her phone. She never imagined she'd be calling up a development tycoon to discuss business, but that's what she was doing.

Derek told her he could get the Trans a low-rate loan. No problem. Starkezahn could arrange everything. Any expansion of the house might have to wait, though. He was keeping Mateo busy at the childcare center and had work for him after that—remaking Bea's villa into a River Road Community Center on the first floor and an apartment for the Moreno family on the second.

Nicole went to discuss the idea with Tran and Thieu. She had drawings from Derek and numbers from Starkezahn. She took her time, explaining step-by-step what was involved in buying a house. She explained mortgages, income tax benefits, home equity. When they seemed interested, she gave them the name of a real estate lawyer Starkezahn recommended who had a bilingual Vietnamese-American assistant.

Tran and Thieu contacted the bilingual assistant the very next day. They told Nicole they were encouraged. She invited them to her house early in the morning before the restaurant opened. "We bring food," Thieu said.

They brought enough to feed Nicole and all her friends for a week. Their son Henry was in the kindergarten program at the community college. Thieu carried baby Michelle on her back. Following Nicole from room to room, they *oooe*d and *aah*ed at everything. Nicole wondered if they'd ever been invited into a native-born American's house before.

Tea, of course, came first—Nicole supplied that. Then noodles, then lots of items that Nicole couldn't identify with certainty as either animal or vegetable. Nicole pointed out where Derek's planned expansions could be. There was a lot of discussion in Vietnamese. "Yes, we would like to buy," Tran said before they left. "Buy first. Make bigger later."

After dinner that night—Nicole couldn't eat much—she told Ralph and Bobby her idea of selling her house to Tran and Thieu.

"Great," Bobby said. "Then you can—"

"Perfect," Ralph said. "So that means—"

"I'd move in here. I mean, if you still want me to."

"Nikki!" He picked her up and swung her around.

Ralph's house swallowed up all Nicole's things without seeming the least bit full. It made her realize how few possessions she had. Bobby was excited to have Smokey as a member of the household. He played with him until Nicole had to remind him to do his homework. Ralph wanted to see all her books, all her clothes, shoes, lotions, jewelry. He set up an unused third bedroom she could have as a "dressing room or whatever." She was installed.

Now for botanical improvements. Nielsen's open-air market now displayed tulips, daffodils, roses, and hyacinths. She bought some of each and got busy planting them in Ralph's front yard. In another month she would plant some azaleas.

"Nice," Ralph said, smiling. That was all, but she was sure he liked them. His face was streaked with plaster, and there was antique white paint on his work shirt. Bobby thought maybe glossy royal blue and gold would be a good motif for the whole house, but Nicole vetoed that. She would have liked to get rid of the orange bean bag chair in the living room, too, but Bobby liked it too much.

She sat at her new desk changing her address for bills, insurance, car registration, and the new board of education contract. She went through everything that had her previous address on it—flyleaves of books, notebook covers, her backpack. Ralph's address was now her address. She called her mother, invited her parents to come from their retirement home in Austin to visit.

Liz brought framed pictures of sunset on the Piskasanet River and the old Capitol building in Colonial City as housewarming presents. It was the first time she'd met Bobby. He entertained her with his impressions of Principal Prosterner and the U.S. President.

It turned out the Trans already had quite a bit of savings. Soon papers were signed. The Trans had their first house.

Nicole still got occasional calls from Andre. This time he wanted her to come see what Derek was having Mateo do to Bea's former villa. The outside looked the same, except Esmeralda had put a wire mesh along the pastel stucco walls and planted climbing clematis, which was already starting to bring back the natural ambience of the original fishing village. Most of the first floor had been transformed into an open space with serving counters along the walls. There was a meeting room in the back and a huge industrial-looking kitchen, which Andre swore had been left just as Bea had built it. Mateo was starting to work on the upstairs where he, Esmeralda, and Juan were going to live. He was finishing an enclosed stairway in the back leading up to their apartment. Guatemalan music blared from a portable radio while he hammered and sawed.

"The agora in classical Greek times served as the center for fellowship and discussion among the citizens," Andre began. "I believe the River Road Community Center can serve the same purpose. I look forward to playing pinochle with Old Man Grayson and his wife again. We'll use the Center meeting room to play until his cottage is finished on the lot behind mine. The Trouts, Derek says, can live on the first floor of the Center until their cottage is rebuilt where it was torn down next to mine. My mother can hold her Happy Patchers quilting sessions in the Center and use that enormous kitchen to prepare refreshments."

Andre introduced Nicole to Johan, ten or so years younger than himself, a handsome, curly haired man with wide, intent, caramel-colored eyes, who hung on Andre's words as if he were actually a Greek philosopher. "I'm very glad to meet you," Johan said. "Andre talks about you quite a bit. You're one of his favorite people."

Nicole felt her cheeks warming.

"**Y**ou look worried, Nikki. Anything wrong? Come here. Whatever it is, I'll make it better." He pulled her onto his lap.

She curled up the way Smokey did on hers. "Have you been thinking, Ralph?"

"Thinking? What do you mean?"

"You asked me once if I would like to have a baby. I said yes. Do you remember what you said?"

"Uh ... not exactly."

"I do. You said, *Huh, something to think about.*"

He buried his face in her hair.

"Well? Have you come up with anything yet?"

He stared at the floor. "I've been sort of waiting more than thinking. Wondering."

"Oh."

"OK, I *have* been thinking maybe we could go to one of those fertility clinics. Do you think we should?"

"We might not have to."

That night Nicole fell into a deep sleep. She awoke slowly, opening her eyes with a sense of déjà vu. The room was dark. A warm hand was caressing her breast. She lay still for a moment, allowing the thrill to course through her body. When she turned her head, Ralph was awake, gazing at her. He whispered her name. "Nikki, Nikki."

Keeping quiet so they wouldn't wake Bobby intensified their pleasure. Finally, they lay out of breath, trying to keep their gasps soft, quiet. Then Nicole fell once again into a deep sleep.

42

Sorkhi-zardi

سرخی تو از من و زردی من از تو

Sorkhi-ye to az man o, zardi-ye man az to.
(Your red into me and my yellow into you.)
—Zoroastrian purification and renewal chant

The next day Ralph came home early. On the dining room table, he fanned out a mix of magazine clippings, computer printouts, and advertisements for baby items. "Sharise had a baby about three years ago. Never threw any of this away." He picked up an advertisement for cribs. "Look. What do you think? Pari says blue for boys and pink for girls is gender stereotyping. Anyway, what do you think of plain white?"

She couldn't believe how excited he was. "Yeah, white's good, Ralph. Let's get a white crib."

Liz seemed more excited than at her own pregnancy. She rushed Nicole to the drugstore to get a test kit—two of them just in case. Positive. Positive. "My OBGYN is great. You should go to her. You beat the clock, Nicole. With time to spare. Maybe you and Ralph can have two kids. Alphonse and I are thinking about that. Did you call your mom?"

"My mom's a little conservative. I haven't gotten up the nerve yet. I will, though. Soon."

Liz couldn't stop herself. "Our kids will be less than a year apart. Think of that, Nicole. How about Bobby? How do you think he's going to take it? He'll probably love having a little brother or sister."

"Well, he likes the cat, so ...."

"Be serious, Nicole. This is 'major,' as the students say. You are 'so' going to become a mother. Let's get some ice-cream."

Andre found out about it before Nicole's mother did. He heard it from Emma, who heard it from Pari, who heard it from Ralph. Andre drove straight to Ralph's house—he'd also heard she moved there. He gave her half a hug, then stepped back. "Sorry. I didn't mean to squish you. I hope—"

"It's OK, Andre. Here, give me a real hug."

He cocked his head and began, "Male primates exhibit a sense that the female of the species—"

"How's Johan? He seems like a nice guy, very polite. Good-looking."

Andre shrugged, flushing. "I guess so. We're happy to-gether. Johan says we should get a dog, but—"

"You should adopt a child. Ever think of that?"

His blue eyes met hers, and he put a finger to his temple. "I've thought of having a child, wished I could have one. I don't know about adoption. To tell the truth, my income, my work ethic as they say, might disqualify me, as unfair and il-logical as that might seem. Maybe Johan would have a better chance. I don't know."

"Well, I'm going to need a babysitter now and then. And, when she or he gets bigger, we'll take him to your childcare center."

Andre had news of his own. He'd helped Willard line up a future job as a personal trainer at Abs 'n Glutes in North-brook. "My friend Charles says there's a good chance he'll be granted parole when his hearing comes up."

Personal trainer sounded better to Nicole than infantry-man or border guard or anything that would put a gun in Willard's hand.

"Also, I want to invite your whole family to a Chahar-Shanbeh Soori celebration at my house."

"Invite my whole ...? Oh. Right. Thanks. What's Cha-har-Shanbeh Soori?"

"Remember the Yaldā celebration? The winter solstice gathering at Pari's mother's house?"

No way Nicole would ever forget that.

"This celebrates the spring equinox—on the Wednesday before it, marking the coming of spring. Johan and I plan to build a fire on the beach. Tell Ralph not to wear his suit. It's informal."

Deep green holly and pine, yellow forsythia, and purple hyacinth dotted the riverside's brown switchgrass with color. Robins dove down from bare catalpa branches to scratch in the dirt, and a lone osprey coasted in a wide, slow arc around the nest it had built the spring before on a piling in the river.

Andre's Chahar-Shanbeh Soori celebration had brought the little fishing village to life. Spanish reggae music blared from the open windows and doors of Bea's villa, where Nicole found Mark and Mastaneh using the huge kitchen to roast kabobs. In what was now a large meeting room, Shahnaz Del-pak prepared a table of Iranian food, all of which began with the letter *s* in Persian. Lentil sprouts, wheat pudding, apples, sumac berries—interesting, Ralph granted, but he gravitated towards the kabobs.

Outside, Bobby, Emma's son Todd, and the local kids Alan, Bill, and Beth followed the older Juan and Jim wherev-er they went. The kids climbed up to the slanting tree house Andre had helped them build in his yard, ran to the beach, paddled near the shore in his sun bleached dinghy. Jim had brought a soccer ball. He and Juan formed two little teams on the beach using lines drawn in the sand as goals.

On the patio behind the villa-turned-community center, Andre's pinochle playing friend sat drinking cans of beer. Mr.

Trout and his wife were living temporarily on the first floor in one of the villa rooms that was closed off. He was talking to Andre's mother, who offered Nicole and Ralph some of her homemade plum wine. Ralph preferred Mr. Trout's offer of a Budweiser.

Mateo had just finished building Old Man Grayson's new cottage and the two of them were toasting with bottles of Dos Equis. Esmeralda came down the stairway from their apartment on the second floor of the villa. Her long hair was damp and gleaming in the sunset. "Ms. Ernst, is wonderful our big new apartment. We have Jacuzzi, big like heated swimming pool. You must visit some time."

Anthony heard and came over, said he'd seen the Jacuzzi. "Bea gave me a house tour once. I didn't try out the Jacuzzi, though." He smiled as if he were keeping something to himself.

A curly haired young man braving the slight chill in shorts and half-open shirt passed by Nicole. Andre's friend Johan. His hands were full of wood, so he gave Nicole a little bow. "So nice to see you again. This is my first Chahar-Shanbeh Soori. Do you know how big the fire's supposed to be?"

"It's a first for me, too."

Shouts rang out from down on the beach. "We can't get it started."

Mr. Trout put his hand behind his ear. "What's that? You need some paper?" He showed a sardonic grin. "Oh, I've got some paper. Anthony, want to give me a hand?"

They emerged from the Trouts' room in the villa, which had formerly been Bea's office, carrying armfuls of the defunct Riverside Paradise brochures.

The fire was blazing up nicely just as the sun went down. Jim's father Reza explained the ceremony. "It's an ancient custom we have. *Zardoshti*, I mean—"

"Zoroastrians," Andre said. But Johan stopped his interruption with a nudge.

"It's hard to explain," Reza said. "Maybe Jim ...."

His son told them the fire symbolized the spirit of light and good coming back into the world. "We jump over the fire saying *Sorkhi-ye to az man o, zardi-ye man az to*. Your red into me and my yellow into you."

"A Zoroastrian purification and renewal chant," Andre couldn't keep from adding.

Jim backed up, ran towards the fire, and barely cleared the blaze as he chanted. Juan gave a whoop and followed, chanting the phrase in English. Then Reza, Shahnaz, Mastaneh, Mark, and Pari in Persian. Nicole noticed Anthony mumbling to himself, clearly trying to memorize the Persian. He jumped mumbling something. "Close enough," Pari laughed.

The younger kids jostled for position in a line they'd formed. "That *sorkhi-zardi* thing!" Bobby yelled as he jumped. The rest of the kids took it up. "*Sorkhi-zardi*!" "*Sorkhi-zardi*!"

Johan pushed Andre to go first. Both of them, laughing, resorted to "*Sorkhi-zardi*!" So did Ralph and Nicole. Andre's mother hadn't come down to the beach, but the old neighbors had. "Your Budweiser into me!" Mr. Trout yelled with a low jump that barely cleared the fire. Mateo jumped and changed it to "Dos Equis!" Nicole glanced at the Iranians to see if any were offended, but they were laughing harder than the rest. Mrs. Trout and Mrs. Grayson held up their skirts and leapt, saying nothing. Esmeralda went last. She soared over the fire singing out the Persian phrase perfectly to a great round of applause.

They stood watching the fire die down to a bed of glowing embers. Anthony said he had an announcement. "Pari and I are going to get married."

Nicole looked at Ralph and realized he already knew.

"June first," Anthony said. "Everybody here is invited.

The wedding is going to be on that island in the river. Pop, our publisher, built a dock there when he expected to build a house on the island. That didn't work out, but the dock's still there. You can come by boat. The wedding will be on the top of the hill overlooking the bay."

It sounded so romantic, Nicole could hardly hold back tears. There were toasts, congratulations, and Old Man Grayson, who had brought his guitar down to the beach, even started strumming the wedding march.

Nicole squeezed Ralph's hand and whispered, "What a wonderful place to have a wedding."

Ralph said, "Maybe we can beat them to it."

CPSIA information can be obtained
at www.ICGtesting.com
Printed in the USA
LVHW051547020819
626315LV00006B/31/P